PRIMARC

THE MARKED BONDS SERIES

BOOK TWO

S.M. STORM

DEDICATION

They say it takes a village, and I know that to be true because I have you.
This is for my village.
I adore you. Truly.
Thank you for loving me through every overthinking spiral and last minute panic.

TRIGGER WARNINGS

Content warning: This book contains explicit sexual content and themes of kidnapping, torture, violence, death, and trauma.

Danielson's Family Bloodline Journal

(Translated from the Elder Script of Etruria)

750 B.C.—The Widow Decima Anu Otacilia, last of her house and mother of a single heir, Augustus Maximus Otacilia, defied the oldest laws of the village of Nerulia. Augustus fell fatally ill, and in her grief and desperation to preserve her bloodline, she reached into the forbidden shadows of the dark arts—practices outlawed since the dawn of civilization in ancient Etruria.

It was then that Decima sought a relic of the heavens: the Sacar, known in later tongues as Cosmos atrosanguineus. This sacred bloom bore eight petals, each vessel of a rare golden-brown hue and a spiced aroma of vanilla, marking its celestial origin. None were permitted to touch the flower; its appearance alone was considered a divine omen of life's fragility, a blessing from the gods.

But Decima's fear outweighed faith. She plucked two blossoms, and at once the petals shriveled and the stems turned to dust. She ground their remains into a fine powder and mingled them with unknown herbs and oils, ignoring the omens of doom that accompanied her trespass.

From the wild fields, she summoned the Hound, a creature long bound to her son's side by unseen threads. She drew its blood and, under the unblinking moon, mixed it with the powdered Sacar.

When she added her son's blood to the concoction, the mixture thickened and darkened, shimmering like night water. Decima chanted forbidden incantations over the bowl, words mortals were never meant to shape. She poured the elixir into Augustus's mouth, binding boy and beast in a single ritual. The Hound drank next, sealing the covenant forevermore.

For three days and nights, Augustus lay between life and death as Decima prayed to uncaring gods. On the fourth dawn, he rose renewed—his strength restored, his spirit changed. The Hound's eyes mirrored his own. Their breaths synced. Their hearts beat as one.

Thus began the Ancient Bond.

Years later, when Augustus took a bride, destiny revealed its full cost...twin sons were born:

One, blessed with the instincts of the Hound—loyal, perceptive, and strong.

The other, cursed by blood—skin cold as twilight stone, fangs like razors, sustained only by living blood.

So, the brothers diverged into legend:

Avont Otacilia—first of the Guardians, sworn protectors who could harmonize with the strength of animal spirits and walk among humankind.

Lunce Otacilia—first of the Blood-bound, whose eternal hunger severed him from the warmth of mortal life.

Tension festered between them, like a wound left to linger. Avont, beloved, lived in the open, unafraid. Lunce, feared, remained in the shadows, bound to a hunger he could not escape.

Their bond was unbreakable, yet their differences spoke louder than loyalty. Avont would always stand as Lunce's protector, while Lunce kept his distance, feeding and surviving in the dark.

In time, Lunce took an innocent maiden as his wife, and from that union came a lineage forever marked. Whether she chose it or was forced into it was lost to time.

Meanwhile, Avont continued to grow his gift, discovering new creatures whose spirits could join with his own. From this, a legacy began to take shape, one that would one day give rise to Guardians tied not only to wolves but to many creatures of the earth.

This bond—the mark of life intertwined and blood transformed—has shaped all descendants of the Otacilian line. Their histories are written in both salvation and suffering, all born from a single act:

A mother who could not bear to lose her son.

And a flower that should never have been touched.

PROLOGUE

4 months ago

The deserted security room smelled like dust and old insulation, a graveyard of forgotten equipment, emitting a dystopian aura. A row of monitors sat dark, cables coiled across the floor, the whole place dim except for the faint hum of a dormant power source. It wasn't ready to protect us yet, not really. But it would do.

Down the hall, muffled voices rose and fell. I could hear Dayken's low growl and Onyx's soft heartbeat beeping away on a nearby machine as they worked on her. Derek's hands were steady as he tried to remove the tracking device embedded in my sister's body. While I was used to scenes like this—my sister unconscious and limp, fragile-looking even though she was far from it—everyone else was not. Which meant everyone's eyes and attention were on the operating table. No one was looking at me.

Good.

I knew my sister was in safe hands. I read all their faces. Chase, Derek, even Alicia—I saw the patterns of their behavior before they'd even set down their bags. I knew they were telling the truth, and I knew they were here to help. Not to mention, Dayken was utterly obsessed with my sister. It didn't take my enhanced perception to know he would rip Derek's eyes from their sockets before he let anything unfortunate befall Onyx. I knew once he shifted, he and his wolf would be completely engulfed in Onyx's well-being, and I could slip out of the room undetected.

I quickly sat in an old, beat-up leather chair and brushed a layer of grime from the keyboard.

I had to move fast.

The machine booted up under my fingers as if it remembered me, screen after screen flickering awake, waiting. Sometimes I even impressed myself with how fast I was. Almost too fast. Too practiced. I should've been out of touch after spending twenty years locked in a laboratory, but my hands knew exactly what to do. Thanks to the mental tests—torture, really—they put me through, and the years spent buried in information technology books. I bet the facility never realized they were preparing me for this exact moment. Encryption. Containers. Distributed systems. Endless breakdowns of cloud orchestration and infrastructure that most people would never touch.

The facility thought it was punishment, giving me dry, boring manuals or dense theory. Enough to dull anyone's mind.

But they had underestimated me.

I didn't skim them; I absorbed them all. Took it apart piece by piece until it stopped being information and became instinct. Something I could move through without thinking.

So, when this moment presented itself, I didn't hesitate.

Directives unfolded in front of me. File trees branching deeper and deeper. Logs scrolled in tight, precise lines, timestamps stacking like footprints. Data streams pulsed in real time, packets flowing in and out like a living thing breathing beneath my fingertips.

I slipped through it all.

Past surface-level monitoring. Past security layers meant to slow someone down.

All the way past its defenses to where the chaos lived.

That was where most people got lost. Too much data. Too many signals bleeding into each other.

But not me.

I filtered it out. Stripped it down to patterns and isolated what didn't belong.

And then I saw it.

A faint pulse was buried beneath everything else. Signals bouncing between nearby towers, overlapping just enough to stay hidden.

I locked onto it and followed the rhythm. Matched the pattern.

And then—

There it was.

My signal.

My chest tightened, but I forced my fingers to remain steady. If they discovered it or knew its exact location, I would be in danger. Worse, if I didn't do *this*, I'd always be a risk to Onyx.

To all of them.

I rerouted. Masked. Scrambled. The signal's heartbeat blinked once, twice, then stilled into silence. To anyone watching, it would look like the source simply died.

Not good enough. I went deeper, syncing code into this ancient system, layering false trails and loops, so if anyone came looking, they'd only find a ghost.

My temples started to throb, but I rubbed the ache away with my fingers.

I didn't have time to cover my tracks as thoroughly as I'd like, but I needed to keep this hidden. No one could know what I just did.

Alarm bells screeched from the other room, carrying down the hall, sharp enough to spear my chest. For one terrifying second, I wondered if I caused it.

Fuck. Something bad was happening to my sister.

I whispered, "I'm doing this for your own good," to no one but myself, and strung together the final line of code.

The monitor blinked black. Silent. Empty.

No one would ever know. Not Chase or Derek. Not Dayken. And not Onyx.

Especially not Onyx.

I stood, tried to school my features, and sprinted down the hall to see what was happening with my precious sister. I knew she'd be okay, though. I'd already calculated her odds for survival. They were good. Really good.

And if anyone noticed something was off and asked about it later?

I'd say I never saw a thing.

CHAPTER ONE

Silver. So, so much silver. Silver-plated ceiling that connected to the silver-coated walls. Everything around me was metal—shiny, cold, and unyielding. My metallic prison. This was new. I was not used to this type of captivity.

Alone, without my sister nearby.

I had a taste of freedom for a short while. I didn't exactly know how many days had passed, but that freedom was beautiful and comforting. I paced back and forth on the hard tiles that also seemed to be made of...silver.

My thoughts of freedom were interrupted by the sudden image of distressed, yellow eyes that seemed to peer straight into my soul. They searched for me, haunted me. Day or night, time was meaningless here, but those eyes were always there, in my mind.

I missed them.

Even more so, I missed my sister, my other half. I could only imagine what she was going through and how she tried to prevent this exact thing from happening ever since we escaped from the facility. She swore it wouldn't happen again, but it did, and it's my fault. I was careless and let my guard down. Now...who knows what fate awaited me or how the consequences of my actions would affect those dearest to me. If asked if I was scared, I'd say no—there was nothing to fear here, no threats, no torture. But I would say I was nervous, because I didn't know why I was here, which made me uneasy. I was also worried about what my sister might do to reach me. She had just started her healing journey with Dayken, had just begun to trust others, and I might have ruined it all.

I paced more slowly now, each step echoing loudly against the walls. The air felt charged, like the room itself knew something I didn't. I ran my fingers along the silver seams, tracing where the wall met the floor. No cracks. No weaknesses. Whoever designed this place knew exactly what they were doing.

My reflection stared back at me through the metal, distorted and ghostlike. Pale skin, bruised eyes, hair knotted from restless nights. I didn't even look like me anymore. Maybe that was the point—strip away one's identity, make the subject forget who they were, before morphing them into a weakened, twisted version of themselves. They taught us that in the facility, *a vampire without confidence is easier to contain.*

I took a breath and forced my shoulders to square. They couldn't take that from me again. I would not be small. Not for them, not for anyone.

The silence hummed so loudly it felt alive. And that's when I sensed it—something shifting in the air, a disturbance just beyond the door.

The metallic click of the lock yanked me out of my thoughts.

The musky smell reached me immediately, assaulting my senses. It was overbearing, cheap, and artificial—like a synthetic cloud meant to hide whatever rotted underneath.

I loathed it.

"Look who's awake," he said, his voice cutting through the silence.

I stayed quiet, as I always did. There was no point in engaging him. He never listened, wouldn't tell me why I was here, and didn't care about what I had to say. Not really. I hadn't figured out his motives or endgame yet, but I would. I was patient, deliberate, and strategic. I would figure him out. I just needed more time.

He stepped further into the room, closer than usual.

"Sky, my dear, you can only stay quiet for so long. You can only *ignore me* for so long. You're going to be here for a very, *very* long time. We might as well become friends." He paused, his gaze settling on me. "I have a sneaking suspicion you'll even grow to love me."

"No, I won't," I said, finally breaking my silence. My gaze locked with his, my rage buried deep beneath a carefully composed expression. My voice was calm, steady, and collected when I spoke. "And I know because when I look at you, I feel sick to my stomach."

"That will change," he said dismissively.

I tilted my head slightly, my tone turning thoughtful. "I suppose if you had food poisoning every day, you'd get used to it. But that's all that will change—my tolerance to poison."

He growled, low and guttural, the sound jagged enough to scrape my nerves. It was nothing like Kolton's growl—his was wild, raw, almost feral in how it tore through the air. The comparison hit me before I could stop it. Gods, I missed it. I missed *him*. Kolton never wanted me out of his sight, not for a second. His instincts were a constant pressure on my back, pushing me to stay close. And when I craved just a little space, just a breath of freedom, I lied. Told him I was going to train with my sister. He must have been full of rage, tearing himself apart over my disappearance. My poor tiger...

The growling stopped, pulling me back to the present. I studied him again, because that was what I was good at. It was an enhanced ability of mine. I could read people's body movements, tone of voice, pulse, or even a slight eye dilation. I could take it all in. But I could not, for the life of me, figure out what he wanted right now. He believed his words when he said he thought I would grow to love him.

"Even poison has an antidote," he said, and with that, he turned to leave.

His heavy footsteps echoed as he headed back to the door, and without a word, he slammed it shut behind him. The sound reverberated through the cold, metallic room. So did the heavy *thud* of a lock clicking into place, sealing me in. And just like that, I was alone again. Only this time, I think I was just given a clue—something to focus on, a puzzle to unravel while I passed the time.

I flopped down sideways on the cushy bed, bouncing slightly on impact. With my arms dramatically flopped to the side, I lifted one hand and brought it to my bonding mark, rubbing it for comfort. I, not for the first time, pulled hard at the bond, putting all my desperation into attempting to summon my Guardian. I pictured his face, I accelerated my heart rate, I made my adrenaline spike, and I pulled at the invisible rubber band that connected us...but nothing. Not even a whisper.

This silver was getting in the way. It was blocking my connection to him. Why though? Why did they want me? Just me, cut off from my Guardian.

I tried again anyway...

Kolton, can you feel me?

CHAPTER TWO

I entered the room and was greeted by a disturbing, yet all too familiar, sight.

Dayken and Onyx.

He was standing behind her with his arms wrapped around her waist. His chin rested on the top of her head. He held her tight, like she could suddenly slip away at any moment. The amount of PDA these two have been flaunting was borderline offensive.

Onyx was in deep conversation with a bear, who was reporting his latest patrol to her. I was trying to eavesdrop when Dayken saw me. His grip on Onyx loosened, but not before he nuzzled her neck, his lips lingering there. I watched uncomfortably as Onyx took in a breath, and her eyes nearly rolled to the back of her head.

Get a fucking room.

"I think it's important to remember that Sky received the same training you did. She knows how to protect herself, and she isn't weak."

"I don't need to be reminded of that, Chase. What I *do need* is my sister back. Now."

"We're working on it—"

Feral instinct surged through me. Not a flicker. Not a warning. A full avalanche rolled through my chest so hard it rattled my teeth. My skin prickled as if my claws were trying to shove their way out, my tiger itching beneath the surface, begging to tear free.

I should have walked away.

I didn't.

The urge to pace, to rip, to move burned too bright.

Fuck them. Fuck this whole useless committee of talkers.

They sat there discussing Sky like she was some jigsaw puzzle instead of the air in my lungs. They planned and strategized and reassured each other while my Sacar was still out there, fearful of the unknown and all alone.

Talk. Talk. Talk.

My tiger snarled against my ribs. None of this was enough. I needed action. I needed teeth. I needed to stalk and hunt and drag the truth into the light.

This diplomatic shit was just that...shit.

My restraint was hanging by a thread stretched far too thin.

After nauseatingly detaching himself from Onyx, Dayken headed straight in my direction.

Fuck.

I was not in the proper headspace to deal with him right now. Not that I ever was.

"Come with me," Dayken said, trying for the—I'd honestly lost count how many times—to get me to step back and take a break.

"No."

"We won't be far. If there's any sign of Sky, the twins will let us know, and we can leave from there." Like I'd ever trust the well-being of my Sacar to the bird boys.

"I don't want to wait for the twins. I want to look for Skylar myself."

"Well, I think we've established that you can't be trusted to do that in a way that won't cause a war." He crossed his arms over his massive chest.

"I had every right to question the Primarc of the Randall Clan."

"You grabbed her by the throat."

"Well, she wasn't being helpful."

"She is the Primarc of the cougar clan in Canada! A highly respected, isolated, and rare clan. She didn't know anything that could help us. And I told you as much before you stormed up there!"

I just shrugged. Details, details...

"Kolton..." he began again, "I think it would be best if you came with me to question Aurora." He immediately sensed my reluctance and followed up with, "And while we're there, I'll let you have five minutes with Crowe. Alone."

My brain instantly started running through scenarios of how to shatter the bulletproof plexiglass of his cell.

Could I fit an impact drill in my coat pocket? Maybe, if I wear a large enough coat.

"Okay. Deal."

CHAPTER THREE

C rowe leaned back, lips curling into that infuriating smile.

"Oh, hey, wolf," the smug bastard drawled as Dayken walked past him on the way toward his sister's cell. I was hot on his heels as I approached Crowe, but he was still vying for Dayken's attention. "I take it you couldn't find any of my spies," he called as we continued down the corridor.

Dayken's steps slowed but didn't falter.

"Pity. Actually, no, not a pity at all. I knew you never would. We've worked together for too long. Loyalty can be so predictable."

"Fuck off," I snapped, forcing him to focus on me. "And tell me what you know about where Skylar was taken." My flaring anger made the words hotter than I intended. I hadn't wanted to take his bait, but here I was, gnashing down on the hook.

"Skylar? What happened to my precious Skylar?" His voice dripped with mockery. Self-satisfaction was twisted into every syllable. "You know she's special, don't you? I worked very hard on that one—"

"SHUT. UP!" My roar cracked through the air like thunder.

Crowe only chuckled.

"But didn't you ask me where she was? I'll give you a clue. To where I think she might be, that is. How about that? Or am I still to 'shut up'?" he said, his tone turning singsong, like a cruel teacher mocking his pupil.

I didn't respond. My claws had already slipped free from my nail beds. My body hummed with the need to rip his jaw free from his face.

His eyes glinted as if feeding off my fury. His voice slowed to a deliberate cadence: "She's not in chains, you can see. No, she sits beneath a crown—golden, gleaming, proud. Too proud. And pride, boy...pride can slice deeper than any blade. Tell me, when has a king ever been content with just one treasure?"

Motherfucker talks in riddles.

All I could think about was tearing through the barrier, wrapping my hands around his throat, and suffocating the smugness right out of his eyes.

"You useless piece of shit. Tell me what you know!"

"I just did. But if you want more details, I'll make a deal with you."

I was desperate to find Skylar. But was I desperate enough to make a deal with the devil? I could see the reflection of my glowing eyes in the plexiglass, casting him in an ominous wash of light. He huffed. "Bring me Peachabelle, and I'll tell you more."

Easy enough. I could do that. "Why do you want her so bad?"

"I'm so glad you asked." Crowe adjusted his posture in an attempt to come off as regal, clearly enjoying his moment of lording information over me. "Peachabelle Clarisse Vaughn is different. Her blood is not that of the ancients, like Onyxiana and Skylar. She was made into what she is—designed. Generations of turning humans into vampires, those cunning bastards figured it out at some point. And her blood holds the secret to all of it. Imagine a world where more vampires could walk the earth, where more bonds could form. Beautiful, don't you think?"

Nah.

It would be chaos. Endless wars. He wasn't fooling me for a second if he thought I'd buy into his bullshit of caring about the clans or vampire dynamics. Half-truths—that's all he ever gave.

"And if I bring Peach here, you'll tell me?"

His smile was pure evil, bone-chilling. My gut twisted with the certainty that bringing Peach here was the wrong move. I didn't want her to be hurt. Skylar liked her. I'd just pluck her from her clan, sit her in front of this glass, and it would be fine...but his smile said otherwise.

"Of course, you bring me Peachabelle, and I will tell you whatever you want."

"Fine. Deal—"

"Stay in wolf form for so long, you know that." Dayken's muffled voice carried from down the hall.

"I'll come back to you later."

I eased down the hall to where Dayken crouched with his elbows resting on his knees. He was in front of what had to be Aurora's cell.

Inside was a wolf I recognized from my childhood—beautiful, majestic, the white fur kissed with darker tones around her face and paws.

Aurora.

Traitorous shitbag.

I shouldn't wonder how long she'd been like that. It shouldn't matter to me. Let her turn feral for all I cared. She almost killed my precious Sacar. That was the absolute least she deserved.

And yet, I wondered how long she'd been in wolf form, anyway. I also started to wonder *why…*

"Fine. Too much of a coward to talk to me? Stay that way." Dayken stood up, his tone even and calm despite the storm I knew had to be brewing inside him.

Why did she do this to us?

Fuck it, I had to know.

I marched down the hall. Dayken whipped his head in my direction as he heard me coming. "Kolt—"

"Aurora! Godsdamn it! Get up right now and shift!" Before I had the chance to control or even think about my actions, I punched the glass. The impact made my teeth rattle. It hurt and didn't do shit to the glass, but it made me feel better. So, I did it again.

"Tell!" *Punch.* "Me!" *Punch.* "Now!" *Punch.* I never broke eye contact with her wolf, not even as fury burned through me, overtaking everything else.

She stirred but still didn't shift. I crouched down like Dayken had and jabbed my finger against the glass, completely lost in my sudden rage. Sometimes, it came so quickly and out of nowhere that all I could do was take a back seat and watch like an out-of-body experience.

"What's wrong? Feel guilty? Frustrated that your stupid fucking idea didn't work? Well, guess what, too fucking bad. Shift back NOW!" My voice hurt my own ears.

"She's not worth it, Kolton. Come on," Dayken said, his hand clamped on my shoulder. "I don't even know who that is anymore."

The whine that came from the cell shut us both up.

The silence was haunting. My raging on the glass didn't do anything, but Dayken's words got to her.

I looked over my shoulder at Dayken, my eyebrows raised in a way that said, *"Do it again."*

He got the hint. "It's true. I don't know you. Because my older sister, my most loving, doting sister, Aurora Danielson of the Danielson Clan, kin to Primarc Dayken Danielson, would never, *never* have done this. So, if you want me to know who you are, to even recognize you, then talk to me. Or I will leave and let this ghost of a person I used to know stay here to rot."

It only took a beat, and then the shift happened.

Before us, through the glass, was Aurora. She sat on the ground naked, her clothes behind her in a heap. She wrapped her arms around her legs, holding them tight and pressing her forehead to her knees. Her light brown hair was the most unkempt I'd ever seen it. The woman I knew had always been so prim and proper. Dayken was right. Who was this?

"Speak, Aurora," I said.

"I'm sorry." Her voice cracked.

"Sorry isn't good enough. I'm going to need a lot more from you than that," Dayken stated calmly, despite the tension in the air.

She dragged in a shaky breath, tears spilling down her face as she kept her eyes fixed on her brother. Dayken's jaw clenched, but he didn't move.

"H–he said they were deadly," she stammered. "He said they carried an infection that made them unlike normal vampires. And when they didn't need blood, when Onyx had those strange abilities, and when Sky read every book in our library within a few days...I thought maybe he was right. Maybe what I was seeing was a unique curse."

"Aurora, you couldn't have been so stupid to—" I snapped.

"Kolton, enough." Dayken's voice cut like a whip. His gaze never left his sister. "Keep going."

Aurora flinched, then swallowed hard.

"I questioned it, but he said he was the only one with the medicine to cure them. That if left untreated, they would start to get odd cravings and inevitably go on a murderous rampage. He said that they didn't feel the bond like other vampires. So, when she kept pushing you away, it just—" Her voice broke. "It just started to make sense."

"Aurora...come on." Dayken's voice cracked, heartbreak bleeding through. I almost felt pity for them. *Almost.* But any shred of kinship I felt toward his sister died on that battlefield the moment Crowe yanked her from his car.

"I thought I was protecting you!" she shrieked. "I thought if they were out of the picture, you would be safe. I realize now that I was manipulated, and I almost got them killed. I will live with that shame for the rest of my life. But that is what happened...I swear it on the clan; I swear it on Mom and Dad's graves."

Dayken inhaled sharply. I, on the other hand, didn't give a shit about a pile of bones rotting in the ground. Her words were worthless. Swearing on graves meant nothing.

"We have one purpose in this world," I snarled. "To protect. And you turned around and did the exact opposite!" Rage continued to burn up my throat, hot and sharp.

"I know!" Aurora sobbed, her gaze snapping to me. "Don't you think I see that now, Kolton? I won't make excuses for what I've done. But you must understand—" She jabbed a finger down the hall. "That *thing* is a monster. And as long as he lives, terrible things will keep happening."

As if we didn't know that already. I wanted to kill him the day we found him. But nooo, we had to keep him alive for questions. Look how well that turned out.

"And one more thing," she said, her voice hoarse. "If he asks about Peach...don't tell him anything." Then she shifted back to her wolf.

CHAPTER FOUR

O nce we got back to the compound, I headed straight to the security room to see if there was an update on Skylar. But instead of getting an update from the twins, I had to deal with Onyx.

It grated every time she insisted that she wanted her sister back more than I did, and it left me wanting to tell her that she was being a selfish cow.

"If you two start fighting again, I am going to shave my ears off my head and jam them down one of your throats, so I don't have to hear this bullshit anymore!" Derek's voice boomed, loud and uncharacteristically angry.

Instead of replying, Onyx stormed out of the security room. I paused, not because I cared about his ridiculous threat—or her temper tantrum—but because I'd never actually heard him yell like that. Not at me. Not at anyone. I must really be pushing him.

But here's the thing: I didn't care. If anything, it was validating to know I wasn't the only one teetering on the edge.

And let's be honest—the edge had a name: Onyx.

Skylar's sister could not be more infuriating if the heavens themselves had crafted her in a lab, stamped "perfect specimen of pure antagonism" on her forehead, and tossed her in my path.

Royal. Bitch.

Yeah, yeah, Skylar would lecture me for calling her that. Something about respecting women, not using words like that, blah blah. But let's break down the definition, shall we?

Bitch: A female dog, wolf, fox, or otter. Or to express displeasure or grumble.

The first part? Hilarious. She's bonded to a wolf, so she's basically halfway there already. The second part? Her entire personality. Always barking orders, always glaring, always in my business. Perfect fit.

Of course, I didn't say it out loud—not unless I wanted even more fucking stress in my life. But it didn't stop the word from gnawing at my skull while the tiger inside paced, hungry for a fight.

"Stop growling; it's distracting," Chase muttered without looking up.

Didn't realize I was, but fine. I'll let them think I'm in control.

I stormed out to grab something to eat. I couldn't remember the last time I consumed anything nutritional, and I knew Skylar would be upset with me about it. So, for her sake, I left the security room and went to the cafeteria.

Once inside, I discovered it bustling with Danielson Clan members, Mack Clan members, and a few Averie Clan members. I could pick them out by scent alone.

I tried to avoid any interactions so I could just grab something healthy to make Skylar happy, even though she wasn't here to witness my good decision-making skills—it still felt right...somehow.

"Sorry, no catnip here," one of the bears mocked, jarring me out of my spiraling thoughts.

I ignored him, because how fucking original.

Also, cats don't eat catnip, you stupid shit.

"What did you say, motherfucker?"

Whoops...guess I said that part out loud.

Well...looked like peace was not on the menu today.

I barreled into the security room and sank into the nearest office chair, causing it to rock back. I looked at the stupid apple in my hand and tore into it. The crunch echoed louder than necessary. I redirected my glare to the screens mounted to the wall and did everything in my power not to think about how the bears in the cafeteria had outnumbered me twenty minutes ago. I swiped at my nose to make sure the bleeding had stopped. A quick check of my hand confirmed my nose was already healed.

Fucking bears...they smelled, by the way. Like musk and swamp mud. I've told Mack that more times than I can count, but she just grinned and waved me off like hygiene didn't matter when you're built like a brick wall. She always was too loyal for her own good. Too bad about what happened to her...I wonder why no one has received word on her condition yet.

I clenched the apple in my hand a little too hard, and juice dripped down my arm as my temper boiled over. Skylar would want me to eat this, so I'd better not destroy it.

I didn't enjoy fighting with the bears—or Skylar's sister, for that matter. But if people would stop constantly testing my patience, it wouldn't have to come to this. It wasn't my fault I'd lost control of the tiger inside me...was it? I never did figure out how that worked exactly.

I resumed glaring at the monitor as juice from the apple continued to trickle down onto the arm of the chair.

Chase lounged next to me in that overly ergonomic seat he insisted wasn't a gaming chair, while Derek stood behind him like a statue, his wings stretched wide as if to make himself look bigger.

I didn't acknowledge them. Instead, I used my feet to roll the chair forward and positioned myself close enough to see the monitors but far enough to avoid being dragged into whatever mess these two were undoubtedly cooking up.

"Is Kolton sick?" Chase asked, almost conversationally.

Oh, wonderful. They were going to talk about me like I wasn't sitting right there.

"Sick?" Derek drawled, feathers fluffing. "I don't think madness qualifies as the kind of sickness you're asking about...at least not technically."

Chase tilted his head. "Yeah...madness sums it up pretty well."

"I CAN HEAR YOU, ASSHOLES!" I snapped, glaring between them.

"Good, then hear this. I mean it in the sincerest way possible: you are criminally fucking insane!" Derek barked back, louder, obnoxious, daring me to snap.

Juice splattered as the apple crumbled in my grip. "You two sound like you're diagnosing yourselves."

Derek smirked. "If the fur fits, Kolton. And don't try any deflection on me; I watch *a lot* of Dr. Phil."

"Sure, but you've got feathers," I bit out, gesturing at his wings.

"And you've got stripes. What's your point?"

"My point is you don't exactly scream *sanity* either, bird boy."

"Derek, stop arguing with him," Chase murmured calmly, but with a flicker of amusement. "You're proving his point right now."

All I wanted to do was just sit here and not talk to anyone. Did that have to be so hard?

But silence never lasted long. Not in my head.

"Why do you do that?"

"Do what?" I asked, though I knew exactly what she meant.

"Just sit here in this hallway, refusing to look at me, talk to me, or engage with anyone, really."

I said nothing. She didn't need to know the storm in my head. Didn't need the weight of the rot inside me. If she ever figured it out, she might carve her marking out of her chest and throw it at me. And I couldn't live with that.

"It's driving me mad, Kolton," she whispered, almost pleading.

Well, welcome to madness, Skylar. Didn't want it for you, but here we are—sharing that little piece of hell. I chuckled at the irony of the memory that lingered like smoke, choking me.

"Hello? Oh great, now he's catatonic."

Chase's voice yanked me out of it.

Act normal. Nod. Don't snap. Just pretend I've got my shit together.

Then her laugh slid in like a knife, bright and haunting. Clear. Beautiful. Mine.

It cut through everything, not in this room, not in this world, but too real to deny.

I had to get her back. Again.

At least...to tell her that I loved her laugh.

The glow of the monitor flickered against my skin. The hum of the fan felt suffocating now. I couldn't sit here. Not another second.

I shoved out of the chair, stormed down the hall into the room Dayken had given me and yanked open drawers. Clothes. Phone. Water bottle. All stuffed into a bag with Skylar's voice in my head, nagging me to "stay hydrated," like she was still there.

Slinging the pack over my shoulder, I strode for the exit. Cold determination drowned out the voice screaming at me to stop.

"Where are you going?"

Godsdamn it.

I turned and found glacial eyes, cold and piercing. Not intimidating—though they were—but unbearable because they looked too much like hers.

"You seem pretty smart, Ox," I muttered, letting the nickname cut. "I think you can figure it out."

Her brow arched, steady and unflinching. "So even though you were specifically told to wait for movement on the live feed, you're planning on heading out anyway?"

"The story goes, Skylar's mother was holding her, and your mother was holding you. You two saw each other, and the mark appeared on the back of

your neck. There is no record of a baby being able to pick a Guardian. It's unheard of and goes against everything we were taught," Mrs. Danielson said as she ruffled my hair. "You are special, Kolton. Don't ever question it."

"No," was all I said, jarring myself away from that memory. I forgot what she was asking me, but no matter what was said while I was lost in my own mind, it was probably a fitting response, given the bullshit swirling around this compound like a toilet bowl.

Onyx didn't miss a beat. "No one, and I repeat no one, wants my sister back more than me. But you can't just storm every clan demanding answers. Trust me, if that were an option, I would have taken it already."

Looked like 'no' was the correct answer.

"Aren't you a saint?" I seethed. Her eyes dilated, turning into those eerie slits.

"Far from it. Now answer me honestly this time. Are you planning on looking for Sky or not?"

I nodded. What was the point of lying now?

"Good," she said after a beat, her voice like steel. "I'm coming with you."

I opened my mouth to argue, but the look in her eyes stopped me cold. Onyx wasn't asking.

Which meant I had two options.

One: pick a fight with her and risk blowing my shot of going after Skylar. Two: accept my fate, keep walking, and hope she gets bored.

The choice should've been obvious.

I chose violence.

CHAPTER FIVE

It's been three days since they took me. At least, I think it has been. Hard to tell with no windows—just the endless silver walls and my own heartbeat to count the time. My captors' intentions are still a mystery to me. They are...nice to me. Too nice. Fresh blood bags, clean clothes, crisp bedding. The whole place gleams, sterile and well-constructed, nothing like the cement cells they left Onyx and me to rot in at the facility. This feels more like a temporary hold than a prison, and that is what unsettles me most. No one builds a cage this polished without specific plans for its use.

So many questions clawed through my brain, too many to catch just one before the next tore through. My mind felt like a storm, but that was fine. The chaos gave me purpose. They don't know I have a secret—my own little ace tucked away, waiting for the right moment to be played. And that moment? It was coming soon. Which brought me to my current situation—

"I could give you the world—you just have to ask," he said smugly, arms crossing over his broad chest. The fabric of his suit jacket stretched taut with the motion. Clearly, he bought it a size too small, and not by accident.

So unnecessary.

When I didn't respond, refusing to take the bait, his posture shifted. Subtle, but there. Agitation.

He tried again, this time throwing his arms wide. "Tell me what you want, and I'll make it happen. You want money? Jewelry? Gems and stones of any size, or is it power you desire?"

He splayed his fingers, flashing the glint of his gaudy rings. I resisted the urge to scoff.

Still, I said nothing.

"Just name it," he snapped, frustration bleeding into his tone.

Situations like this required precision. When someone spoke from emotion, not reason, that's when you had to read them carefully.

Reading people was one of my strengths—one that complemented my other, more hidden talents. It wasn't just about body language. You had to feel their aura. Study what they didn't say. Trace the tension in their silences. Decipher the truths buried between their words.

Take him, for example.

He was asking what I wanted—not because he actually cared. He wanted leverage.

But he already had leverage. I was his captive. That alone gave him power over me—and more importantly, over my family, who were no doubt trying to find me.

So why did he need more? Why me, specifically?

Because there was something I had that he needed?

Something only I could give?

Perhaps.

I'd need to keep playing along if I wanted to find out.

"A book," I said confidently, squaring my shoulders for my all-too-familiar request.

"What?" He looked genuinely thrown.

"A book. I would like a book. It is very boring here, and since I doubt I'd be able to physically escape, I'd like to escape into a story." My tone was flat, almost bored, masking the intricate web I was starting to weave.

My request seemed to offend him further.

"Oh, am I boring you? Isn't that rich?!" His golden eyes flashed, a warning I wasn't about to heed. Provoking an enemy could be precarious, but I needed to throw him off guard. I wanted to know what I was working with, how far I could push him.

"If you do not wish me to be bored, you could always release me," I said. "I could return to my family."

"Not an option." He smirked again, as if this was all a game. "But fine; I'll play. You want a book? Let's make a deal."

Now *this* was familiar to me.

Dangling my request like bait. The monsters at the facility used to do that all the time.

If I behaved and let them take what they wanted—blood, tissue, organs—then maybe I'd earn the next book in whatever series I was reading.

"What's the deal?" I asked, deadpan.

No emotion. Just like how I survived before.

"Say something nice about me. And in exchange, I'll give you a book."

Surely this was some sort of trick. What game was he playing?

I stared at him. Said nothing.

A flicker of uncertainty crossed his face before he could mask it. He lifted his chin and arched a brow. He was serious, and that quick flash of doubt told me everything I needed to know. As strange as it seemed, he really was just trying to get me to like him.

Now that I'd figured that out, I just needed to determine why.

I squared my shoulders, stood tall, and exhaled slowly before I said, "Your eyes are a nice color."

Pride and satisfaction flickered there, his pulse quickening just enough to notice.

But instead of closing the distance between us, he turned to leave.

He could have forced himself on me, or at least tried, but he didn't. I misread his intentions again. That unsettled me more than I wanted to admit.

He left without another word, but his footsteps echoed longer than they should have after the door closed behind him. I studied the sound, measuring the weight and the pace. Any detail could be useful later. Every detail was a weapon.

When a different set of footsteps approached, heavier and less certain, I recognized them before the door clicked open. It was the man who stood guard outside my door. I didn't have a chance to get a good look at him before now, but I recognized the long hair he kept tied back. He had a book clutched in his hand.

I watched him as he crossed the room and handed it to me without a word. I normally would have thanked him—manners got you further than defiance—but I was too busy studying him.

He avoided eye contact, shoulders tense, jaw tight. The book wasn't heavy, yet his arm strained like it was.

Why did I make him so uncomfortable?

I turned the book over in my hands as he retreated and the lock clicked back into place.

Origin Story: The Original Brothers.

I sighed.

The title pulled me back to when I turned an old office at the compound into a library. It had been pitiful—schematics for outdated servers, a vacuum manual, and half a set of twenty-year-old encyclopedias. Still, I wanted it to feel like Dayken's library someday, filled with the same kind of history. I remembered sitting there in silence, devouring those ancient texts.

How Lunce, in an act of desperation, found a way to change a village girl into a creature like himself and convinced her to bear his children. Every one of them was born cursed, just like him.

Lunce was fascinating, but Avont was the brother who caught my interest—the first to bind his life force to animals, an echo of the ritual their grandmother used on their father.

It made me think of my tiger, causing an ache in my chest.

I tossed the book to the foot of the bed. I'd read it before.

I hated when that happened.

CHAPTER SIX

A lot of people wondered why I was so "crazy." They didn't always say it out loud, but I could feel it in the way they looked at me, their unspoken judgment like an itch under my skin. It didn't help that I looked the part with my unnatural hair and bright eyes. I was often accused of dyeing my hair or wearing contacts.

Neither was true.

My tiger gene just ran abnormally strong. As for being unhinged, the truth is I didn't know when that started, or why.

Maybe it was always there, like the gene mutation that causes Guardians to go feral. Maybe they were connected. I was no scientist, so

I couldn't pretend to theorize. But what I did know is that I was the only living tiger—a rare species among Guardians. Chosen as a Guardian at an unheard-of age, my discipline and strength training began as far back as I could remember. After my parents died, the Danielsons took me in. They fought for me so that I could be assimilated into a wolf clan, the only way for me to survive at the time.

Then the DeStephano lion clan came sniffing around. Fresh off the boat from Italy, they came to carve space for their clan in Detroit's auto industry. Leo's father was the Primarc at the time. He wanted the lone tiger, badly, but the Danielsons knew the entire clan was trouble. They shielded me, stuck their necks out for me. The lions made offer after offer, all of which were rejected. The DeStephano Clan claimed I'd be better off with them. The Danielsons disagreed wholeheartedly.

Maybe the lions were right. But the way they escalated things? Putting a hit out on Dayken's parents? That was enough for me to know I'd never be one of them.

It was my fault they were dead. Dayken would never say it out loud, but that's when things really started to splinter. That's when I started to...shift.

Wolves growled. I hissed.

They whined. I purred.

They used their claws as tools. Mine were a retractable weapon.

The differences were small, but they added up. Little fractures that widened over time until I became a stranger among my own pack. An outcast from the start.

When I finally went searching for Skylar, what had been a slippery slope became an icy cliff. Everything I did to find her pushed me further into madness. And the worst part? I knew it was happening. I watched myself slipping, powerless to stop the fall.

Now, lying here, staring at the ceiling, it was all I could think about. Sleep would not come. My body was tired, but my mind kept pulling me backward, dragging me to places I'd rather not revisit. Onyx was right to suggest we wait to leave, despite the brawl it caused, I was man enough to admit she was right as we gathered more information and waited for nightfall. It was also unnecessary of her to remind me of my previous failures in trying to find Skylar...but despite that, she was right. even though I would never give her the satisfaction of admitting it. It was hard enough admitting it to myself, especially after she kicked my ass earlier when I couldn't shut my mouth about her trailing after me. Moving in the dead of night made sense. Animals hunted in the dark, while humans were armed, alert, and far more dangerous in the daylight.

Maybe that was why I couldn't look at humans the same way anymore. It wasn't guilt that ate at me. I didn't see their faces in my dreams, nor did I hear echoes of their screams. What I felt wasn't regret. It wasn't even hate. It was something colder.

And maybe that was what unsettled me the most. That quiet absence of remorse. It was the reason I was still awake. The reason I will never let Sky all the way in. Because underneath everything else, one truth remained.

I liked it...the darkness.

"Kolton?"

I jerked upright.

That voice. I knew that voice.

My room was gone. I wasn't in bed anymore.

I was barefoot on...sand.

Not Michigan sand. It had the wrong texture, wrong color and lacked the familiar pebbles and rocks.

This was finer. Paler. And the breeze smelled like salt, not pine.

California.

I blinked slowly. Huh. *Guess I fell asleep after all, just lucid and aware.*

A wave crept up the shore, curling close to my toes before slinking back. I watched the foam retreat, the hiss of it louder than my heartbeat.

"Kolton."

There it was again. Her voice. But I didn't look.

Didn't want to.

Instead, I studied the rhythm of the tide. One wave. Then another. It was hypnotic, almost peaceful.

"Kolton!"

"Repeating my name over and over again is so unoriginal," I muttered, gaze still locked on the water. My voice sounded tired even to me. I could dream better than this...

"Oh, good, you can hear me."

Her voice was closer now, like she was whispering straight into my ear.

I tensed but didn't move.

I just let the next wave roll in. Let it almost touch me. Let it remind me I was somewhere else, somewhere peaceful, even if only for a moment.

I heard a sigh, frustrated and familiar.

Anxiously, I turned to see the source of it. But I moved too fast, nearly slipping in the sand and almost falling to one knee.

There she was.

Skylar.

"What the hell," I breathed.

"Oh good, you can see me, too." She beamed, those perfect little fangs showing.

Gods, I loved when she smiled like that.

I scowled, glowering down at her. "I need to wake up. This is absolutely fucked."

"Well, nice to see you too." She huffed, hands going to her hips.

And that's when I noticed what she was wearing.

A nightie.

White and silky, almost sheer in the moonlight...

Why? Why of all the things my damaged brain could conjure, would I imagine Skylar on a beach in a white nightie?

It clung to her, made her skin glow. Like moonlight incarnate.

"Look, I don't think I have long, but I need to tell you—"

"Wake up, wake up, wake up," I chanted, backing away. Smacking my head like that would work. Desperately clinging to some sliver of sanity.

She sighed, exasperated. "Stop hitting yourself. Or else I'm gonna do it for you. Would you please just listen for one second?"

My smirk was instant. The shift in my mood immediate. The memory of the time she slapped me flared bright in my head. Her fire. Her fury. The way she stared me down. Or up, I suppose, since she was so short. Then I felt the sting of her palm colliding with my cheek.

"Oh, Skylar," I said, voice low, teasing. "I love when you're rough with me. You're not threatening me. You're tempting *me."*

I could admit that to her here; this was just a dream. I could speak words I never dared to in real life.

Her eyes brightened, pupils dilating into slits. Her breath caught. I watched the pulse in her neck thrum harder and harder. Her reaction made my tiger purr with delight.

"Oh, you like that little secret?" I took a step closer. "Would you like to hear more about what I like?"

She nodded once. Then she blinked and shook herself out of the daze she'd unwittingly slipped into. "Kolton, listen," she said, as if I wasn't already hanging onto her every word. "I'm okay. I'm slowly figuring him out. When the time comes...I need you to control yourself. Okay?"

I had no idea what she meant. No idea which "him" she referred to. Didn't care. I was so close, already reaching for her. My thumb brushed the strap of her nightie. I liked dream Skylar. Hell, I liked the real one, too, but here I could touch her skin.

It was soft.

"Kolton, please."

That didn't sound dreamlike. That felt...real.

I yanked my hand back instantly, locking eyes with her. She looked frantic, panicked, like her gaze could say everything her words couldn't. The look gutted me. This wasn't how I would dream of her, and I wanted to fix it.

Before I could speak, the dream shattered.

The fluorescent lights above my bed were still on.

My *dream* was over, but somehow it felt like I never slept at all.

CHAPTER SEVEN

I couldn't take it.

I thought my mind might finally break.

Skylar was haunting me.

Literally.

She was invading my dreams now. And she didn't belong inside my head.

That's where I kept the dark shit. The bad memories. The violence.

They lived there, caged within a vault in my mind, so only I could enter to pay a visit to my demons.

Skylar didn't belong anywhere near it.

Sometimes the darkness won too. And when it did, I remembered things I swore I'd locked away.

The chair groaned as I pressed down on it with my knee. I braced myself on the backrest with my free hand while my other hand tightened around the hilt of my blade, still slick with blood. His muffled screams had become background noise, just ambient buzz in the room. I wasn't even sure what I was asking from him anymore. Answers, confessions, apologies all blurred together after a while. What mattered was control.

I pressed the steel against his skin, slow enough that he felt every drag as his flesh opened. His breath hitched, short and shallow. The sound filled the room, a melody only I could appreciate. I leaned in closer, so close I could smell the sour sweat rolling down his neck. Close enough to hear the small, broken noises he tried to swallow.

"You think this ends when you break," I whispered. "But I don't want you broken. I want you aware...for every thought. Every nerve ending. Every sound. And most importantly, every feeling."

The tiger in me purred at that, deep and hungry. There was a sick satisfaction in knowing how long a body could tremble without completely giving out. How much agony a mind could take before the person begged for mercy. Mercy he was never going to get.

I shook myself. The vault slammed shut, and the memory vanished, leaving nothing but the echo of his screams ringing in my ears.

No...Skylar couldn't get anywhere near that.

I didn't know why my subconscious decided now, of all times, to conjure her face. I never dreamed of her before. Not once. Not in all the years we had been bonded, which was extremely long and uniquely early, apparently.

Unheard of.

So rare.

They'll be unstoppable...

All that crap. And yet...

Not a single dream.

Maybe because I couldn't picture her face. It was always just a pull I felt instead. A need. An ache under my skin that screamed, *Find her.*

And I did.

Finally.

Only to fucking lose her again.

Such a failure.

Before I could stop myself, I smacked my forehead. Hard.

Too hard, honestly, but it silenced the thoughts. For a second, at least.

Now I just felt the sting of a welt forming. And then the image of her from the dream came back. The way her icy eyes stared through me.

The bond always seemed to burn hotter in memories of her looking at me that way. Like fire pressing against my ribs, demanding I move, demanding I find her *now*. It made me want to claw my chest open, just to ease the ache.

I started pacing, rubbing the bond mark at the back of my neck. My incessant need to keep checking that it was still there in the mirror temporarily subsided with the gesture.

The presence of the mark was my only way of knowing that she was alive, because if she wasn't, there would be no eight-petal flower on my neck.

Too soon, my fingers began to twitch, desperate to yank at my hair, anything to feel something other than this misery crawling through my bones. misery for losing her again, misery for my violence clouding my memories, and misery for feeling utterly helpless.

A jarring beep cut through the air, pulling me from my spiral.

Right.

I forgot that I had gone into the security room. Which meant Chase probably saw the whole thing. My downward spiral, in real time. Whatever. He had seen worse. I had done worse in the short time I was here.

I was pretty sure I came here to see if Derek was ready to leave to get more intel from a nearby clan. But thoughts were jarred by a loud sound coming from a speaker attached to a security monitor.

"What the fuck is that noise?" I demanded. Not exactly the sanest of greetings, but there we were.

"The gate," Chase said.

I waited for more.

Nothing.

I shoved into his space, leaning toward the monitors.

A truck.

Not *the* truck. But familiar.

"Titus?" I asked.

"Yes," came Chase's clipped reply.

The fox. Of course. Arms dealer. Weapons master. Sly bastard who always seemed to walk away unscathed. What the hell was he doing here? It was like three o'clock in the morning. Did he not realize we were in the middle of a full-blown crisis? Now was not the time to peddle weapons or make trades to increase his profit margins.

Titus had a reputation. Charming. Clever. Dangerous. Every rumor painted him as always being one step ahead of his adversaries, and I hated him for that alone. Men like that never broke. Never bled. Never woke up haunted by laughter that wasn't theirs to keep.

I stormed up the stairs, ready to tell his greedy ass to fuck off; never mind I had no authority to do that, only to discover Onyx already intercepting him at the loading dock. Of course. No doubt her obnoxious hearing picked up the rumble of his engine before the cameras even caught his arrival.

I still wasn't used to that. It was unsettling when someone told you things before they happened.

Onyx was unsettling.

If I were being honest, she creeped me the hell out.

But I pushed my ill-willed feelings of Onyx aside and walked over to the docks. I tried to stay still but ended up pacing back and forth between the massive metal doors that stretched into the ceiling, listening to the conversation unfold.

"Tell me what you know," Onyx demanded.

Titus, to his credit, didn't skip a beat in making his own demands.

"First, tell me where Peach is."

I shoved down a hiss that tried to crawl up my throat. How dare this motherfucker come to the compound and make demands.

"I already told you, she's fine. She is with the Mack Cl—"

"Without her Guardian!" Titus bellowed.

I had to raise an eyebrow at that. Where was this rage coming from? Did the fool fall in love or something? He was acting like he had a stake in needing to keep Peach safe, and since they weren't bonded, that only left two options for Titus.

Feelings or money.

I was getting the vibe that this wasn't about a weapons deal.

Gross.

Feelings were something I neither had the time for nor gave a fuck about. The way I saw it, the fox had information I needed, and it was time for him to hand it over. Even if I had to hurt him to get it.

"Speak now, fox, or you start losing body parts. I am a big fan of removing ears first," I said as I stepped outside, claws splayed. I probably should not have disclosed that fun fact, but that was fine. Apparently, I was unhinged enough that no one batted an eye at my confession.

Yay me.

Titus inhaled a steadying breath. "We will be discussing why Peach needs to stay here later." He pointed a finger aggressively at the ground where he stood before continuing. "But for now, I came here to tell you about a conversation I just had."

CHAPTER EIGHT

Titus spoke softly, in a hushed tone, as if he were afraid to admit what he came here to say.

"I was on the phone with Leo earlier today. He sounded...off. Rushed. Distracted. Not his normal, calculated self. Then I heard muffled voices in the background; someone was definitely talking about needing to make a run to the hospital."

He paused, jaw tightening as his mind worked.

"At first, I brushed it off. But the more I thought about it, the more it didn't sit right. We don't go to hospitals."

His eyes met mine—cold, calculating. His light brown irises practically glowed as he carefully chose his next words.

"Anything we need, we handle in-house. Medical aid, rehabilitation, even trauma response. We're set up for everything."

The words landed heavily. There was a physical shift in the air that could be felt; everything became too sensitive, too heightened, the fluorescent lights of the dock buzzing a little too loudly against the silence.

My stomach bottomed out as realization punched through me.

My tiger began assaulting my mind, roaring with fury.

A low, animal rumble filled my ears even though nothing else moved.

"Blood," I said with a deadly calm I didn't feel.

Onyx froze at the word. Not a breath. Not a sound. Just a shared silence as the pieces clicked together, fast and sudden.

"That motherfucker! Are you sure you heard everything correctly?" Onyx asked.

It was a valid question. I didn't trust the fox as far as I could throw him.

And honestly? In fox form, I could probably toss his smug little ass across a football field—so maybe not the best metric. But I still didn't trust him. Not one godsdamn bit.

Still, the logic was sound, especially after he doubled down on what he heard.

And I couldn't think of a reason for lying to us that would benefit Titus; we had made deals and were mutually benefiting from each other.

Because...of course it was *him*.

Leo. Fucking. DeStephano.

That slick-haired, gold-chain-wearing, walking STD of a lion. Just the thought of his greasy, manicured fingers anywhere near Skylar—

My brain short-circuited. Thoughts and questions scrambled in a thousand different directions, but one kept coming back loud and clear...

What if he touched her?

No. Worse—what if he hurt her?

I'd be on the news. Massacre-level rage. Full-blown village wiped off the map type of vengeance.

"Kolton."

I could bury the bodies. I've got claws. I was good at digging.

"Kolton."

Graves didn't need to be that deep if no one was looking. I knew that well enough.

"KOLTON!"

Onyx's voice cracked through the haze in my head, snapping me out of my bloodlust.

"WHAT?!" I snapped, blinking hard. Why was I the one getting yelled at?

"We need to go."

Right. Yes.

I just needed Skylar.

Wait—no. I needed her back. I needed Skylar back.

I clenched my jaw and turned to the fox. "Agreed. Where is he?"

"Leland," Titus said, curt as ever. "That's where he usually holes up. But I doubt he'll make it easy."

"Then let's make it hard," I said. "Send the falcons to scout ahead. We find him. We end this."

"Do you know for a fact that he's in Leeland?" Dayken asked as he turned the corner. He must have sensed the adrenaline spike in Onyx because the concerned look on his face was enough to make me puke. "I know he has more than one property on Michigan's west side: Manistee, Bear Lake, that ugly beach house in Onekama. Why Leeland?"

"Because it's the furthest away from the clans. He hasn't been spotted at any of those other locations in some time, and I keep tabs on all my business dealings. That is the one location I can't get to. He keeps that peninsula heavily guarded, and the tourists give him solid cover. So, it's a simple process of elimination."

"Well, the faster we get this mission in the air, the faster we can find out if he is in Leeland," Dayken said as he pointed at nearby Averie clan members posted up in nearby trees. Dayken thanked Titus for coming to us with the information, and then the fox was back in his truck, driving off the property. As we made our way back inside, I couldn't help but notice our footsteps sounded crisper than usual on the narrow shaft of stairs leading down into the compound. There were barely any lights in this stairwell, intentionally kept dark for security reasons. My tiger didn't mind the darkness, though; it adjusted effortlessly. The others followed suit, and honestly, I didn't mind the company this time.

I didn't trust myself to go on this mission alone. I'd leave a trail of bodies that rivaled my time in California. And we didn't have time for the type of attention that would come from that level of violence.

So instead of admitting my homicidal tendencies, I simply nodded when Onyx suggested that Derek and Chase's cousin fly to Leeland, gather any intel she could, and then report back.

It was easy enough. But of course, Onyx couldn't leave easy enough alone.

"Did we just agree on something?" Her tone was almost playful in her disbelief. "Is it possible for us to have finally found common ground, Kolton?"

I didn't want her to get her hopes up, but a bit of shame hit me. I didn't know why Onyx bothered me so much. At the end of the day, we had the exact same goal. Keeping Skylar safe. And at that moment, getting her back. Immediately.

"I'm sorry for always calling you a bitch," I muttered, head hanging low, unable to meet her eyes. The confession came out before I could stop it.

"Wait. What? How many times have you ca—"

"I'll be in the lobby, waiting for the falcons' return," I said, cutting her off before she could finish her question. "And she better hurry."

Instead of pacing like I really wanted to, I sank into a cushiony chair that looked like it didn't belong in the warehouse-style compound. But I know who wanted it here. I know she wanted it, and I know how much its presence meant to her. So, I ran my hands up and down the arms of the chair without even realizing it. Like that gentle touch could somehow translate into the words I could never say. I care. More than I should, about her happiness...I tucked my head back against the headrest, closing my eyes to compose myself. Onyx and Dayken would be back any second with reinforcements.

CHAPTER NINE

Leo sat casually in a plain, leather chair near my bed. The chair was a recent addition to my prison cell, probably brought here for this exact reason. I sat cross-legged on the bed with my back against the headboard, watching and waiting. Sitting like that, in the nightie they kept me in, I was well aware of the amount of exposed skin on display, but I refused to appear modest. In this situation, it felt like modesty would somehow be seen as a sign of weakness. Weakness was not an option. At this point, I planned to treat every moment, every interaction, between us as a power play.

So, there I sat, bare and exposed, in nothing but the thin, nearly see-through attire they gave me—in front of the Primarc of the

DeStephano Clan—trying to piece him together like a puzzle. But it felt like I was missing the corner pieces, failing yet again to understand *why*.

Leo sized me up from his seat, purposefully showing mild interest. I didn't get a sense of desire from him. More like, from what I was reading, I was a means to an end, there to satisfy his goals in other ways. That was the energy he gave off during all of our interactions. Disinterest mixed with need. So complex, and so difficult to figure out. So, a new plan formed. Let's see what happened when his disinterest was mixed with anger.

"Are your needs being met, my dear?" He casually twisted one of his gold rings, adjusting it so it lay properly on his finger. "Anything I can get you?"

"It's quite ugly in here." I let my gaze guide his to the bland, silver-plated walls. "Pretty lame, actually."

"E–excuse me?" My abrupt comment succeeded in catching him off guard. Perfect, now I got to analyze a different side of him. "First I bore you, now; all of this is ugly?" He gestured his hand around the room.

"It's just *so* shiny, and yet so dull," I said in a mocking tone.

"This took years to craft. Do you have any idea what you are sitting on?"

A clue. Time to start ruffling his mane.

"A shame. I can only guess it was expensive. I would have at least gotten my money's worth if it were me." I pat the bed for emphasis. "Even the bed I had, in a previously abandoned building, that they got from who knows where, was much more comfortable than this."

Rage flashed in his mocha eyes. His pupils dilated into thin slits, similar to Kolton's. They weren't as thin as Onyx's or mine, but it was enough to accentuate the unique color of his eyes.

"Then I shall get you a used, donated mattress, since luxury doesn't appear to be your taste," he fired back.

"No need; I like the floor plenty enough." I smiled, letting my fangs show. Peach always told me how cute I looked when I did that.

Frustration replaced his rage. He stood abruptly, the chair sliding back with the momentum of his movement. He stared at me with fury, and I prepared for a strike. I could handle that. I had been struck across the face more times than I could count. I didn't even know if I would feel it at this point.

Instead of the sound of a crack across my cheek, his feet started moving, and he stormed out. I let myself sink back against the bed, eyes closing as I tried to steady my breath and take inventory of all the information I extracted.

He didn't want to physically harm me and...

"Years to craft."

His words pinged around in my head.

Why would you spend years building a place like this?

I couldn't have been the intended prisoner since I was locked up in the facility. Right?

My mind raced with different scenarios. I wished I had someone to talk to. Technically, I did, but that would require sleep, and sleep was not an easy thing these days. I had to remind myself that it wasn't about rest. No. Instead, I was attempting to hunt down Kolton in the only place I could reach him—my dreams.

In Dayken and Aurora's library, I had found a text that changed everything. The bond wasn't just something granted to a Guardian by their Sacar; it was a living, breathing thing, deeper than anyone realized.

Matching heartbeats...shared essence. Those lines had burned them-selves into my memory.

And what better way to test the strength of the bond than in REM sleep, when the body slows and the heart finds a steady rhythm? If his heart was tethered to mine, then maybe, just maybe I could follow the connection straight to him.

I planned on calling it REM jumping and mentally recording my success thus far. Because, you know, science. But the unsettling thing about REM jumping was the lost sense of time. Minutes could stretch into hours, and hours could vanish in a blink. Drifting in that liminal space felt like gambling with reality.

So, I lay still, willing my thoughts to quiet, listening for the echo inside my chest that wasn't entirely my own. My body relaxed, and I was taken to another place. Transparent, mine to mold.

I pulled, and then I tugged on the bond again.

But the longer I was alone in the static, the more I started to worry that he might not be sleeping tonight.

I pulled one more time, ready to wake up when his form began to solidify, as real as if he were here with me in the silver room.

"There you are! I've been waiting forever."

Kolton looked just as wild as ever—untamed, feral—my unpredictable tiger. A flutter stirred in my chest. I enjoyed not knowing what he'd say or do next, or even what type of mood he'd be in. It made everything feel alive, electric. And those eyes—those strange, bright yellow eyes were magical and lured me in every time.

His scowl deepened as he took me in, like I was something dangerous and unfamiliar to him.

"Why are you haunting me right now?" he muttered, raking a hand through his unruly orange hair. "Seriously. Why now? Is my guilt conjuring you?"

"You don't think I'm real?" I asked, confused. Surely, he could feel this—feel me—*like I felt him. I stepped forward and placed my hand on his chest, right above the steady rhythm of his heart.*

"You don't feel this connection?" I asked, looking up into his eyes. But instead of looking at me, he just closed his eyes. I watched as his jaw tightened. He didn't speak. Instead, he lifted his hand and held it over mine, pressing my palm deeper to his chest. Like it hurt, but he wanted more anyway.

His eyes slid open, just barely, and he took a deep, steady inhale, as if to breathe me in. "You can't be real. You wouldn't let me touch you like this if you were."

I smiled gently. "That's just silly. See?"

I slid my hand up to his shoulder. His hand stayed firmly over mine, following along, and then, once I was sure I was steady, I rose up on my toes and kissed his cheek—soft and slow. I let my lips linger just long enough so he could feel it. Just a whisper of contact. Enough to prove I was really there.

His eyes flew open. Gone were his human eyes, replaced with his tiger's slitted ones instead. His mouth parted slightly, revealing the large fangs on top and the smaller ones along the bottom. I couldn't help but admire his beauty. How deadly and wild it was at the same time. When I was stuck in my cell at the facility, I loved reading about tigers. I learned so much about them, and it made sense now—my bond to him was being fulfilled through reading. Or so I told myself.

"The Skylar I know would never be bold enough to kiss her pet tiger," *he said, voice low, husky.*

"Well, this Sky wants her tiger to pay attention. So, I'm willing to do whatever it takes."

"Whatever it takes?" he purred. The sound was soft and rough at the same time—part human, part animal—and it made my breath catch.

He finally let go of my hand. With a confident grace, he gently trailed his hand down my body, lower and lower, before slowly brushing it over my hip and curling his arm around my waist with unexpected tenderness…then yanking me against him with a force that knocked the air from my lungs. I slammed into his chest, hands rising instinctively to brace myself.

"Tell me," he whispered against my ear. "Tell me what you're willing to do."

I never saw this side of Kolton before, this tender yet demanding part of him. Did he yearn for physical touch more than he was letting on? Without second-guessing myself, I ran a hand along his cheek. He leaned into it like a cat begging for attention—unthinking, instinctual. His purring grew louder. The sound was so at odds with the tense lines of his body and the overpowering grip he had on my hips. It made my chest ache, knowing how much he warred with himself.

"I'd do anything to get your attention, Kolton. Because I want this rescue mission you're planning to actually work," I said, trying to stay on track. Trying, and probably failing, to focus on something other than the thrill he was currently giving me.

He inhaled sharply, still letting me stroke his face. I gently threaded my fingers into the soft hair behind his ear. Little wisps stuck out at odd angles as I tried to gently tame them down.

"I'm listening," he said thickly. "Just don't stop touching me."

Finally feeling confident that I had his full attention, I said, "Listen closely, okay?"

He barely nodded in acknowledgment.

"When you come here, don't storm in like a savage. Come like you intend to ally yourself with Leo. I'm close—so close—to figuring out why he took me. There's more at play here, something bigger than just us."

He locked his eyes with mine; they were glowing. Hungry. "Whatever you say."

"I'm serious, Kolton. I need you to be on your best behavior. Strategic. And I know Onyx won't like it, but you should come here without her."

He nodded, but I could tell he wasn't absorbing a word I was saying. My fingers stilled.

His frown deepened. "Why'd you stop?"

"Because you're not listening."

He scowled. "But it's my dream. I want you to keep going. Why isn't it working?"

"Because this is real, you stubborn-ass jungle cat."

He blinked.

"Wait—you swore. I wouldn't have you swear in my dreams."

His eyes went wide, as if I'd just sprouted horns. He stumbled back a step, throwing his hands up in mock surrender as if to say, I didn't touch you.

"I can feel you," he breathed.

"No shit, Sherlock."

"This is real..."

"Yes! Damn it, Kolton. You are infuriating."

He looked like he might actually puke.

CHAPTER TEN

I snapped awake, breathing ragged, like I'd just run a marathon. I shot up from the chair as if it was on fire.

Fuck. Fuck. Fuck.

That was really her.

Skylar.

She found me in my dreams, of all places. How the fuck did she do that?

I let her touch me.

My hand rose instinctively to my face, where her soft, perfect lips had been just seconds ago.

She'd hate herself for that if she knew about the darkness living inside me.

"Please, please! I have a family!" Blood poured from the gash above his eyebrow. The kitchen lighting made the falling drops reflect off the tiled floor.

Head wounds...always so dramatic.

The smell of iron thickened the air, hot and metallic. I pondered his words. It was something they all claimed at this stage of the torture.

"I suppose I could have a family too." I let my claws jut from my nail bed, directing one at his eyeball. "If you motherfuckers didn't mess with them!"

She could have tainted herself with that one innocent kiss.

"What's your problem?" Onyx asked. Dayken was at her side with the twins trailing close behind.

Great. A welcome party. Just what I needed during the most unique emotional crisis of my life.

And for me, that was really saying something.

So instead of answering, I just stared.

"Oh, he's broken again," Derek offered, ever-so-helpful. "Try speaking slower. Let me. What. Is. Your. Problem?"

Does Skylar like him?

I couldn't remember anymore. She might be the only reason I hadn't killed him yet. And my restraint was getting thinner by the minute.

Speaking of Skylar...

Fucking hell, I let her touch me.

I touched her.

We touched.

"It didn't work," Chase muttered. "Is it just me, or does he look like he's about to puke?"

"Kolton!"

That was Dayken—using his godsdamned Primarc voice. Annoying as hell.

There was a time when he and I were close. Brothers, in a way. When I was younger, I stayed at home while he and Aurora went to school. I used to wait for them to get back, pacing in front of the window until I saw their silhouettes coming down the road.

We lived like that for a while, until we both lost our Sacars. Then everything just became too much...

"It's Skylar—"

"What about her?!" Onyx cut me off before I could finish.

"She...she came to me. In a dream—"

"Oh Jesus. Guys, we've lost him." Derek again. "Check his pants for wet spots."

Why did I even bother? For one second, I thought maybe, just maybe they'd actually listen to me.

So stupid.

"Wait, Derek. Stop," Onyx said, holding up a hand to silence the obnoxious bird mid-rant about wet dreams and needing to euthanize me.

Her voice softened. "Tell me, Kolton. Please?"

The plea in her voice hit me hard, yanking me out of my self-loathing.

I looked at her—really looked, and she was staring back at me like I held all the answers.

Like I, and I alone, could find Skylar.

"Somehow our minds must have connected. It's the only thing that makes sense. Why else—how else could she have come to me like that? Talking to me. Telling me when to find her. What to do when I did."

Onyx's eyes narrowed. "Did she confirm that Leo has her? That they're in Leeland?"

"So, you believe me?" I asked pathetically.

"Of course. There's more to Sky than any of us understands. And your bond—" She hesitated, studying me like she could see it written across my skin. "It's rare. Nothing like it has ever been documented."

Oh, believe me, I know.

Besides being reminded of that fact almost every day by some jackass, I lived the truth of it in every breath I took, every thought I had. Even when she was first captured, she never really left me. Not once. I didn't need a face to feel connected to her—just the memory of a girl I couldn't forget. She was always there.

I shifted, jaw tightening. How was I supposed to tell Onyx that I couldn't confirm anything because I'd been too busy drooling over her sister to hear a thing she said? Yeah…that wasn't happening.

"I don't know if she's in Leeland," I said. "But it all adds up. That riddle Crowe gave me—kings and pride. He's been working with Leo. And after what Titus overheard? It's a done deal in my book. She also mentioned something about me coming as an ally. Whatever that means."

I turned and headed for the door. I couldn't wait and talk about this for another minute. I couldn't wait for intel or confirmation; I just needed my Sacar with me. I needed to claw my way back to the tiny scrap of sanity I could cling to when I had her nearby.

I heard Onyx behind me, analyzing and mulling over her sister's words about being an ally. But I couldn't listen anymore. I just wanted to be alone with my thoughts of Skylar.

What if he was forcing her to drink from him? She did not need to feed that often, but her fangs were for me.

Only me.

I remembered the way she dug them into my flesh, the soft, hungry pulls she took while she lay half-unconscious just a few weeks ago.

If he were force-feeding her, I would slaughter his entire clan. I would leave him for last and tear every limb from his body.

"Oh gods, why is he growling now?" Derek asked, exasperated.

"Who knows. Take to the air and intercept your cousin, then track us down along the coast to give us an update on what has been discovered," Dayken said with a shrug before Derek shifted and did just that. "Chase, you good to stay back and man communications, or do you want to go with him?" he asked, taking command like the Primarc he was.

"We have other Averie Clan members at the compound and around the forest who can assist with comms," Chase said. "I want to rescue Sky."

A tangle of rage, jealousy, admiration, and respect knotted over my heart. I wanted to beat against my chest until it sorted itself out, and I felt just one clear emotion. That didn't work. So, I settled for the most irrational one, like any sane, normal Guardian would.

Jealousy.

It pulsed like a live wire under my ribs as I spun on Chase.

"No. I will rescue Skylar. She is mine. *Mine.* Not yours."

To his credit, Chase didn't flinch or even blink. He stood stoically, like I was a toddler throwing a tantrum.

And maybe I was.

But I still wanted him to understand.

Baring my double set of fangs, I hissed at him.

Chase simply raised his hands and pointed them to the ceiling as massive, curved talons jutted out from his fingertips. They looked sharp enough to carve marble. I braced myself, ready for a fight. There was a chance I would be shredded to pieces with those knives at his disposal, but I was ready to stand my ground.

However, Chase simply said, calm as ever, "I'm coming with you. End of discussion."

All right…. Fine.

But only because I liked his dagger nails.

Instead of responding, I turned and left, letting the metal doors slam behind me.

The compound's front steps echoed under my boots. The building itself loomed behind me, all steel and concrete, quiet except for the hum of security lights that cast everything in a cold blue light. The air outside smelled like wet pine and gun oil, a mix of forest and fight.

I made my way down the long driveway, approaching the gate. It didn't open, no doubt because Chase was flexing on me or just wasn't in the control room to do his job. So, I paced back and forth, feeling like a literal caged tiger.

The rest of the group took their sweet time before finally appearing at the end of the drive. Before I could bark at them to move faster, a little ball of brown fur shot between my legs.

Son of a bitch.

Dayken didn't call in reinforcements from *them…*

Did he?

Chapter Eleven

I thumbed through another book about Avont, reading how he used his blood to create predator-like Guardians to protect his brother's children. My mind absorbed the words at lightning speed. It was a skill that quickly became the facility's favorite to test. They would place a book or magazine in front of me, time how fast I could read it, then quiz me on the accuracy of my retention.

If I passed their tests, I would get more books.

If I failed, they made my sister watch as they amputated something.

That always hurt more than whatever body part they took—seeing her pain. Hearing her scream for them to stop, begging them to do it to her instead. I used to tell her I was fine, that it didn't hurt, that I'd be okay—just to quiet her cries.

The door burst open, slamming against the wall and ripping me out of my dark thoughts. No knock. No warning. Just raw, untamed energy radiating from my unwelcome guest.

Leo marched toward my bed. His blonde hair was slicked back, and he was dressed in a suit as always. He didn't bother pretending he was attracted to me anymore, even though he still insisted I wear clothing that barely covered anything.

I read a magazine once that had an article about the backstage drama at a Victoria's Secret runway show, and the outfits he forced me into made those photos look wholesome.

"Come now, Sky. Time to go outside."

He extended a hand, too casual, too familiar, like I should be grateful for the gesture. It enraged me and made me want to snap every tiny bone and tendon in that hand. But I tilted my head at him instead; something in what he said intrigued my curiosity.

Time to go outside.

The phrasing tripped me up. My mind dissected it instantly, searching for the motive behind his words. It wasn't a suggestion; it was a command. A signal that something was about to happen.

I took his extended hand, deciding to play nice and see what would happen next. He obviously had some sort of scheme in motion.

He gripped my hand tightly, and I followed along as he led me down the long, extravagant hallways.

The entire place was flamboyant and gaudy. Gold smothered everything, as if its excess could pass for power. To me, it was just noise. The glare of yellow stabbed at my eyes, too harsh, too hollow. It wasn't the intense shade of yellow that woke my blood while simultaneously making me feel safe and cherished. No. This wasn't my yellow at all.

We approached two sets of tall French doors; the glass panes glistened, radiating the outside light into a shower of crystals. We passed through the first set into a small vestibule, then the second set, and suddenly I was outside for the first time in days. The air hit me all at once, cool and brisk. I inhaled deeply.

Michigan.

I'd know the scent anywhere. The air never lied here. I had the timeframe right too. It had to have been about a week, given that there was no drastic seasonal change in the surrounding forests.

I suddenly felt a rubber band tug at my heart. I recognized it instantly. I pulled harder, letting the person on the other end know where to find me.

Leo inhaled deeply, taking the air into his lungs as if scenting something.

"Good. Right on time," he all but purred.

I caught a flash of orange hair in the sunlight, vivid and impossible to miss.

That sight confirmed all my suspicions. This *was* planned.

I think I just made a mistake.

Had I overanalyzed the situation? I told Kolton to come as an ally in my dream, but there was no way Leo could have known that...so what did he mean when he said, "right on time?"

I thought this was just about me, but it was about Kolton too...why? Why did they want him?

Before I could assess the situation any further, I was hit with the severity of my miscalculation as the rest of Kolton became visible—broad shoulders and that lean, powerful frame. His clothes clung to his body like they were fighting to contain him. He moved with purpose, every step deliberate, dangerous, alive.

My heart jolted hard enough to hurt. The bond snapped taut as he drew closer, syncing our rhythms until I could feel his heartbeat pounding inside my own chest.

Kolton.

He crossed the lawn with a calm determination that was far more terrifying than rage, each stride bringing him closer until the air itself seemed to bend around him. By the time he reached the steps, the world had gone silent.

He was breathtaking—feral and radiant in equal measure. The bright blaze of his hair, the wild gold of his eyes, the way the sunlight lit his skin—he was the impossible, yet violent, person I was missing while locked here.

And then I saw it. The anger. The betrayal. The rage building behind his expression.

He was furious.

I knew that look well. I'd seen it in battle. The raw determination that could level anything in its path. Only this time, it wasn't aimed at an enemy. It was aimed at me.

My hands trembled, though I couldn't tell if it was from fear, relief, or the unbearable ache of being near him again.

CHAPTER TWELVE

T he late winter air was crisp and earthy as I pushed through the sand and trees of Lake Michigan's unsalted coast. I couldn't shake my fury. Every time I tracked her, I ended up with godsdamn sand clinging to me, my boots, teeth, and nails. It took me back to San Diego, where I tracked an agent along the boardwalk to a beachside coffee stand, with sand *everywhere*. By the time I ripped his arm off, it had coated my tongue. Sandy grit, combined with blood. I could still taste it—

The bond slammed into me so suddenly, it was like a live wire. A jolt straight through my chest that burned down to the bone.

Skylar.

For days, it had been nothing but a whisper, a ghost pressing on my ribs. Now it sharpened, tightening with every step. I was closing in.

Gods, it felt good.

I felt as it was yanked taut, a rubber band stretched to the limit. Instinct made me tug back, curious. A reckless part of me insisted I test its limit. Pain tore through my chest, searing and hot.

She was pulling back. My Skylar. My Sacar.

She was safe. And she was calling me to her.

"Kolton?" Onyx's voice cut in. She noticed the shift in me. She noticed *everything*. Irritating as hell.

My walk turned into a jog, and before I even thought about it, I was running.

Of course, Onyx was quick to join me, gliding along like it cost her nothing. Her speed...irritating. Always irritating.

"Kolton, if you sense my sister, tell me now." She wasn't even winded.

I vaulted over a fallen tree, shot her a glance, and gave a single nod. That was all I had for her. My focus tunneled. Skylar. I needed to get to Skylar.

Faster.

"He's got her!" Onyx yelled over her shoulder.

Among all the sounds invading my senses, I picked up a unique, tiny, almost scuffling noise. Then, the falcons dropped from the sky, wings snapping into limbs, bodies shifting mid-air before they hit the ground running. They landed a few paces ahead, trying to cut me off.

I blew past them before they could open their mouths. If they'd just shut up and followed me, they'd have their answers soon enough. No need for tea, crumpets, or a godsdamn interrogation.

Before I knew it, I was at the edge of the forest, my chest thrumming with the strength of the bond. Peering through the trees, I spotted a sprawling estate rising behind manicured lawns and a few overgrown maples that were nearly stripped bare. Its façade was all polished stone and money, the kind of place built to make lesser men feel small. White columns framed double doors, wide enough for a car to drive through. DeStephano Clan members, shifted into their lion forms, stood guard across the grounds, more for show than anything else but still a threat.

Well...here goes nothing. Hopefully, they don't shoot me in the head on sight.

How embarrassing would that be?

I stepped forward, only to feel a sharp grip on my shoulder.

"Wait, asshole. What's your plan here?" Onyx demanded.

"Don't have one." I pressed forward.

"Well, make one! That's my sister in there!"

And people thought *I* was the problem. At least I wasn't screeching outside enemy territory, risking being heard and blowing our cover.

"Let go of me before I detach your hand from your body."

"I'd like to see you try." Dayken came from out of nowhere. His timing was impeccable. Always popping out of the shadows like the wolf he was. He handed Chase a metal box, which he immediately started fiddling with.

"I don't have a plan," I growled, the hair on my arms prickling. "All I know is I'm going in. Alone. And I'll get her out. Even if it costs me my life."

"There are no signals nearby," Chase muttered.

Good for him and the non-existent signals. Maybe they could whisper sweet nothings to each other while I went and got my Sacar.

Onyx released me, and I didn't waste a second. Heading straight toward the estate, she started to protest behind me, but Derek cut her off.

"Don't bother. Bullets will bounce off his thick fucking skull anyway. Trust me, I'm a doctor."

"If he endangers my sister with his reckless behav—"

I tuned out her pathetic attempt at a rant as I stepped out from the cover of the trees.

Not one lion rushed me. No one even looked surprised to see me.

Which was…unsettling.

I continued forward across the dead grass. The brittle, cold-murdered stalks crunched under my boots. Then I saw it—the outline of a figure ahead. I would know that silhouette anywhere.

My lungs forgot how to work. My heart stuttered. The world narrowed to *her*.

She was perfect.

She was mine.

Every step dragged her into sharper focus—not just the sight of her, but the bond itself, thrumming through my bones, pounding in my blood.

She turned, just slightly, like she felt it too. Her expression gave me nothing. No smile. No anger. Just a blank stare that cut me deeper than any blade.

We didn't speak.

Onyx and her merry band of fuckwits had hung back behind the tree line.

That had been the right call, though. Leo needed to believe I'd come alone; it was the only way to get close. Still, the distance, even though I was getting closer, scraped raw across my insides.

She stood near the front steps of a garden, framing the estate's extravagance, and illuminated by the golden light spilling from the doorway. Something suggested her placement was intentional; Sky would never opt to stand out on display. Being the center of attention just wasn't her style.

Then my gaze caught the thin slip of fabric Leo no doubt forced her to wear. Skimpy. Inappropriate for the chill in the air. My stomach turned molten. That bastard knew exactly what he was doing, parading her around like a prize, forcing her into clothes that drew attention, meant to tantalize.

My hands curled into fists at my sides, claws threatening to punch through my skin.

The lions stationed along the courtyard steps straightened as I approached, their eyes tracking me with the patience of ambush predators. But I only had eyes for Skylar. Every instinct screamed at me to close the distance, to hide her from their sight, wrap her in something warm and shield her from the cold. From their stares. From Leo.

The bond yanked harder, urgent, demanding.

I forced my gait to stay steady, refusing to give Leo the satisfaction of seeing my desperation claw me apart from the inside out.

"Kolton, welcome." Leo's voice cut through the tautness of the bond, snapping the rubber band. The sting felt like a physical blow against my skin.

"Leo." My only greeting. I tried to hide the fact that he just severed my connection to Skylar. I also tried, and most likely failed, to hide the hatred for his clan that flowed through every fiber of my being. I was just a child when they slaughtered my family. I had no photos, no memories, nor keepsakes to cherish. All I had was the knowledge that his pride of lions played a role in dismantling my life. And that knowledge made me want to spiral into a rage I could not leash. Being robbed of the life I was meant to have fueled a different kind of hatred.

"Grab him," Leo commanded.

The lions moved in perfect unison, following their Primarc's orders like the obedient machines he molded from flesh and bone. Submission was beaten into them, both figuratively and literally, exactly as his family's reputation promised.

I stood my ground, refusing to meet Skylar's eyes. If I looked now, I would give too much away. She was my purpose but also my ultimate weakness. A gap in the armor I spent years forging. I wanted them to see only a strong, loyal Guardian, here to retrieve his Sacar. Nothing more.

If I were honest, which I was not, the truth was that I wanted, more than anything, to feel her in my arms. To breathe in the proof that she was alive. To feel her chest rise and fall against mine, the way her muscles shifted with each breath. My tiger demanded it. My tiger demanded too much. The man inside me refused to indulge in such fragile comfort.

Two lions seized my arms, their grips so tight it was as if they expected me to resist. But I didn't. Skylar told me to play nice. I still didn't understand why, but I'd do as she asked.

For now.

"What will you do with him?"

Her voice lashed through me, shattering my control. My head snapped toward her before I could stop myself. She held Leo's forearm. Too close. Too familiar. It sent my instincts into a frenzy.

"Uh, boss," one of the lions said in a thick Italian accent.

Leo ignored him, his attention locked on the angel beside him. I couldn't fault him; she was completely captivating. But I still wanted to bash his face in with my fists.

His lips curled into a smug grin.

"Do not worry, amore mio. I will show him the same kindness I have shown you." Came Leo's reply.

Kindness?

What fucking kindness has he shown my Sacar?

A growl tore out of me, deep and raw. When it died, I was met with ice. Ice-blue eyes that cut straight through me.

That look said one thing.

Don't.

But why? Why could I not rage? Why couldn't I take her and leave? Instead of asking, I bared my double fangs and hissed at her, letting my frustration bleed into the air between us. The hair on my arms started to prickle, an indication that my tiger was clawing its way out.

"Boss..." The lion at my side tried again.

"Yes, yes," Leo drawled. "I have failed to introduce this tiger to my clan. DeStephano Clan, meet Kolton Teegra, the feral Guardian who has twice now lost his Sacar." He laughed, and his pride joined in.

It did not matter. The only thing I cared about was standing right next to him. But she was not moving toward me. She was chuckling nervously at his side, and it made my blood boil.

I was going to lose it.

"So feral, in fact," Leo added, "that he hisses and snarls at his very own sacred one." The pride nodded in response, like disciples. Leo placed his hand over Skylar's, where it rested on his arm. "Is this what you want, Sky? This feral tiger?"

She looked up at him with a smirk. I knew that look. I saw a quip coming. I waited for it like her words were the only reason I was still breathing. Of course she wanted me. She chose me. Only me.

"No," she said, her tone sweet as a delicate pastry. "He is not what I want."

The words ran me through like a sword. Sweetness wrapped around a blade.

No...

What was this feeling? Why was my stomach twisted in knots? Was this rejection? No...it wasn't rejection.

It was worse.

It was betrayal.

Leo's chuckle rumbled low, pleased. "Perfect. Absolutely perfect." He leaned down, his next words meant for her but loud enough for me to hear. "So, even you see how unfit he is to be your Guardian. Even though you chose him, you regret it?"

She didn't answer, just gazed into his eyes.

For some reason, I couldn't read her expression. I couldn't tell if she was looking at him with affection or admiration. But both made me sick.

"Take him to the underground level. West side. Not east."

The lions' grips tightened, bruising my arms, but I barely felt it. Was this why she said those things? To play nice? To behave? To *trap* me.

Before I could scream at her, the lights went out.

CHAPTER THIRTEEN

I followed behind Leo, surrounded by his entourage.

The sound of their boots echoed against the marble floors, and every step carried me deeper into his domain.

I should've seen it sooner, and I was so mad at myself for missing it before now. I thought Leo only wanted me, but he needed Kolton too. And that changed everything.

I led Kolton straight into a trap. Told him to come in peace.

And oh, Kolton was furious about it. Big, big mad.

But he couldn't honestly believe I would do that to him. Could he?

With Kolton, anything was possible. His mind ran wild, feral, untamed. He didn't trust easily, and why should he? We hadn't had the luxury of time to build something solid between us. A bond didn't just bloom overnight.

Well, technically, ours did. Our ancient bond was forged long before we consciously understood our choice. But bonds only promised connection, not trust. I needed to fix this before he burned everything to the ground and took innocent lives in the process.

The hall stretched on forever, more walls smothered in gaudy artwork framed in thick, gleaming gold. Portraits, landscapes, saints, sinners...I couldn't tell which was which. The ostentation was almost grotesque, like someone shoved too much wealth into too small of a space.

Was this what art galleries looked like? Gods, I hoped not. If so, I'd rather never visit one. But maybe, someday, I could go for real. Walk through one that didn't reek of power seized through death and destruction.

And maybe Kolton could come with me.

Though I wasn't sure which would shock me more: Kolton in an art gallery or him being there and not scowling the entire time.

"Sky, my dear, I think it's time for you to rest," Leo said, suddenly stopping and turning to face me. His entourage stopped in lock step with him, almost as if they anticipated his every move.

I stopped as well, and Leo stepped toward me. I stood firm, holding my chin high. My confidence came easily, as he did not intimidate me in the slightest. I made sure to soften my features so as not to appear defiant. The closer he got, the more his intense scent invaded my senses. It made my brain foggy; it was that musk mixed with a hint of something else.

He reached out a hand to toy with the blunt edge of my hair, tucking it back behind my ear. It was just long enough to stay.

"My precious, precious Sky. This must have been just so exhausting for you."

I nodded once, not trusting my voice to conceal the anger I felt.

He paused, tilting his head.

"Shall I keep you company tonight?" he asked with a genuine tone. Not smug or gross, but his eyes revealed the truth. I read them quickly, and they lacked emotion. To those listening, it might seem like he wanted to comfort me over how Kolton acted, but didn't they know...I adored that side of Kolton.

"No, that's all right. I would very much like some rest."

A plan immediately formed as one of Leo's brown-haired clan members ushered me toward my room.

The joys of my ability came to the rescue once again.

"But, if you would like to sit and chat for a few minutes, I would not be opposed."

He smirked, as if he had already won. I let him believe that as he followed me into my silver-plated prison. The door was nearly shut when he stepped closer, eliminating the space between us. His hand hovered near me, his eyes searching my face as if weighing how far he could push. For a heartbeat, I let him think I might allow it.

"Although," I added, just as he was about to touch me. "You may not want to. You already look tired. I would hate for your clan to think you were preoccupied with me when your focus should be on Kolton."

The effect was immediate. His smile fractured, the smugness gone in an instant. His hand dropped, his jaw tightened, and he muttered a curse under his breath, low and venomous.

"Are you calling me weak?"

I widened my eyes, letting a note of softness creep into my voice. "No...of course not. I'm merely suggesting that your clan might see it that way if you linger here with me. They expect their leader to be focused on the tiger, not..." I paused just long enough for the word to sting. "*Distracted* by me."

His jaw clenched tighter. I intended to question his leadership, indirectly at least, and he reacted exactly how I expected him to.

He spun on his heel, shoulders rigid, and slammed the door on his way out, the sound ringing against the metal walls.

I pressed my ear to the door, straining for the sound of footsteps. I wished for the hundredth time that I had Onyx's extremely heightened senses. Only silence answered me. I waited a few more minutes before testing the handle, certain that Leo's arrogance would work in my favor.

Sure enough, he hadn't bothered to lock the door. Perfect. He wasn't behaving rationally. His fragile ego made sure of that. Easy to predict. Easier to play.

I cracked the door open and spotted a man standing guard. He was broad-shouldered and casually dressed, with his long brown hair pulled into a low ponytail. He had tan skin, dark features, and a presence that screamed *leave me alone*. Which meant I was going to do the exact opposite.

"Did Leo tell you what I'm supposed to do?" I asked.

The guard blinked, caught off guard. "No...he didn't." He opened his mouth, likely to tell me to get back in my room, but I leaned in, dropping my voice just enough to make it sound urgent.

"Did you see how angry he was? Trust me, we should go now, before he thinks we're the ones wasting his time."

"Go where?"

I winced, pretending it pained me to give him the information he should so clearly already have. "To the tiger, obviously. He wants me to..." My brain scrambled, searching for words that would resonate with a lion. "Assert my dominance. Leo clearly isn't happy about the lack of respect the tiger showed me. I have to set him straight. Right now."

That gave him pause.

He reached for his comms device, but I quickly interjected. "We need to beat Leo there, or he is going to come back even angrier," I said, adding a sense of urgency to my voice.

His lips pressed into a thin line, and then he nodded, reluctant but convinced.

I tried to hide the shock that my plan actually worked as intended. Lions were easier to figure out than I originally thought.

CHAPTER FOURTEEN

I followed the lion with long brown hair. His steps were steady as he led me through corridor after corridor, then down a long flight of stairs. The air grew colder the deeper we went. The basement was unfinished—concrete walls that were damp and unwelcoming. There was a metallic tang of rust clinging to the air. Metal lined the walls, row after row, until I finally saw it.

Bars.

A cell door.

And behind it, an eerie yellow glow, and lethal eyes that locked onto me like they could pierce through my soul.

There he was, standing right in front of me. His scent thickened the air, pulling me closer, coaxing me to take deeper breaths until it filled every part of me. Citrus tangled with wilderness, uniquely his, like everything else about him. Memories of how he held me in our dreams flooded my mind, and it suddenly felt very warm down here, despite the lingering chill in the air.

"Just give me five minutes," I murmured to the lion. "Leo should be here before I finish." He nodded, leaving me to face the cage alone.

My pulse thrummed as I approached. The thrill of never knowing what to expect from Kolton hit me full force. I wrapped my hands around the cold bars and opened my mouth, but he spoke first.

"Where do you keep going? I can't feel you sometimes." His voice was sharp, desperate. "I don't like it. Whatever you're doing—*stop it.*"

I froze. His worry for me was palpable, and it was clouding his beautiful intensity. My fierce tiger was stuck in this cell because of me. There was a small cot behind him, no window, just bars, stone, and smooth concrete—the sight of it shattered me. He didn't belong here. He belonged with me.

I suddenly felt sickened by it all. It was fine when it was just me in this prison. But now I had dragged Kolton into it too, and I just felt…. It felt like…

"I–I need a hug…please." The words were out before I could think better of it.

His brows furrowed, and he jerked his head back as if I'd struck him, though his feet remained rooted to the floor. Quickly recovering, he tsked and said, "I'm not hugging you, Skylar."

"Why not?" I whined, genuinely curious, despite the unintended question slipping passed my lips.

Silence stretched between us. I was convinced he wasn't going to answer me as the seconds ticked by, but then he said, "Because. I ca—I can't touch you. My hands are too dirty."

I looked at his hands. They were clean as he tightly gripped the bars of his cell. He was wearing a simple black V-neck and jeans, but he might as well have been bare before me with the way he was looking at me, his eyes pleading with me to drop this.

"Fine," I said, squaring my shoulders. "Then I'll touch you with mine."

I slipped my hand through the bars, brushing his cheek. His pupils narrowed to slits, and his eyebrows shot up so high they nearly touched his hairline, eyes wide, unblinking. But he didn't pull away. I took the opportunity to gently rub my thumb along his cheekbone. His eyes fluttered shut. A purr rumbled from him.

"Stop that, Skylar." His voice wavered, but he didn't move.

"I've missed you. And if you're done being mad at me, I have things to tell you. We're running out of time."

That broke the calm. His eyes snapped open, feral again. The soft moment between us gone in a flash. I dropped my hand from his face.

"Go on."

"You can't feel me because Leo has me locked in a silver room. It blocks our bond. I'm still trying to figure out how he knew to use it against us."

A hiss burst from his throat before I could finish.

"Would you stop that?" I snapped.

"Sorry. I can't control my tiger right now. It doesn't like this. *I* don't like this."

"Well, I need you to keep a level head if we're going to get out of here. I'm being held surrounded by silver, but believe it or not, I'm being treated well."

Another hiss.

"Kolt—"

"How well?! Has he touched you?"

I glared. "No, you idiot. Would you just listen?"

He said nothing, just stepped back from the bars, took a steadying breath, and crossed his arms over his lean, muscular chest. He then dared to arch a brow at me, as if to say, *Go on.*

Grinding my teeth, I pressed forward. "I thought he was using the silver to keep me away from you. But then he brought you here, and I can't figure out why. He's treating me well because he needs me to be happy and complacent, for some reason. He dotes on me and gives me gifts. I need to figure out his next move. Which means I need you to behave. Please, Kolton."

"He didn't bring me here. I came on my own. And no, Skylar. Surprise, surprise—I don't agree with your stubborn-ass idea."

"I'm not going to fight with you on this, Kolton. I will protect you, and I will get us out of this."

"No, Skylar. I'm going to protect *you.*"

Why did everything have to be an argument with him?

Defeated, I backed away from his cell. There wasn't going to be any reasoning with him. Not right now.

I took another step back to see if he'd say anything to try and stop me.

When he didn't, I turned and headed back down the hallway with my heart in my throat. As I approached the lion who escorted me down here,

I paused and said, "Looks like Leo must have changed his mind. If you see him before I do, tell him I told the tiger off."

He nodded, and I followed him as we headed back to my silver-plated prison cell.

Chapter Fifteen

Images of Skylar's delicate hand kept flashing in my head, the memory of her touch burning my skin. Need pressed hard and insistent, greedy and restless. It was a low ache that refused to be ignored. Gods, her touch was life itself, warm and undeniable. It woke something inside me that I had forgotten how to quiet. It left me hollow and starving for more.

But it was becoming too much. I needed to maintain the barrier between us, to hold the line before my wanting turned reckless. Whatever this was, whatever her touch threatened to stir, I couldn't let it blur the lines between her and me. Not now. Not when the cost of wanting her would affect so much more than just me.

I pressed closer to the bars, watching as she walked away with a long-haired lion. Her small frame shrank with every step down the hallway. I watched her pale legs, still bare beneath the back of her nightgown that was barely more than air. All I could think about was how if anyone so much as brushed against her, they'd feel that silky-smooth porcelain skin. Skin that was mine to protect. A roar tore out of me before I could choke it back—loud and furious.

Skylar's steps didn't falter. She slipped through the metal door, and it slammed shut behind her.

Gone.

For now.

I roared again in frustration.

The only reason I wasn't tearing this place apart was because I finally knew where she was, and causing a huge commotion might risk them moving her. But so help me, if one of those greasy fucks laid a hand on her, I'd have a fresh collection of lion heads for my wall.

The patter of tiny feet snapped me out of the dark place I was sliding into.

A sliver of brown fur darted past my boots. It dove under the cot, back out again, then under once more before slipping through the bars.

"Would you calm the fuck down?" I whisper-yelled.

It came back, stopping at my feet, and chirped at me.

"Yeah, well, you tell her she can kiss my ass if she thinks she'll do a better job than me." I gestured around my cell like it was some kind of prize. It wasn't. But I pretended it was.

The rodent squeaked again.

"I really wish different species of Guardians couldn't talk to each other in shifted form right about now."

More high-pitched chirps.

"That doesn't make sense. Ju-just tell them no, I don't need backup. Tell them where I am, that Skylar's unharmed, and that I've clocked about fifty lions in this house, probably more outside."

Chirping. Squeaking.

"I'm not answering that. And no, I don't know *exactly*. But if they're ready to go to war—and for the record, my vote's yes—they'll need everyone from the Danielson, Averie, *and* Mack Clans."

The little menace nodded, darted back under the cot, then zipped back through the bars and up the wall before vanishing into a vent.

"Well, goodbye to you too."

Fucking mongooses.

The little shit either had great hearing or impeccable timing because the metal door at the end of the hall slammed open again. I peered through the bars and saw that long-haired lion pick something up before sitting in a chair. Skylar wasn't with him anymore. Which meant someone else was watching her.

"Did she make it back okay?" I yelled down at him.

Silence.

Dick.

"I said, did she make it back okay? Did anyone try to hurt her?" There was panic laced through my voice, despite my best efforts.

He just held up a middle finger and crossed his ankles as he leaned back in his chair.

"ANSWER ME!" I roared. My tiger broke free, joining my shout. The sound rattled the walls and reverberated through the concrete floor. The air itself felt like it shook with the force of it. Silence pressed in afterward, thick and heavy. Like even the shadows were holding their breath.

"Yes, she's fine." The reply cut through, abrupt and clear, and my shock was instant.

I don't know why, but I wasn't expecting a response.

She was okay, though, and I could find peace in that.

Chapter Sixteen

Typically, when a Sacar bonded with their Guardian and spent every waking moment together, the two started to feel like extensions of one another. Like family, in most cases parents, siblings, cousins. Or for Peach and Alicia, best friends who shared everything but blood.

Romance, however, was never supposed to be part of it. The bond between a Sacar and their Guardian ran deeper than physical or sexual attraction—it was spiritual, biological, and ancient. The bond wasn't meant to support that kind of intense emotion. Mix love with duty, and it twisted into something dangerous.

Onyx and Dayken were the exception. They met as adults, having matured separately and already grounded to who they were as people, strong enough to survive the strain.

Romantic, I guess.

Good thing I didn't have to worry about any of that. My Guardian seemed to have a permanent case of emotional frostbite.

If he would stop being stubborn for just two seconds—

"Why won't you look at me?" Leo's voice was soft. Too soft.

I kept my gaze fixed on the wall.

"Are you thinking about *him* right now?" His tone turned insidious, the pretense of gentleness gone. "You think I don't know that you snuck down there to see him?"

"I'm sorry," I murmured, careful to lace my voice with guilt. "I needed to be sure."

"Be sure of what?"

"That I truly am disgusted by him."

His eyes narrowed. "And?"

I let the words slip out slowly, as if each one weighed on me. "I am. He wouldn't speak to me. Or even take my hand." The truth cut deep, but I forced the pain down, turned it into something else. "He backed away as if I were tainted. It makes no sense. How can he protect me if he can't even bring himself to look at me? Maybe our bond was always broken, and that's why it doesn't work."

Leo's expression shifted. His suspicion cooled into something worse: *interest.*

"Do you know why you were able to bond with him as a baby?"

"No." That was the truth; I had no clue. There was never a bond like ours before, and I checked. I snooped around Titus's place while we were there making weapons. I checked through Alicia and Peach's compound. I scoured every shelf in Dayken's library. Nothing. Not one record of a bond forming that young.

Which made me realize that Leo had to know *something*. I wanted to ask him why he needed Kolton here too, how he knew when he was going to arrive, and what was to come. But Leo didn't want to play those games with me today.

"Well, that's a shame," he purred. "A bond forged that young is so unpredictable, so...strong. Some even surmise that it could survive death itself."

He tried to come off as skeptical, like he didn't believe his words and was merely spreading gossip. But I caught the flicker of truth beneath his act.

His scent was still overpowered by the cologne he wore—intentionally, I realized. Somehow, he knew about my ability to read people, so he masked himself to cover his lies. The smell was a mix of spice and smoke, making it difficult to inhale, harder to reach the foul, sour note that came with deceit.

So many layers to this man in front of me. So many secrets he tried to keep hidden.

But peeling back layers was what I did best.

So, I made my move.

I slid my legs slowly off the side of the bed, letting the hem of my nightgown rise just enough to expose the top of my thighs. I stood, unhurried, and crossed the short distance between us. His eyes followed me, watchful yet almost bored, like he already knew what I planned to do.

That was fine. I could still find a way to surprise him.

I brushed my fingertips down the front of his tie, gently catching the silk before pretending to straighten it for him. The backs of my fingers flittered over his chest, and I felt the sudden intake of his breath. He went rigid but didn't pull away. When I looked up, his rich mocha gaze was no longer bored—it was alive with curiosity, a low hum of hunger simmering beneath the surface.

I had his full attention now.

He might not desire me, but I could feel his want. The faint spark of attraction he tried to bury.

"Surviving death seems a bit extreme for a bond," I said softly, letting my tone flirt with disbelief. "I'm sure that's just a bedtime story meant to inspire Sacars to pick a Guardian when they're young," I added a wink for effect.

His hand shot up, gripping mine tightly and halting my movements. The softness in the room evaporated.

"This isn't a game, Sky," he said, his voice low and controlled. "If you think he can't protect you, you need to consider the possibility that fate made a mistake."

"Possibly. But there's nothing to be done about it now." I patted my chest, right above my mark, letting the gesture linger just long enough to make a point.

Rage flickered in his eyes. They swirled with a fury he couldn't quite hide.

My mark angered him. That much was clear. And with that reaction, another piece of the puzzle fell into place.

Interesting.

Very interesting.

"You are not to go down there unless I permit it, do you understand me?" Leo commanded.

My options were either to ask him why and listen to some made-up story about my safety or play nice by accepting his demand.

I got more information from him when I played dumb and compla-cent, so I kept up the act.

"Of course," I said, nodding in agreement.

That seemed to please him.

What he didn't realize was that he could never truly stop me from connecting with Kolton. Although this silver blocked our physical con-nection and we could no longer feel each other physically, it did not impact our mental bond—a connection that does not appear to be documented in history. A first of its kind...so unique. But now, I just needed that stubborn-ass tiger to fall asleep...

CHAPTER SEVENTEEN

I lay on the shitty cot with my arm under my head, terrified and excited, to fall asleep. I had a feeling that once I did, Skylar was going to appear in my dreams. Now that I knew it was really her, I had to figure out how to face her while still maintaining the barrier I had erected between us. Yet, at the same time, I *needed* to have my eyes on her. I needed to make sure she was okay.

The familiar sound of soft, scurrying feet dragged me out of my dilemma. I cracked an eye open and looked down. The annoying little brown menace was back. Only this time, it had something tied around its body.

Propping myself up on an elbow, I stared at it, waiting for an explanation it clearly wasn't going to give.

It hopped onto the cot, squeaked at me, and shoved its tiny paws against my chest.

I untied the string and grabbed the small pouch it was carrying. I emptied it into my palm just as the pesky little rodent leaped from the cot and, without warning, shifted right in front of me.

Brown fur evaporated. Limbs stretched. Suddenly, there was a very tiny, very naked woman standing in the cell with me. She was around my age, with brown hair hanging just past her shoulders. Her amber-brown eyes were wide with excitement.

"Hi! I'm Bailey Urva!"

I knew who she was; we had met already at the Danielson compound. Also, she is supposed to state which clan she is from in standard guardian introductions. Even I knew that protocol.

"What is this?" I asked, instead of addressing her mistake, caring more about the item in my hands than her odd behavior.

She beamed, like a kid showing off a new toy. "Um...hi! I was told to tell you that the little silver thing makes it so you can talk to the fox!"

I blinked down at the object in my hand.

The fox?

Fuuuuck, why him?

I looked back at the chaotic little creature standing before me only to remember it wasn't a mongoose I was dealing with anymore. It was now an overly enthusiastic, very *naked*, woman...I probably wasn't going to get any answers from her.

Then, my mind drifted somewhere it shouldn't.

If Skylar were to walk in right now...

Would she think there was something happening between me and this woman? That I somehow lost every shred of my self-control and decided to make friends with a naked stranger? What if Skylar assumed there was some attraction on my end...how would that make her feel?

Jealous? No, that would be insane. She wasn't wired like that. I would explain that I only just met Bailey, right before making our way to Leo's estate. That she had come to help the rescue mission and that this was *not* whatever it looked like.

"You're the tiger, right?" Bailey asked, eyes wide and unblinking. "They told me to get to the tiger, and I did! I did it! This place is so cool!"

Did she already forget that she had been in here earlier?

Shit...how was *I* the mentally stable one right now?

She tilted her head, eyes bright and unbothered. "You're cute. In an unconventional, just escaped from the circus, kind of way. Hey! Look! There's a crack under the bed!"

Stay calm. Stay cool.

Skylar would want that, right?

"Did you know you had a crack under here?" Her voice was muffled, having dropped to all fours before crawling under the cot. I now had a full moon staring me in the face.

Please don't let Skylar choose this moment to visit me again.

"No," I ground out. She talked faster in her human form than she did as a mongoose. "How does this work?" I asked, referring to the small device she brought me.

"Oh, right, that." She pulled herself out from under the cot and plucked it from my palm, turning it over until it caught the dim light of the room. "Has anyone ever told you that you're kinda cute?"

"How. Does. It. Work?" My voice came out part tiger, part human hiss as I pointed to the device and tried to get her to focus.

She blinked at me. "So grumpy. Just slip it into your ear canal," she said while unnecessarily poking my right ear.

"Yes! I know where my ear is." I tried not to yell as I swatted her hand away.

"Chase—the super hot, hot guy with the big arms—he said, um, oh yes, he said his brother will take it out later."

"Do I have to turn it on?"

She crouched down again, peering under the cot as if she discovered a hidden treasure chest.

I tried to be patient. I really did. Instead of growling, I smacked my hand on the cot to get her attention.

"Nope," she chirped.

I slipped the tiny device into my ear, feeling it attach itself inside the canal. It felt uncomfortable, like I needed a Q-tip to dig it out.

I hated it.

Before I could ask how long it would take to start working, Bailey shifted back into her mongoose form and darted under the cot. She popped up again in the middle of the cell, scratched her head with her back foot, and darted into another cell like a pinball.

"Mic check one, two, three." *Oh, dear gods, no.* "Hello, Scranton, Pennsylvania!"

I think it might actually be time for me to seek therapy.

Chapter Eighteen

KOLTON

"You're avoiding me."

I wasn't shocked to find Skylar waiting for me and for her to see straight through my bullshit. There was no hiding anything from her—even if we weren't bonded—she was too smart for that. Intimidatingly so, if I was being honest. But her mind...her mind was just as captivating as the rest of her.

She stood there in a light, almost transparent camisole. It was similar to the nighties she wore earlier, but the fabric of this outfit was so thin it moved *with her every breath. The whisper of cloth clung to her waist and brushed against shorts so tiny that they barely fit the definition. I shouldn't have looked, but I did. The outline of her stomach, the subtle curve of her hips, her belly button—it was all right there, on display. It was all I could see, all I could think about.*

That's when the truth hit me. Hard. I wasn't just drawn to her. I wanted her.

The sudden realization caused me to stumble backward.

No. No, I can't. I can't be attracted to her.

Or could I?

Attraction—that wasn't too bad, right? It was just a normal fucking thing, something normal people felt all the godsdamn time.

Only...I wasn't normal.

"Kolton? Why were you avoiding me? And why aren't you talking to me right now?"

"Chase and Titus had an earpiece delivered to me." I tapped my ear for emphasis, trying to keep my mind away from those insane thoughts and focusing instead on the situation at hand.

"I can keep them updated on how much longer this will take and feed them intel."

"Good. That's good."

She subtly inched closer to me, and I took a step back. She noticed and let out a sigh.

"You're exhausting, you know that?" she said, her voice carrying a hint of despondence.

I just shrugged to avoid taking the bait. She didn't need to know about the intrusive thoughts popping up inside my head, or the distance I wanted to keep between us. She definitely didn't need to know about how much I wanted to run my fingers under that slip of see-through fabric to feel the soft skin of her stomach before trailing my hands up until they brushed along the edge of her bra—the one concealing everything I shouldn't be thinking about right now. I could easily slip a finger beneath one of the cups and—

My dick was suddenly hard as a rock. I turned, giving my back to Sky and adjusting myself before I did something I'd regret.

"Listen," she said softly. "I know you're mad at me, but I didn't know he was trying to lure you here. I swear."

That snapped me out of my frenzied, inappropriate thoughts.

She thought I was mad at her? How could I ever be mad at her? She was too enthralling, too overwhelming, too much. I couldn't rely on a single emotion to describe my feelings toward her, let alone an emotion like anger.

I wanted to hiss at her for even thinking *I could be mad at her.*

Also, I had already figured out this was a trap before I arrived. How had she not noticed that sooner? Oh, right, she had been imprisoned in a room full of silver and didn't know that Leo and his family had wanted me in their clan and under their control ever since they learned of my existence.

I supposed it was time to give her a lesson about my personal history.

"Did you know that my grandma came over here from Korea?"

Skylar shook her head. She looked stunned by the sudden change in topic but didn't interrupt. It seemed like she was afraid of spooking me, which was adorable. She didn't have much of a poker face. I stepped closer, trying to see if I could get another reaction out of her. She didn't back away, so I started slowly circling her. My Sacar tried to follow me with her eyes as I rounded behind her.

"My grandma was a rare—coveted—Siberian tiger. Even when she came here, to America, and planted roots, she was still rare, but she was no longer sought after for breeding purposes."

I was standing behind Skylar when I happened to look down. I regretted it immediately. The shape of her ass was fucking perfect. My mouth started to water, and I had the urge to bite it, mark it as mine. My fingers flexed instinctively as I resisted the need to grab it and squeeze—to let her know who it belonged to. Fuck. I smacked my head hard to shake the thought away, grateful that she couldn't see the movement while her back was still toward me.

"Until?" Skylar prompted, smart enough to realize there was more to this story.

"Until the Guardian gene skipped my mother. Then I was born, and the DeStephano clan found out about me.

"Guardians need time to mature into our abilities, as I'm sure you know. Babies aren't born strong. The older you get, the more you build your strength and hone your senses. The fact that we were able to forge a bond at such a young age is part of the reason why our connection is such a mystery. It's part of what makes us so special, but it also created a giant fucking target on my back for the entire twenty-five years of my life.

"I'm not mad at you, Skylar. I'm pissed at these fucking lions, who have been hunting me my whole existence. But now I'm ready to fight back. I'm ready for war. So, tell me, my precious Sacar...why shouldn't I start it now that I'm here?"

Chapter Nineteen

This was the most I had ever heard Kolton speak. He never shared anything like this before. It felt like there was something shifting between us. Like the hard line he'd drawn to separate us was finally starting to blur. It didn't mean that he'd suddenly become a different person, though. He still stood there, trying to convince me that we needed to go to war with the DeStephano Clan.

"War isn't necessary, Kolton. Not right now," I said. My voice came out small, almost pathetic, against his powerful presence. I reached for the hem of his shirt before I thought about it, a clumsy, useless anchor. He didn't

stop me. His eyes went distant for a second, like he was watching something only he could see.

"Leo wants the DeStephano Clan to go down in history. I can make that happen. I'll drench these walls with lions' blood. I'll mount their heads on the front door of every clan compound so they will be remembered as the poor, lost souls they are, weak and worthless. I will carve their names into stone and song until the DeStephanos exist as a warning told to children in bedtime stories. A warning about what happens when you cross a rabid, fucking tiger."

Heat rolled under my skin, and there was a metallic taste in my mouth. He was a hurricane, primed for destruction, and for the first time, I understood how close to the edge he truly lived.

I tugged on his shirt, pulling him closer to me, and looked up into his bright yellow eyes.

"I'm right here," I whispered.

"Yes...yes you are," he murmured

I saw him raise a hand from the corner of my eye. Then, with a confident swiftness, his hand was at my neck, his grip rough, eyes fierce. I felt his thumb brush over my esophagus. The gesture suggested he was contemplating whether or not to squeeze it, but his eyes...his eyes held hunger. And not hunger for violence.

Was it hunger for me?

I opened my mouth, about to reiterate that there was no need for violence yet. I wanted to promise him that he could avenge his family and Dayken's, as soon as we got out of here.

But something in his eyes stopped me. His gaze held me frozen as his thumb continued meticulously stroking my neck.

"There's something bigger going on here, Kolton. This is about more than just us. I can feel it."

"I don't care. You are mine, Skylar. Mine to protect. Mine to decide what to do with. Mine."

The tiger was forcing itself forward, cutting through in his voice.

My stomach felt like it was flipping. My fangs extended from my gums, and my vision narrowed as my eyes shifted into slits.

Kolton growled. "You like that you are mine? Do you like me touching you, Skylar?"

Was this really Kolton...had this side of him been here the whole time?

If I nodded yes, would he stop? Did he want me, or did he just want to torture me?

He leaned in, tightening his grip. "War is inevitable, Skylar. They took you from me, and that was the last straw."

I was breathless. I prided myself on being intelligent and rational, but my mind was mush right now. This feral tiger had me completely enraptured, in every sense of the word. I was helpless to say or do anything about it.

Hell...I didn't want to do anything.

He leaned closer and inhaled deeply. His eyes went wide, nostrils flaring in rage. His irises practically glowed with his fury.

My breath hitched as his grip tightened ever so slightly.

"Why do I smell him on you?" He growled so low, so deadly, it caused goosebumps to spread across my skin.

I opened my mouth to reply but couldn't.

I saw the realization across his face once he came to his senses and registered where his hands were. He practically snapped his hand away from my neck. He threw both his hands in the air as he stepped away.

"No one is to touch you but me. Do you understand?!"
And then he was gone.

CHAPTER TWENTY

He was there again.

Same stance. Same bored expression. Same long ponytail that brushed his collar whenever he moved. For days, he stood outside my room like part of the décor—silent, watchful, pretending not to listen.

He stood there decorated in his comms and weapons.

"Do you ever get tired of standing there?" I asked, peeking out from behind my unlocked door. Leo must have decided there was no reason to keep me trapped inside, convinced I was no longer a flight risk. Convinced I actually felt safer with him than with Kolton.

Idiot.

He didn't look at me as he replied, "It's my job."

"Right. Standing. Breathing loudly. Pretending you don't hate this."

His jaw ticked. I smiled. "See? There it is. Proof you're not an insentient being."

"Maybe keep your theories to yourself," he muttered.

"If we're going to spend all this time together, I should probably know what to call you. Guard Number Two feels impersonal."

A pause. Then, quietly, "John."

I tilted my head. "John," I repeated, letting it roll off my tongue. "Simple. Strong. I like it."

"Don't," he warned, still not meeting my eyes.

"Don't what? Use your name?"

He exhaled. "Don't make this harder than it has to be."

"I'll try," I said softly, though we both knew I wouldn't. "Goodnight, John."

He didn't answer, but his mouth twitched—small but enough.

Now I had a name.

A few days later, John came into my room and leaned against the door with a phone to his ear.

He covered the mic with his palm before asking, "You ready for your daily walk?"

I popped up from the bed, ready to stretch my legs. My bare feet kissed the cold silver-plated floor, reminding me that while they had been giving me more freedom lately, I was still their prisoner.

"I'll be there in a moment," he whispered, his hand still over the mic. He was still by the doorway, so I just nodded and slipped into the hall.

Leo had slowly loosened the security around the compound too. Over the days, I've noticed fewer and fewer lions filling the halls.

My fake complacency must be working.

I walked along the corridor, this particular one being the longest in the house. A narrow tunnel of gold moldings and dim sconces that sucked up more light than they gave off. My bare feet whispered against the marble floor. Even that felt too loud. I breathed in, counted my steps, and let the silence settle.

Then a voice. Low. Hushed. Urgent.

I froze.

"Tell him I've been following all of his instructions." Leo's tone vibrated with fury, each word sharp enough to cut.

"I don't care that he's locked up. You've been getting messages to him up until this point. Keep doing it."

I pressed flat against the wall, one hand covering my mouth, careful not to jostle the picture frame beside me. My pulse hammered in my ears.

There was a pause. Then his voice returned, lighter but still menacing. "Yeah, that's right. Tell him she doesn't want anything to do with him anymore." He paused briefly before adding, "And get this, when he arrived—just like I expected—he hissed at her. Once a savage piece of shit, always a savage piece of shit." His laugh was menacing, twisted with disgust.

It was quiet again. I could hear someone murmuring back, but too softly to catch.

If I could just get a little closer, maybe I could hear who was on the other line.

Leo laughed again. This time the sound was warm but empty, the kind that made your shoulders tense before you knew why. "Of course, the flower is here. She trusts me. Don't worry. I'll be able to take his place in no time."

The words scraped through me like glass.

Flower.

Take his place.

My thoughts fractured, racing ahead, calculating and recalculating. Every variable. Every mistake. The chip in my head throbbed, as if I could feel and see a red light blinking behind my eyes.

I clutched my head.

Take his place.

No.

No.

No.

Air rushed from my lungs just before I took off running.

I went back the way I came, turning down a set of stairs that led to the kitchen and dining room. I couldn't risk running past Leo's office and being seen, so I opted for the longer way.

I sprinted through the next golden hall, my steps, normally so light and calculated, were instead heavy and weighted with fear.

I busted through the double doors that led to the basement—hitting the stairs two at a time. The lighting down there was dim and cast shadows on the steps as I ran.

I hit the bottom of the stairs. There was no one guarding this space. Not viewing Kolton as a threat anymore.

And now I knew why.

As I rounded the corner and shouted, "We have to get out of here—now!" My voice echoed off the concrete walls.

I turned the last corner as Kolton shot up from the cot. "What happened?!"

I ran my palms along the wall, searching, pressing at the seams of the cement blocks, hoping one might shift, reveal a key, a latch, *something*. But no luck.

"Skylar! What. Happened!" His voice snapped like a whip.

"I-I heard him," I stammered, my breath short. "I heard everything. All of it. This is bad. Really bad."

I hadn't anticipated this. Yet *another* mistake that I made. A rough hold caught my wrist before I could move again. Kolton's hand shot through the bars, clamping around me like a vice, dragging me closer.

"Heard what?"

"Leo," I whispered. "He's—he's going to sever our bond. He knows how. He wants to make me bond with *him* instead."

Kolton's face turned into a mask of pure fury, and flashes of the tiger slipped through. I flinched when his grip tightened enough to bruise.

"Kolton, you're hurting me."

The second the words left my mouth, he let go—jerking back like I burned him.

The sound that tore from his chest wasn't human. It shook the walls, rattled the ceiling, and vibrated straight through me until my knees threatened to give out. I didn't know if the outburst was from accidentally hurting my wrist or the news that I'd just given him, but it was primal. Wild.

Then he roared—

"BAILEY!"

For a heartbeat, I froze.

Did I hear that right?

Another woman's name.

Before I could make sense of it, something brushed my ankle. A blur shot past me, fast enough to stir the air, and in the next blink—a woman was standing there. Naked. Smiling like she'd been summoned.

"You're so cute!"

I blinked. "What the hell?"

"Did you know that cheetahs aren't actually the fastest—"

"Bailey," Kolton growled.

She froze mid-lecture, eyes lighting up like she'd just been praised. "Yes, Master. Wait, no, you're not my master. Yes, Tiger?"

My mouth fell open. She was tiny, beautiful, and completely naked. She stood there without even a hint of shame. Her body was flawless—slender curves, skin glowing under the dim light.

Kolton didn't even *look*.

Of course, he didn't.

Still, heat flared up my neck anyway. Something hot and foreign curled through me.

Kolton's jaw flexed, and his voice came out low and controlled, like he was wrestling the beast inside him. "Plans have changed. We need to escape. Now."

Bailey clapped her hands like a child at a carnival, bouncing on her toes. "How exciting!"

I stared, stunned. "You've got to be kidding me."

"Where are the keys?" Kolton demanded. "Who has them? How many lions do I have to kill to get out of here?"

She crouched low, sniffing along the edge of the cell, muttering something about vanilla. She suddenly shifted back into a mongoose and bolted through the bars and out of sight.

I folded my arms, glaring at Kolton. My eyes burned, my fangs itched, and my pulse was too fast to be normal. I didn't need a mirror to know my pupils were slits.

He rubbed the back of his neck, looking—of all things—*sheepish*.

"I tell you we are in grave danger, and you summon a naked woman to your cell. One who just called you cute before calling you *master*," I said, each word clipped. "Care to explain, Kolton?"

The corner of his mouth twitched. "I'm not so good with emotions, but just checking—does this mean you're jealous? Or are you actually asking who she is?"

Insufferable. Fucking. Asshole.

I spun on my heel and stormed back down the corridor. Fuck it. I'd just kill Leo myself. I was not dealing with this.

"Skylar!"

I continued up the stairs, rage coursing through me. It felt foreign—unfamiliar, raw. I couldn't seem to remain rational; I wasn't used to emotions like this. Having been captured and kept away from society most of my life, I never learned how to mask my feelings or blend in with others. I was able to fake it better than Onyx, but that wasn't saying much. Despite all the magazines and books they gave me to keep "educated," I still had no idea why I was so upset at the moment.

All I knew was that I didn't recognize myself.

"Skylar!" Kolton roared again, still trapped in his cell.

"It's *Sky*!" I snapped without turning back. "Only the people at the facility called me Skylar."

My voice cracked as it bounced off the walls, raw with something I didn't want to name.

CHAPTER TWENTY-ONE

Sometimes, getting answers to the random questions that popped into my head was not worth finding out.

For example, I wonder what Skylar looks like when she's pissed?

I had seen her annoyed, defiant, assertive—but this? This was different. I didn't even know someone could radiate that kind of fury while still appearing calm.

"Will you stop stomping off!" I roared through the bars, my voice nearly cracking the stone.

Nothing.

Where the hell is that damn mongoose?

No way was I calling Bailey's name again. Once was bad enough.

"Skylar." I tried again, softer this time. "Wait. I can explain. It's not safe. Will you please just come back here?"

Her footsteps stopped.

The silence that followed was worse than her anger.

I pressed my forehead against the bars, breathing hard. The cold bit into my skin, grounding me just enough to not lose my mind completely.

How could I make Skylar understand? I *needed* the mongoose—I didn't *want* her help. I didn't want anyone's help, really. Not in this moment. Not when everything inside me was torn between wanting to rip this place to shreds and wanting to pull Skylar into my arms, just to prove that she was real. That she was safe.

I am not well.

"Please," I said again. The word came out rough, dragged out of me like it didn't belong there.

Her shadow stretched across the corridor before she appeared. When she finally turned the corner, the sight of her nearly undid me. She approached my cell again, back to the spot she stood before Bailey left. Eyes blazing, shoulders tight, lips pressed thin—she looked ready to kill.

Somehow, I'd never seen anything more sexy.

And like any rational tiger, I reached through the bars and wrapped my hand around her throat—not tightly, just enough to keep her from walking away again.

That only fueled her fury. She hissed at me, fangs bared, eyes flaming shards of ice.

My dick got instantly hard.

Fuck, that was hot.

"Skylar," I growled, the bars biting into my chest as I leaned closer. "My precious Sacar. You just told me that the piece of shit who's spent years trying to ruin my life is now planning to sever our bond—*our bond*—and make you his. You are not walking away from me again. Do you understand?"

Her pulse thudded against my palm. She didn't flinch. Didn't back down. Her hand came up slowly, fingers curling around my wrist, not to push me away but to hold me there.

I couldn't have been more stunned until her grip tightened, firm and unrelenting, as she ground out, "Who is she?"

It wasn't a question. It was an accusation.

In that moment, I finally got to see what jealousy looked like on Sky. And I kinda loved it.

I was torn between adding fuel to the fire or trying to douse the flames. I chose the latter.

"Bailey," I said, forcing my tone to remain calm, steady. "She's a mongoose. A shifter. Sent here by Titus and the falcons. She's the one who brought the earpiece."

Her eyes narrowed, still burning. "So, she just...shifts into a naked woman for fun?"

I swallowed hard, trying not to grin. "Apparently."

Her glare was hot enough to set the entire place ablaze. I almost hoped she would.

"Skylar," I said quietly. "You have nothing to worry about. There's no one else I ever want touching me."

The words slipped out before I could stop them, but I meant each one.

Her grip loosened on my wrist, the fight draining from her, but I didn't let go. I couldn't. Part of me was terrified she'd turn and walk away again.

Then her eyes widened slightly and flicked toward my ear. "That earpiece...are they listening right now?"

I nodded once.

If Skylar could blush, I swore she'd be bright red right now.

"Tell her no." Came Derek's voice, low and smug in my ear, with a faint snicker.

I closed my eyes and clenched my jaw tight. Of course, he'd pick *now* to talk.

"Well, wonderful. Let's get one thing straight. If she does that again, you take that sheet off your cot and use it to cover her, you understand *me*?!" Skylar said, mocking my tone with infuriating accuracy.

I nodded, resisting the urge to smile.

Before I could stop myself, I tightened my hold on her neck, pulling her closer. A quiet *oof* slipped past her lips as I drew her in, slowly this time, until her cheeks were pressed against the cold bars between us. Her breath caught as she stared at me.

Then I did something completely and utterly fucking reckless.

I smashed my lips against hers.

She kissed me back without hesitation, as if she was merely biding her time for this exact moment.

It was soft at first, but I felt when her instincts took over. Her fingers curled into my shirt, and she tried to pull me to her, harder, rougher. My heart pounded wildly, and the air between us felt molten. Every breath I dragged in tasted like her, perfect and dangerous. My pulse continued to hammer, so loud I could feel it under my skin. Hell, I could feel it under hers. Her tongue twisted around mine, and I was groaning with need. Then—

Footsteps.

Heavy, quick, and getting closer.

By the time I tore myself away, the lion, whose name she said was John, was already rounding the corner. His eyes widened in disbelief before curdling into something uglier.

"You're playing him?" His voice cracked like a whip. "You're fucking playing Leo."

The words hit like an explosion. Sky flinched. I saw it—the flicker of fear beneath her calm exterior. John shook his head, disgusted, and then turned to leave.

Something primal snapped inside me.

"*Stop.*"

The word ripped out of me before I could think, raw and instinctive. The command wasn't loud, but it was laced with something deeper. Power. Control. Magic.

And he stopped mid-step. His whole body went rigid, muscles locking as if an invisible chain wrapped itself around him and pulled tight.

Skylar inhaled a sharp breath and lifted her hand to her chest, like she could feel the pull too. She looked at me, eyes wide with shock.

My heart slammed once, twice, before the truth hit me.

Fuck.

Fuck.

If Skylar realized what just happened—and her look suggested she did—she didn't say anything. Which I was grateful for. I would process this later.

I nodded toward her, indicating that she take care of John.

"I'm not playing him. I just don't agree with what he's doing."

"He's trying to *save* you from that maniac! What is there to disagree with?" he asked, bewildered, like that wasn't some blatant lie Leo fed his clan members.

Save her?!

All he did was endanger her by taking her away from the one person who was bound to keep her safe.

Me. And only *me*!

Before I had the chance to scream at him, Skylar round-house kicked him in the head. I watched in awe as he crumpled to the ground. The move happened too quickly. She turned back to me without a single hair on her head out of place. If it weren't for the unconscious body on the floor, I would have sworn it never happened.

"You are terrifying, you know that?"

She just shrugged in response.

CHAPTER TWENTY-TWO

John lay unconscious on the floor while we waited for Bailey to return.

"Why do you call me Skylar, anyway?"

She sat on the ground, my least favorite spot for her. She deserved luxury and comfort. All things I couldn't give her. Her back was to me, so I leaned against the bars, trying to press my back to hers. It wasn't exactly a comfortable position, but I needed as much contact with her as I could get.

I didn't want to answer her question. It was complicated. A jumbled mess in my head. I was worried, and suddenly self-conscious, about how it would come off if I said it out loud.

I let the silence linger...until she said, "You know what, it's fi—"

"Because your name is so much more than just Sky. It never made sense to shorten it. You are the moon, the stars, the sun itself." I raked a hand through my hair, unsure if I was articulating my thoughts accurately. "You are the entire universe. You hold everything together for me. So, calling you 'Sky' never felt...right. But I will, if it makes you happy."

She sucked in a breath, as if my words knocked the wind out of her. I felt her shift, and I knew without looking that she was staring at me.

Call me a coward, call me a chicken shit, I didn't care, but I could not face her. The confession was too sudden, too raw, and I wasn't sure if I felt relieved it was out there or regretted that she finally knew the truth.

So, I kept staring at the wall in front of me, feeling Skylar's gaze on my back like a caress.

"Knowing that my name affects you so strongly makes me happy." She paused, choosing her words carefully.

I was suddenly scared, and curious, to see what she had to say. I turned my head slightly, hoping to catch her profile.

"So...is that...is that why you won't touch me? Because you think so highly of me?"

I laughed. I couldn't help it.

That was not at all where I thought she was going.

"No, that is not why I won't give you a hug at incredibly stupid times." I was mocking her, but I needed to deflect.

She reached through the bars and pinched me.

Bailey chose that moment to return, scurrying into my cell so quickly I barely registered her before Skylar shot up, like a daisy ready for war. Her eyes flashed, fangs half-bared. I grabbed the sheet off the cot and held it out before Bailey could finish shifting.

Once she was human again, she tilted her head at the sheet, unconcerned.

"Did you know you have a crack under your bed?"

"Here. Cover up."

She nodded, wrapping the sheet around herself, then finally noticed Skylar.

"Oh, my goodness—hi! You are so, so pretty. You're my new friend now, okay? I'm Bailey."

Skylar blinked, stunned, just as John started stirring on the floor. The reminder hit hard that we needed to move.

"Are you sure now is a good time to get out?" Titus's voice said through the comm in my ear.

Somewhere upstairs, a door slammed, followed by fast, heavy footfalls. They weren't near the stairs to the basement, but the sound was enough to remind us of exactly where we were...and what the risk of staying could be.

"Yes. It is now or never."

"Okay, but we just got back. We're outside of Sparta, about one hundred and fifty miles away. It took a lot of coaxing for Onyx to leave the forest. She spent days there with Dayken, waiting for an update. It is going to take us a few hours to get back to you."

"That's fine; I will leave a bloodbath in my wake. You can clean it up once you get here."

"Who are you talking to?" Skylar asked, brows furrowing.

"Oh, it's okay," Bailey said cheerfully. "Master does that sometimes."

"I am not your master," I hissed.

Titus's chuckle rumbled through the line, low, deep, and infuriating.

I could feel Skylar shooting daggers into the side of my head.

"Bailey, where's the key?"

She appeared deep in thought for a moment. Then she shifted back into a mongoose. I watched her streak down the hallway, a flash of fur with a purpose. A soft ding echoed a moment later, and Bailey reappeared inside my cell with the key to my freedom...a key that could erase this lion clan from existence.

But only time would tell.

"Who are you talking to?" Skylar asked again as she extended her hand through the bars, silently asking Bailey for the key. Bailey, to no one's surprise, shook Skylar's hand in greeting.

"Hi, I'm Bailey."

"Titus," I gritted out.

"What is he saying?" Skylar asked, grabbing a hold of the key as Bailey finally handed it over.

"He's giving me their location. They are still a ways out but should be able to catch up with us once we get outside of town."

She nodded in agreement, her expression both calculating and adorable.

CHAPTER TWENTY-THREE

I slid the key into the heavy metal lock and fumbled for only a moment before finding the right angle. The mechanism clicked, unlocking the door to Kolton's cell.

The satisfying thunk that followed was short-lived. Kolton nearly knocked the door off its hinges and sent it slamming into me as he forced his way out.

Gods, he could be rude and irritating. Flashes of his kiss cut through my mind, demanding my every breath, taking it into his lungs like possessing me wasn't enough. It's a stark reminder that there were sides of him I didn't know as well as I thought.

He grabbed my arm, pulling me down the corridor, when it hit me. A sweet smell, like vanilla. I quickly dig my heels in.

"Wait, where is that smell coming from?"

"Yes! Yes, did you know there is a crack under the cot?" Bailey said excitedly, her tiny fangs on display as she beamed.

The scent lingered—sweet, floral, too pure for this place. Wrong.

I tried to pull my arm from Kolton's grasp. "I want to look—"

"For fuck's sake, not you too. Come on! We've got to move."

Infuriating asshole.

I let him tug me along, despite having all the means to kick him off me. Whenever the facility would train us and put their hardened mercenaries in the ring with Onyx and me, I learned quickly that my legs were my strongest, most effective weapon.

So yes, I let him pull me.

But that smell was so familiar. I needed to figure out what it was.

We hit the stairs and burst through the door. Bailey somehow maneuvered ahead and was leading the way. Terrifying as it was to be led by this very odd woman, toga sheet flowing as she ran, she was shockingly efficient. Almost as if she had navigated these halls a dozen times.

Once we reached the main floor, chaos erupted.

"Hey, stop!"

"She's out of her room!"

"The tiger's loose!"

"Alert the Primarc, quick!"

That was when Kolton shifted into his massive tiger form. I was in a flimsy outfit and barefoot, my standard DeStephano attire.

Oh well, I'd have to make do.

I ran at the first man I saw and sent a knee flying right into his groin while I took his head and smashed it into the ground.

Men shifted into lions, but some stayed human to use weapons instead. I chose those men as my targets, not confident in my ability to take down a lion without a weapon in hand.

I went to attack the next man, but Kolton was already making bloody work of him—the man already bleeding out from a neck bite.

Bailey somehow managed to get a weapon. Also terrifying.

She was shooting men as they piled into the hallway by the dozen.

"Go, Master! I will be fine. Get my new best friend to safety, please."

As much as I disliked this woman parading naked in front of Kolton and calling him master—which I fully intended to dig into later—I didn't like the idea of leaving her here by herself.

"Well, bestie, news flash, that's not going to happen."

I darted down the hall and bashed one man's head against the corner of an ornate gold picture frame, blood spraying the artwork like a masterpiece of its own. I kicked another in the head and then used the wall for leverage to fling myself into the air, getting a better angle at the man behind him. My blow to his temple was instant death. On my way down, I grabbed another man's shoulders and wrapped my legs around his throat, squeezing with my thighs. I quickly turned him over to use his body as a shield—only just realizing no one was shooting at me. Or Kolton.

Whatever Leo had planned, he clearly needed both of us alive.

I decided there had been enough killing. Roughly dropping the man to the ground, I dashed to the front foyer.

I shouted, "Let's go!" to Bailey and Kolton as they slowly made their way toward me.

Unfortunately for Bailey, it was clear that they didn't need her alive, as they continued to shoot in her direction, so I shielded her with my body.

"Let's go, bestie," I mocked, grabbing the back of her neck and ducking her out of the path of a stray bullet. I used the momentum to steer her toward the massive double doors of the estate's front entrance.

There was a giant chandelier with crystal droplets that reflected light all over the floor of the foyer. We needed to make it past the first set of double doors, through the small vestibule, and then the other set of doors. Once outside, I was sure we'd be met with more guards.

My brain flipped through all the different options for escape like a Rolodex, and there was only one that was likely to have the most success.

Speed.

We needed to bolt and just risk any shots we might receive in the back.

"Kolton, run!"

He didn't listen, shocking as it was.

Man, he pissed me off.

He hissed from where he was, paw digging deep into a lion's thigh.

I must have said that out loud.

"Damn it, Kolton, now or I'm leaving without you!"

I would never, but maybe he'd believe the empty threat anyway.

That got his attention. He abandoned his leg-dismemberment and was quickly by my side, charging through the massive double doors, sending them flying with a headbutt.

They tore off their hinges with a crash, crystal raining around us like broken stars. Kolton shoved me through the gap, his shoulder smashing into me, and for a heartbeat, the world narrowed to our pounding pulses and the sharp metallic scent of adrenaline. We made it onto the massive terrace, and then the cold hit us, air so frigid it cut. It must have snowed at some point in the last few days, as a thick, fresh blanket covered the grounds.

The guards outside started shouting. They scrambled to grab us, but we couldn't risk engaging them or even fighting back. We just had to push through and then run as hard as we could. I jumped off the edge of the terrace, and my bare feet sank into wet leaves and half-melted snow. The moonlight illuminated my path as I took off in a sprint. We headed straight toward the tree line, where the shadows would shelter us, concealing our escape and covering our tracks.

A quick flash of brown fur streaked past me. Bailey had shifted back into a mongoose and kept pace with our mad dash. I watched her dodge the bullets aimed in her direction; she was born with an agility that was perfect for this kind of situation.

Behind us, the estate erupted into chaos, with men shouting and pops of gunfire. Still, my focus was entirely on Kolton at my side—pure heat and muscle. I could feel the steady thump of his tiger heart echo against my own ribs. The impossibly bright thread of our bond pulled us forward until the trees closed around us and the world went wild and quiet all at once.

Chapter Twenty-Four

We broke through the tree line and were swallowed by the dense forest. The darkness and gloomy chill in the air made our temporary safety feel even more like an illusion, but it didn't matter. We had to keep moving and fast.

"Bailey, are you okay to head south and intercept the others?"

I knew it was a lot to ask of her, but she seemed committed to helping us and had more agility and stamina than Kolton. Still in mongoose form, she nodded enthusiastically and bounced around in a circle. This little creature had energy for days.

"Great. Kolton and I will head southwest along the lake. Splitting up should help throw them off our trail."

We said our goodbyes. Well, *I* said goodbye to Bailey. Kolton didn't shift back or say much of anything. I watched Bailey's form become smaller and smaller as the mongoose darted through trees and fallen branches. She blended into the forest beautifully and disappeared before I could even process it.

"You ready to run, you grumpy butt?" My voice was lighter than I felt.

He answered with a hiss, lips curling back just enough to flash those massive tiger fangs. A warning to anyone else, but it only made me smirk.

He didn't want to run, but he'd do it anyway. If I had to guess, he probably wanted to go back and keep fighting the lions.

I ignored his objection and sprinted in the direction of the lake. I was not as fast as my sister, but I was faster than almost anything else I'd encountered.

And apparently, Kolton was too. His massive paws pounded behind me, the rhythm steady and controlled. Our bond kept him close, but he would never quite match my speed. He didn't need to, though. He was always there, just a step behind me, a shadow with claws.

We ran along the west coast of Michigan. Snow eventually gave way to slush, then to damp, dark soil. The sun was slowly rising, casting beautiful hues of pink and purple into the sky. The dewy earth smelled alive again, rich and heavy under the clean bite of the cold lake air. My lungs burned with each breath, but the sting was a strange kind of comfort.

When the scents around us started to change—burnt wood, cooked meat, detergent—I slowed.

Human territory.

As I jogged, the bare pads of my feet made almost no sound against the ground. Kolton's pace matched mine until we stopped. His body was coiled tight, fur bristling with restrained energy.

I listened. There was nothing but the steady thump of our matching heartbeats and the faint echo of lake wind through the trees. We locked gazes. His cat eyes were predatory and angry. It was the kind of look that left you wondering if the tiger was going to stalk away or attack you.

"Are we going to talk about how you kissed me?" Yes, I asked the question out of nowhere, but it was clearly on my mind.

He stared at me for a second, then turned away without so much as a grunt.

The audacity.

He veered off through a break in the trees, heading in a completely different direction. I followed him with my eyes, disbelief twisting through me.

"Seriously? You're literally taking the coward's route right now?" I called after him, sharp enough to sting. I wanted him mad enough to face me, to stop hiding behind fur and silence. Just wait until he shifted back, and then we'd see if I punched him or hugged him first.

But Kolton Teegra of the Danielson Clan, the lone tiger who never did what anyone expected, had his own agenda. With a huff, I followed after him as he continued through the thinning trees until a building emerged in the clearing up ahead—an old church, half-eaten by time. The roof sagged, and there was a pile of collapsed bricks to one side where the wall had given way long ago.

I should have let him go. But curiosity, and something else far more dangerous, kept my feet moving. I watched him leap onto the mound of debris and disappear through a hole in the wall. He didn't even glance back. Arrogant bastard knew I'd follow.

And fine, he was right. I would.

I noticed the difference in the air the moment I stepped inside. It was thick with dust and the scent of rot. There were cobwebs draped over broken pews, and the altar was cracked. Hymnals and church papers were scattered everywhere, like ghosts of old sermons trying to escape. The early sunlight filtered through the cracked, but still intact, stained-glass window, painting the dust in a strange kaleidoscope of colors.

Kolton was at the far end, sniffing around a side door near the altar, the muscles of his tiger form flexing instinctively as he investigated the space. I crossed the room quickly, my bare feet carefully avoiding pieces of broken glass that were scattered across the ground.

"Seriously, stop being a dick and tell me why you kissed me."

He froze, spine stiffening. The air in the room changed. Then his bones shifted, fur retracted, and within seconds, the tiger was gone. Kolton stood before me, fully human, in all his naked glory, but I couldn't focus on that because he was also angrier than I'd ever seen him. His chest rose and fell, every inhale a barely contained growl.

He jabbed a finger in my face. "Because you were running your mouth and losing your temper, and it was the only way I could think to shut you up."

I stared at him, stunned, then scoffed and crossed my arms. "Well, I'm about to lose my temper now. You gonna do it again?"

His eyes flickered with that strange glow, light threading through them as they morphed into his slitted cat eyes.

"Sky," he drawled, his voice low and rough in that dangerous way only he could manage. "There is so much more I want to do to you. A kiss should be the least of your concerns."

My breath hitched, then I swallowed hard, caught completely off guard by his words. His gaze dropped to my chest, lingering where the built-in bra of my nightie clung to my skin.

Then his eyes traveled back up to my face, slow and deliberate. The look he gave me wasn't confusion or irritation anymore. It was hunger. Real, raw hunger.

Kolton wanted...me.

Me.

The knowledge hit me so hard that everything else disappeared. My brain went silent except for that single fact.

I realized two things at once.

First, Kolton stood there, bare, beautiful and tangible. And second, I wanted him too. Gods help me, I wanted him.

Badly.

Maybe I always had, but everything had been too chaotic for me to stop long enough to notice. My life was still chaotic, but at least it was just him and me right now. I inhaled deeply, taking in his scent. Despite being trapped in that cell for who knew how many days, he smelled alluring. Like scorched earth and wildflowers.

I was face-level with his chest. I broke eye contact with him to take it in. He was flawless—his nipples were pale, and I had the sudden urge to lick them. His chest was powerful in a way that was defined but not bulky. The lower my gaze traveled, the more that raw, sculpted muscle appeared. Abs carved from marble. A perfect V that led to...

Holy fucking shit.

He was huge. My fangs punched through my gums before I could stop them, a reflex I couldn't hide from him.

"Fuck," Kolton hissed under his breath—once, then again, as if he was trying to exorcise the thought. "Sky, do not look at me that way. I am warning you now."

"But you just said you wanted more."

"I don't get everything I want." His voice was quieter now. Steady but strained. He took a step back before adding, "And what matters more than any of that is keeping you safe."

The silence that followed was heavy—the kind that made the air feel too thick to breathe.

He took another step back. I stayed rooted where I was, heart hammering in my chest, still trying to decide if I should be furious or flattered.

Maybe both.

Because right now, I didn't know if I wanted to fight him or kiss him again—and that was becoming a problem.

CHAPTER TWENTY-FIVE

I looked inside a small room that, given the stack of books, crosses, and wardrobe strewn about, clearly belonged to the church's former priest. There was one small mattress, the bedframe had long since collapsed and gone.

"I'll take the floor." I grabbed an abandoned pair of pants to throw on before I started stacking the rest of the clothes, making a pile for me to sleep on.

"No."

"Yes."

"I'm not arguing with you. There's plenty of room on the mattress," Skylar said in response. The sass in her tone, the fire in her words...it made me burn. She was doing things to me I couldn't control, but I shoved it down.

"No."

"Fine, I'll take the floor then."

She knew damn well I wasn't going to allow that. I didn't even like it when she sat on the floor, let alone sleep on it. She deserved much better than that.

"Don't start this shit, Skylar. I am not in the fucking mood."

"No! *I'm* not in the mood! You are *not* sleeping on the floor! We've been through too much, and we will BOTH rest more comfortably on the godsdamn fucking bed. Understand?!"

Stunned. It was like she smacked me again. Only this time with words.

I stepped up to her, and she dug her feet in, crossing her arms over her chest.

"What. You going to kiss me again?!" she mocked in a sassy tone.

As a matter of fact, I think I might.

I shot my hand out, clasping her around the nape, and pulled her against me so I could inhale the side of her neck.

"I see you've gotten over your hang-up about touching me," she said in an attempt to push my buttons. But her voice was sultry now, distracted. The sass was gone.

"It was never a hang-up. I just didn't want to dirty you." She tried to tilt her head at my words, but my grip was too firm, holding her in place.

Damn, I said too much.

"You can't dirty me with a touch, Kolton."

"Well, either way, I clearly don't care about it now." I did care, but I was also a selfish prick, after all. I ran my nose along her neck again, watching goose bumps blossom across her skin.

I pulled away to look back at her face. She was too beautiful. Too perfect. I didn't deserve the look she was giving me. She was warmth and light. She was hope. She was everything I wasn't.

Outcast. Murderer. Insane.

You name it. That was me.

But she was good, kind, and smart. I couldn't risk tainting that.

"Kiss me," she whispered soft, seductive. I wanted nothing more than to comply with her demand. Because that is what it was. A demand.

"No."

This time, she growled in frustration.

I shouldn't have enjoyed this as much as I was. I shouldn't even be touching her, but the softness of her skin was too addictive. And now that I knew what it felt like beneath my fingertips, I needed more. So much more.

My tiger roared, "Yes," in agreement.

But now wasn't the time. We had a pride of lions after us. The residential area we passed would no doubt throw them off our trail, but not for long.

"Why not? I can see in your eyes that you want me."

She looked directly into my strange eyes, eyes that others struggled to meet. The reason I always wore sunglasses in public was so I didn't blow a gasket when I got asked if I was wearing contacts for the hundredth time. But Sky met my eyes head-on, and she didn't seem to mind them.

"Because we are being hunted. I need to keep my senses alert and free from distractions right now."

What I wouldn't give for a weapon. Like a chainsaw or something.

"You are a weapon...and so am I. You don't have anything to worry about."

Shit, I must have said that part out loud.

The fact that she didn't bat an eye at my internal thoughts made me wonder if maybe, just maybe, she wouldn't mind the dirt, blood, and gore that tarnished my hands.

I reached down, grabbing whatever clothes lay at my feet, and stepped away from her. I needed to put some distance between us before I did something stupid, which was likely, given my nearly non-existent self-control.

I strolled back into the main part of the church, passing some empty, run-down confessionals. I searched for anything that might make Skylar more comfortable. Some type of soft curtain, a used pew cushion, anything, but it all looked worse than if she just slept on the old clothes on the floor. I cracked open a door on the far side after the last confessional. I looked over my shoulder, making sure my Sacar was still there. Whether it was out of paranoia or general care remained unclear.

She was still there, sitting on the mattress, pretending not to stare at me. For as brilliant as she was, she sure didn't make a great actress.

I fought a smirk.

Once I checked all the doors, I had no choice but to return to Skylar's alarmingly enticing presence, empty-handed. I arrived and immediately saw that she had moved my makeshift pile of clothes to the mattress and was, in fact, planning to sleep next to me.

In one bed.

With me.

Someone who had almost no self-control in every aspect of his life.

"Have you heard from anyone?" Skylar asked.

Her voice cut through my spiraling.

Her voice soothing and grounding.

I blinked, dragging myself back to the present.

"Yeah." I kept scanning the room, unable to settle even with four walls around us. "Dayken talked to me while I was shifted. Said Titus updated him on Bailey breaking us out. They're coming, but it'll still be a few hours before they get here."

I glanced toward the doorway again before adding, "They're going on foot to intercept Bailey first. They're supposed to rendezvous at a predetermined location, then reconnect with us once they know where we are. It's too hard to stay in constant communication while any of us are shifted."

She nodded, calm like that update was enough.

"I'll keep watch and make sure no one is coming."

"You will stay right here with me. I can hear perfectly fine, and we'll have plenty of warning if someone comes."

I crossed my arms over my bare chest and arched a brow. I also felt my dick stir in my pants.

She remained silent. Just stared at me, waiting for me to challenge her. I always felt so torn when I was in her presence. When she wasn't around, all I wanted was her near, within reaching distance. And then when she was close, I wanted to keep her at arm's length.

Skylar finally broke the silence, ending the momentary standoff we were in.

"I have something to confess to you."

I didn't like her tone. Not one bit.

"Go on then." I motioned for her to continue. She didn't like that for some reason.

"Sit. Down." She tapped the mattress for emphasis.

"You are awfully bossy tonight, Sacar."

"And you're extra arrogant. Now, I have something important to tell you, and I don't want to keep craning my neck to look up at you. So, sit down. Please."

"Only because you said please."

I chose the floor instead of the mattress, attempting to keep some distance between us. I sat, legs stretched out, hands on the floor, bracing myself so I could lean back and stretch. When she didn't speak, I looked up to glare at her. Silently asking, *what is it?*

"When we first arrived in Michigan, Dayken found us and took us in, but the people from the facility kept finding us. So, Derek and Chase helped to find and remove a tracking device from Onyx."

"Okay...good to know."

She inhaled deeply. "When they scanned me for trackers—"

I sat up straighter, suddenly very concerned with where she was going with this.

"They couldn't find one." Skylar cleared her throat. Her voice was soft as she continued. "Because they didn't scan my head."

I waited for her to go on. She winced, almost looking like she was preparing for me to yell at her. But I didn't understand what she was saying.

"Scan your head? Like a brain scan?"

"Correct." She nodded. "They couldn't find a tracking device on me, like they did on Onyx, because...it's in my brain."

I—I think I might puke. The church was suddenly spinning.

CHAPTER TWENTY-SIX

Now that it was out in the open, I didn't feel any better. Kolton looked like he was going to be sick, and I hadn't even finished telling him everything.

"Kolton, do you need some water or something? I'm sure I can find—"

"No. No—nope. I'm good." He tried to regain his composure but wasn't successful. "So what, we need to find a brain surgeon? I don't blame you for not trusting Derek to go digging around inside your head."

"No. Here's the thing..." I inhaled deeply for what had to have been the hundredth time. "I'm not willing to get rid of the device."

"WHAT?!"

His rage was ferocious and immediate. He went from a sick kitten to a feral tiger in a blink. His eyes slitted, veins bulged in his neck, and faint stripes began forming along his arms.

"Calm down." Which I quickly realized was the wrong thing to say.

"No, I will not calm down! You have a fucking tracking device in your brain. YOUR BRAIN! And you just told me that you *like* it! That is beyond fucked up, Skylar! And that's coming from someone who is very *fucked up*!"

"I'm not going to say it again," I warned evenly. "Take a deep breath and just listen."

He hissed at me but shut up. I ground my teeth, forcing myself to ignore the flash of fangs aimed in my direction, and continued.

"The device helps me, and I know how to disable the tracker so long as I have access to a computer."

Kolton growled low in his throat. The signs of a shift were still there, but at least he wasn't shouting anymore.

"The device allows me to absorb information, make calculated decisions, assess risk, and read people. I can't function without it. I've had it for as long as I can remember. It's a part of me, just like my beating heart or the breath in my lungs."

Time to rip the bandage off.

"But I'm pretty sure the only reason Leo managed to send one of his guys to get me is because I screwed up while updating the chip. I was trying to strengthen it for my own protection, but in the process, I accidentally disrupted the compound's security. I shut the old safeguards down too early, and for a brief period, the gate code could be bypassed. It was bad timing, but it gave him the opening."

"WELL, THAT'S NOT VERY CALCULATED!" he roared.

"I know!" I shot back. "I'm not claiming I'm perfect. But I need this chip. For the most part, it *is* safe. And I'm telling you now because I want trust to be part of our bond. I couldn't live with myself if I kept this from you any longer."

"Well, aren't you *so* thoughtful!"

"Oh, grow up! You're being childish about this."

"*I'm* childish? Says the vampire who's clinging to a tainted brain implant like it's a pacifier!"

"You insufferable asshole!"

I stood up and started pacing. This wasn't going at all how I thought it would. I thought maybe he would see things my way, if even only a little bit.

"So what—you kept this from your sister too? Dayken? Does anyone know?" He cut in, interrupting my thoughts.

"No. They don't know. Just you," I said, not wanting to look him in the eyes as the words left my mouth.

I saw Kolton freeze out of the corner of my eye. When I finally looked at him, I caught the rage flickering in his eyes, uncertain now.

"You...only trust *me* with this information?"

The shift in his demeanor was so sudden it nearly gave me whiplash. And I loved it. The way I never knew what was coming next. I prided myself on being able to predict outcomes, but Kolton was impossible to read—unpredictable, untamed.

When he asked if anyone else knew, I calculated what to tell him. Did I try to win him over and make him feel special? Or did I tell him the brutal truth and make him understand why I hadn't told anyone?

"The device helps me read people's motives, anticipate attacks, and process information faster than others. I'm sure my sister's noticed there's something different about me, but she's never asked, and I've never told her. I'm telling you now because I want you to start trusting me, to understand that, even though I'm small and look fragile, I'm not."

He stared at me for a long beat.

"You think I see you as incapable?" He tilted his head, eyes sharp, like a predator studying his prey.

"Sky, you are the most stunning, capable, intelligent person I know. I've done nothing but think of you, search for you. I've—I've done unspeakable things trying to find you. When you tell me that you want to keep something dangerous inside you, it makes me want to do unspeakable things all over again."

His voice dropped, low and broken. "I just want you safe and healthy. And this doesn't sound like either."

Kolton's confession of how he viewed me left me stunned. And I couldn't help but wonder about what kinds of unspeakable things he did to find me. I lowered myself onto the floor, so we were at eye level. Watching and waiting for anything from him.

"Lie down and close your eyes. I'll keep watch. And I'm not arguing with you about it," he finally said.

I nodded, disappointment washing over me, but I accepted my fate. His earlier words still echoed in my mind.

"Okay. Goodnight."

I climbed back onto the mattress and lay on my side, hand tucked beneath my cheek. My feet rested near where Kolton sat on the floor, his back against the wall. We were cramped, but it was cozy—the coziest I'd felt in a very long time.

CHAPTER TWENTY-SEVEN

KOLTON

I watched Skylar sleep.

I knew if I pretended to close my eyes, she would eventually relax enough to rest peacefully. So I lay on my side, perfectly still, not wanting to shift into my tiger yet because my view was too perfect. I wasn't ready to stop staring yet.

Her chest rose and fell in a slow, gentle rhythm.

She was sleeping on her side, facing me, and the short pieces of her hair had fallen into her face.

I had the sudden, irrational urge to brush them away.

I didn't.

Touching her felt...wrong.

Not because I didn't want to.

Gods, I wanted to.

That was the problem.

She was the kind of beautiful that stole the air from my lungs, almost painful to look at for too long. Snow-white skin. Thick black lashes resting against her cheeks. If her eyes were open, they would be staring straight into my soul with that calculated, ice-blue gaze. Her brows were perfectly shaped, dark, and flawless, and I had the strange urge to run the pad of my thumb over them, just to see if something so precise could actually be real.

My hands flexed against the blanket as I forced myself to stay where I was. These hands had done things. Torturous things. Evil but necessary things. Blood had soaked into the lines of my palms more times than I could count.

Hands like mine weren't meant for someone like her.

My gaze drifted across her face again, memorizing the curve of her cheek, the soft part of her mouth, the steady rise of her breathing.

My own breathing started to turn uneven.

And then, inevitably, my gaze went to the place in her skull where that device still lived.

The thought of it sat in my chest like a stone.

Everything in me hated that thing. It was Crowe's handiwork, a reminder that he had gotten close enough to carve into her mind and leave something behind. Every instinct I had screamed the same command.

Remove it. Destroy it. Erase whatever piece of him still lingered inside her.

But Skylar had looked me straight in the eye earlier and told me she wanted to keep it. Said it made her stronger.

And I trusted her. Because she had trusted me with that information.

Me.

Not Dayken. Not Chase. Not Derek.

Not Onyx.

Me.

Trust.

Not a word people usually attached to my name. I was honored, and it made my chest swell with pride. But the reality of the situation was harder to swallow. Every protective instinct I possessed still rebelled against the idea of that chip in her head. A darker part of me kept imagining pinning her down long enough to rip the damn thing out myself if that was what it took to keep her safe.

I would never actually do that.

But the fact that the thought crossed my mind at all left a bitter taste in my mouth. Because respecting Skylar's wishes should have been easy. Instead, it felt like another battle I had to fight with myself.

And lying here now, watching the girl I'd spent half my life trying to find...

How was I supposed to be the Guardian she actually needed now that I had her again?

My jaw tightened.

And yet every time she shifted, every time her scent drifted across the small space between us, the tiger inside me pushed harder against the cage.

Mine.

The word whispered through my mind like a curse.

I shut my eyes.

Because the truth was becoming harder to ignore. I didn't just want to protect Skylar.

I wanted her.

And wanting her felt like the worst kind of betrayal.

Chapter Twenty-Eight

I awoke to the feeling of softness engulfing me. Cushioned and velvety. My eyes snapped open, panic flooding me as I half expected to see the silver walls of Leo's prison. The sun was high overhead, trying and failing to break through the thick clouds. Instead of pitch black, I was surrounded by a dull gray cast.

Realization dawned on me. I was tightly wrapped up in the embrace of my tiger. I was still on my side, only now, my head rested against thick fur instead of a pillow. One of his massive paws stretched out beside me, and the other was draped heavily across my waist. It weighed me down, but in the best possible way. My smile was instant.

I squirmed, trying to turn so I could face him. It wasn't easy, but I managed to shimmy around until my nose was pressed to fur. His face was a masterpiece of white, black, and orange stripes. His eyes were closed, breathing slow and even. Gods, he was beautiful.

My fingers slipped through the thick scruff of fur around his neck. The deep rumble caused by my movement vibrated through my bones. I couldn't help the quiet giggle that escaped.

"My happy kitty," I whispered into his fur, nuzzling closer.

His purr grew louder. The sound filled the room and my chest all at once.

Suddenly I didn't want the tiger anymore.

I wanted Kolton. His skin. His warmth. The wild, chaotic mess of his hair after a long night.

"Shift," I murmured, fully aware of what I was asking—and that he'd probably ignore me. He never listened.

Except this time, he did.

In an instant, fur became skin, claws became hands, and I was once again left stunned by his absolute unpredictability.

His naked body was wrapped around me, touching my exposed skin. I looked into his eyes, seeing raw hunger in them.

For me.

I ran my hand down his chest. He didn't move, and I was shocked by his stillness, unsure if he'd snatch my wrist and make me stop.

He didn't, so I kept exploring, trailing my hand lower and lower, before allowing my eyes to follow it. There was no purring, no rumble from his chest, just warmth and silence. When my fingers traced the V of his pelvis, I looked up to see if I'd made a mistake. I didn't know if his lack of reaction was good or bad, and I suddenly felt self-conscious.

But when I looked into his eyes, they conveyed everything.

Hunger.

Fear.

War.

Without warning, he flipped me over.

I was pinned to my back, both wrists caught in his grip, Kolton's naked body poised on top of me. His double fangs were fully extended, and his pupils had become such narrow slits that the yellow of his eyes was practically glowing.

"This is a bad idea." His chest rose and fell like he'd been running.

"I disagree."

His jaw clenched.

"You don't understand what you're doing," he said roughly. "I am meant to protect you, and I've lost you twice. It feels wrong to give in to desire, knowing what a failure I am. And there are things you don't know about—"

"Stop."

I would have silenced him with my finger, but my hands were still held over my head.

He pushed himself off, dragging a hand down his face like he was trying to physically pull himself back from the edge.

I didn't want to hear another word about his so-called failures. Anyone would have failed going against Crowe alone. He was too young, and he had too much on his shoulders at such a young age, and whenever I reminded him of this, he just ignored me.

I was done.

Done with pity. Done with self-loathing. Done with him thinking he wasn't good enough.

My voice softened, but the meaning in my words was still there. "You didn't fail me. You survived him. And you never stopped looking for me."

I dug my nails into the tops of his bare thighs, applying just enough pressure to prove my point before sliding them slowly upward. My hands were dangerously close to his very hard, very large erection.

I couldn't help but lick my lips as I stared, and when I looked up, he was watching me.

His eyes were tormented now.

"Sky...I—I can't control myself," he heaved out.

"Good," I whispered. "Don't."

And then his lips were at my neck, nuzzling it, kissing it, trailing up toward my ear. He laced his fingers into my hair, roughly pulling my head to the side, exposing my neck further to give him more access.

I moaned, bucking my hips against him. I could feel the hard length of his shaft, with only the thin material of my nightie separating us. The friction felt so good. I wanted more.

I tried to turn my head to meet his lips, but he had such a firm grip on me, I was helpless in his grasp.

He moved lower. Nipping at my collarbone, then kissing to make it better. I kept squirming and moaning, unable to control myself. I was beginning to feel feverish, but he just kept me pinned in place.

"Kolton"

"This is a bad idea. Bad, bad idea," he breathed against my skin, but his tone suggested he didn't care.

"I like bad ideas. More. Please."

He pulled the bra cup down and exposed my nipple. He ran his tongue over it while looking up to watch my reaction. I moaned loudly, and I made sure not to look away from his gaze. I wanted him to see exactly what he was doing to me. I wanted him to see how much I wanted him. To see that there was nothing to be afraid of. That he couldn't hurt me.

And it worked. He grabbed the back of my thigh and moved it so he could grind into me harder.

I nearly screamed with pleasure.

"I could fuck you right now, and you would let me, wouldn't you?"

I nodded enthusiastically.

Yes, yes, I want that! I want to experience that right now!

He loosened his grip on my hair and moved his hand, roughly pinning my hip to the small mattress and stopping me from rubbing against him.

He feathered his mouth lower, down my breasts to my ribs, nipping and then kissing, giving me a combination of mild pain then gentle care, like he was silently communicating that this was who he was. Rough came naturally to him, being gentle didn't. I didn't care; I wanted every sharp edge, every rough angle, even the parts of him that could cut me.

Sliding the thin, nearly see-through fabric out of his way, he took his time as he continued lower down my stomach.

I arched my back at the sensation of his lips against my navel, my skin feeling extra sensitive there.

I tried to buck again, but I couldn't move. This was beginning to feel like torture.

I whined, and he chuckled, low and throaty and sexy as hell. I was so turned on. I wanted more. Badly. And while this was a foreign feeling, it was a welcome one.

"What's the matter, my Sacar? Need something?"

"Yes. I need more. Please."

"More what?" he growled.

The sound sent a shiver straight through me, short-circuiting every thought in my head. How did I put words to something that lived entirely in my body?

"Relief..." I pleaded between panting breaths. My fingers dug into the mattress, hips lifting without my permission. "Please. I need relief."

His smile was slow and unguarded, genuinely beautiful. His fangs became visible as his features softened, relaxed in a way that made my chest ache. He looked pleased. Confident. Dangerous.

I was utterly captivated by him.

In that moment, I knew he had the power to destroy me—mind, body, soul—and I would let him. I would thank him for it if it meant I got this moment.

He resumed his lazy pursuit of my body, his touch deliberate, yet unhurried. Every inch he touched felt like a promise.

Lower.

Still lower.

Until he was there. Right at my core, where wetness and pressure had been building as he took his time exploring the rest of my body.

Heat rushed to my face. I suddenly felt exposed, aware of every reaction my body was giving him. And yet, I didn't stop him. I couldn't. The need was stronger than the instinct to hide.

"Ever been touched here?" he asked, lightly pressing the pad of his thumb to the spot in question.

The contact stole my breath. My head fell back as a broken sound left me.

"No..."

His eyes darkened.

"Good," he said, his voice dropping in satisfaction. "Then I get to be the first. And the only."

His words wrapped around me as he began to move his thumb, slow and intentionally, circling my bundle of nerves. The apex of my desire. He lit every nerve at once, and my body trembled helplessly beneath him.

It felt so...right.

Perfect.

My legs shook as my body coiled tighter, pleasure stealing my breath. I gripped his arm, nails biting into his skin as my head thrashed back.

"Do you want me to stop?" he murmured, far too amused.

I forced myself to lift my head and look at him. Whatever he saw written across my face was enough of an answer for him. He chuckled softly and resumed the unbothered, confident strokes of his thumb. Heat gathered low in my stomach, thick and overwhelming.

My hips began to move on their own, chasing his touch, begging for more pressure. More friction. More of him. That seemed to please Kolton. His thumb moved faster, harder.

I cried out, unable to stop myself.

"That's it. Fuck. You look beautiful when you're about to cum," he said as his smile turned predatory. He leaned closer, his warm breath ghosting across my skin.

"I can't decide," he purred, voice low and unhurried, "if I want to drag this out...or give you what you're asking for."

The pressure built until it bordered on pain. My body strained toward him, every nerve screaming. And then he slowed. Just enough. Too much.

The torment made my vision blur.

"Please," I cried. The word tore out of me, raw and desperate.

He exhaled like he was succumbing, giving in to something danger-ous.

"Fine," he said at last. "But only because I want to do it again."

I barely had time to register his words before he moved. The mattress dipped beneath his weight as he shifted lower. His hands were on my thighs, steady and secure, holding me open as he settled his face between my legs.

His tongue grazed the sensitive area of my swollen clit, slow and deliberately, just enough to make me gasp. He nuzzled closer to me, kissing and pressing against my core in a way that felt almost reverent. The onslaught of sensation ripped a sound from my throat, raw and unrestrained, echoing up into the rafters.

Then he pressed harder. His rhythm picked up, relentless now, pur-poseful. I had no chance to catch my breath before everything shattered.

Stars burst behind my eyes. A moan ripped free, part scream, yet pure ecstasy. My body arched helplessly as my release crashed over me in waves, breathless and shaking.

When I could finally breathe again, I started laughing. He was nuz-zling the inside of my thigh now, and I raised myself onto my elbows to look at him.

"Kolton," I said, my breath catching. "That was absolute torture."

He froze.

His entire body went rigid, like my words had struck him instead of teased him. He snapped upright, shaking his head violently, as if arguing with something only he could hear.

"No. No. No."

Then he smacked his own head, hard and sudden, before doing it again. I jolted upright and grabbed his wrist.

"Stop. Stop hitting yourself," I cried, voice breaking. "What happened?"

He pulled free from my grasp and backed away from me, putting distance between us like the space was the only thing keeping him in control.

And just like that, the moment was gone.

What just happened?

My heart hammered as I stared at the spot on the mattress he had just abandoned, heat still humming through my body while confusion clawed its way in.

What did I say wrong? Was it his name? Had that done it? Should I have said it was amazing instead of torture?

The questions piled up faster than I could process them.

"Hi, best friend! Goats are here!" Bailey suddenly sang from the doorway, cheerful and oblivious.

CHAPTER
TWENTY-NINE

I blinked, still trying to breathe. "Bailey? What?"

She squinted, correcting herself without missing a beat. "Wait. No. Not goats. Lions." She smiled like she hadn't just dropped a bomb on us. "Yeah. Lions are here."

The last echo of warmth drained out of me.

Of course, they were here.

I scrambled up and shifted my clothing back into place. My hands were still shaking from the aftereffects of my orgasm as I tugged the fabric back where it belonged. Kolton had already shifted back into tiger form and was out of the small room, heading for the hole in the church wall. He was massive and silent as he moved. Bailey shifted as well, and we followed after him. She was a quick blur of motion as she climbed upward, scaling stone and disappearing in the rafters leading to the steeple.

I ran along the wall, keeping my body close to the cold stone, avoiding the open area near the center of the church.

I reached the sanctuary doors. Well, one door. Nails and a single board held the other in place. It was crooked and splintered like a rushed afterthought.

I paused and listened, holding my breath.

When I didn't hear anything outside, I slowly pried the wood loose and watched as the door fell to the ground...loudly.

Very subtle, Sky.

I listened again for movement. Silence answered me, so I knew they hadn't made it to my side of the church yet.

I peeked past the decrepit door frame and looked around the corner to see a man scanning the church grounds. There was nothing unusual about him except for the fact that he had a comm attached to his ear.

"We have eyes on the tiger."

"But where is the girl?" Came a different voice.

I ran at him with every ounce of speed I had. A roar tore through the air, powerful enough to shake the trees and rattle my chest. I pushed harder, my swiftness allowing me to catch the man completely off guard. I swept his legs out from under him, and when he hit the ground, I brought my heel down hard on his sternum. The impact reverberated up my leg, but I was already moving again.

Cutting along the side of the building, I caught sight of my tiger lying motionless on the ground, with a tranquilizer dart glinting under the headlights of the vehicles that surrounded the church. The dart jutted out of his left shoulder, and the sight of it made me want to scream.

Lions and mountain lions I'd never seen before circled him. Their tails flicked, muscles tense, while a few men stood behind them, watching.

"Grab him," one ordered.

I could take the men, but I didn't know how my strength compared to that of a lion, let alone an entire pride of them.

Only one way to find out.

I moved to lunge into the fray, only to have my arm yanked back as a solid body appeared behind me.

Instinct took over.

I drove my elbow hard into his side.

An oof came from a familiar-sounding voice as the grip on my arm loosened. I spun around to find Titus.

My chest heaved, my heart pounding so hard it felt like it wanted out. I didn't have time to remind him not to sneak up on a vampire, no matter how sly he thought he was.

"What the hell! Why'd you stop me?" My voice came out rough with adrenaline.

"I was trying to keep you from committing suicide. And you thank me by cracking my rib?" He rubbed his side, wincing.

For a moment, I really looked at him. His skin was smooth and flawless, the deep, rich color of dark chocolate. When his eyebrow arched, it wasn't just an expression—it was an accusation, like he knew exactly what I was thinking and was silently daring me to try it anyway.

"I need to save Kolton."

The air between us thrummed—his stillness against my fury.

"And you're going to help me."

"This is a terrible idea," Titus murmured for the hundredth time.

I ignored him, because no, it wasn't.

No one outside of Dayken's inner circle knew that Titus had recently allied himself with the Danielson Clan. That little secret lived safely in the *classified* section of Dayken's clan files.

I knew, because I looked.

Couldn't help it.

Titus sighed, his patience thinning, but he still followed my instructions.

He placed his hand over my mouth, pretending to muffle my non-existent shouts. It was all for show, after all.

I gave a quick nod.

He stepped out from the corner of the church we were hiding behind, one arm locked tight around my waist, pressing my back against his chest.

"I've got her!" he shouted. His voice echoed off the stone walls, demanding attention. "This little bitch put up quite the fight!"

The lions didn't look impressed. I'm pretty sure I heard one of them mutter, "That fucking fox."

Poor Titus. I might be the only person outside of his clan who actually liked and trusted him. I gave Peach plenty of insight into what I got when I analyzed him. She didn't know about the chip in my head, but that didn't matter. He was still a great friend, and I was happy to advocate for him.

"Give her to me," one of the lions said, reaching for me. I gave Titus's arm a slight squeeze, providing him the signal we'd agreed on.

He shifted instantly. His fox form was a blur of motion as he ducked and weaved beneath the lions, cutting through two of their Achilles tendons with precise, effective strikes.

But I didn't let him do all the heavy lifting. I was in the thick of it, too, landing a solid blow to the man in front of me, then slamming my head back into the one who tried to grab me from behind.

That only left two men standing between my tiger and me. I moved in a wide arc, circling them without giving them my back and positioning myself directly between the lions and Kolton.

Titus's black fox reappeared, latching onto one man's throat while I disarmed the other before he could fire, slamming my elbow into his nose. The melee lasted less than five seconds.

I crouched in front of Kolton before I could even retract my arm, yanking the dart from his shoulder. I peeled back his eyelids, checking for dilation, trying to get a sense of what they'd hit him with.

His pulse was slow but steady. The toxin was strong but not fatal. I could work with that. I moved back to his shoulder, feeling around for the injection site. Once I found it, I lowered my lips to the tiny puncture mark. I began sucking the poison from the wound and then spit it out.

It was bitter, leaving my tongue numb, but my body was healing through the effects quickly enough that I felt confident I could keep going.

A shadow moved across the ground in front of me.

"Easy now," a man's voice said from behind me, calm but with enough authority to slice through the noise in my head.

I spun on my crouched heels, giving Kolton my back, and spread my arms wide to protect him. Instinct took over before rational thought could catch up.

I looked up to see a man standing a few paces away, hands raised in mock surrender. His confidence did not seem to come from arrogance. It was measured. Controlled. The kind that told me he was the one in charge here without him needing to say it.

"Here," he said calmly, holding something out to me. "Primarc DeStephano would like to speak with you."

Chapter Thirty

The man pulled his phone from the front pocket of his combat vest and jutted the screen in my direction, close enough that I had no choice but to look.

Leo's face filled the screen, arrogance etched into every line. He looked unaffected by the fact that we had just taken out a handful of his men. He stared at me like I was still under his control. Like I was nothing more than an impenitent child throwing a fit that he fully expected to put an end to.

"Amore mio, what is this?" he asked smoothly, lips curling into a familiar, infuriating smile. "Come back to me, and I will forgive your transgressions against my clan."

"Get fucked," I spat. The words came easily, sharp and unfiltered. I was done pretending. He wanted to take Kolton from me, to dissolve our bond and replace one of the most important people in my life, as if it meant nothing. The realization hit hard, hot, and violent. He could get fucked in hell, now that I really thought about it.

"Ah, there she is. He told me there was more to you than meets the eye," Leo purred through the phone, his voice rich with satisfaction. "Well, nonetheless, I have something you want. Something you will be dying to see. You'll be back here before you know it, and I will be waiting for you. With open arms."

"Caleb, where is that fucking fox?" Leo demanded, his tone turning harsh as he addressed the man holding the phone.

The video disappeared abruptly as Caleb lifted the phone to his ear and turned away, walking off as if I were inconsequential and he had already accomplished everything he needed to.

I looked around for Titus but did not see him anywhere. Just Leo's men sprawled out in random heaps across the damp, cold ground.

Something you will be dying to see...

Curiosity tugged at me, sharp and insistent, but so did the logical part of my brain. The part that loved to calculate odds, outcomes, and consequences.

Leo was wrong. I would not be back. I was not going to risk being separated from my tiger. Not again. Not ever.

Kolton stirred, a low sound rumbling in his chest. I ran my hand through his fur, slow and steady, grounding both of us.

"Shhh, shhh. It's me, Sky. It's okay," I murmured. "I got the poison out of you."

I lifted my head, scanning the area for a quick escape route, already assessing our exit strategy. Every shadow, every tree line, every possible path out.

"Can you shift?" I asked softly. "I need to know where my sister is. Where everyone is."

I kept my voice low, quiet, like anything louder than a whisper might shatter what little calm he had left.

A grumble escaped him, part growl, part groan, vibrating beneath my palm.

The sound rolled through his chest and into my hand, thick with pain and barely restrained fury.

And then, before I knew it, I was running my hand down the bare skin of Kolton's back and shoulder as he lay naked before me.

His skin was warm, too warm. It was also damp with sweat as his muscles twitched under my touch. Like they couldn't decide whether to fight or fold.

"You okay?" I asked.

My fingers stilled, waiting for his answer, like my touch might tell me more than words ever could.

"No. I'm going to kill those fucking lions..." He swallowed loudly. "Right after I puke my guts out."

Despite everything, the corner of my mouth tipped up. Trust Kolton to still sound lethal while half-poisoned.

"Come on, tough guy," I said, trying to help him up. "One of Leo's goons left their truck this way."

I braced myself, anticipating the amount of his weight I was about to shoulder.

"Seriously, though, I've never been taken out by a tranquilizer before, and trust me, they train you for that shit growing up in a clan full of animals." His voice was rough; his pride bruised as badly as his body.

"I couldn't tell you what Leo's been up to," I said with a shrug. "But it left my tongue feeling numb, too."

The memory of it still lingered, metallic and wrong. Like whatever poison he used wasn't designed for just one species.

I hauled Kolton toward the truck, supporting his weight while he protested the entire way, claiming he didn't need my help.

I opened the door to the giant black truck, knowing full well it was likely loaded with tracking devices. But that was fine. I just needed it until we could get to my sister.

"Have you heard from anyone?" I asked as I pointed to my ear.

"Just Dayken saying that they were close, but he didn't know the exact location of the church, so it was hard for him to give me an exact arrival time."

Relief and frustration tangled tight in my chest. Close wasn't close enough, and I desperately wanted to be reunited with my sister.

I helped Kolton into the passenger seat and closed the door while he insisted that he could drive. I enjoyed the sound of the heavy thud cutting off his ridiculous claims of being capable. I went back to one of the dead bodies that Titus had taken down. I undid his boot laces, slid them off, then quickly took off his belt and shimmied his pants down. I felt tiger eyes on me the whole time. No time to unstrap the chest harness and weapons, but I grabbed a few from lifeless hands and skipped grabbing Kolton a shirt. Pants and boots would have to do for now.

I could feel something heavy in the pocket of the jeans I held and could only hope it was a key. I opened the driver's side door and ignored

Kolton's glare as I tried to figure out how to turn the damn thing on. I really didn't want to have to search more bodies for the key to this thing. Ignoring the animosity coming from the passenger princess next to me, I took a deep breath, hit the brake, and pressed the start button, hoping like hell the key was somewhere in this truck. When the engine purred to life, I exhaled slowly. A small win, but I'd take it.

Screens blinked on across the dash, though they didn't all turn on at once.

One flickered first, the low glow bleeding into the dark cab. Then another followed, and another, until the dashboard was alive with the shifting lights.

Too many of them. Digital maps littered with routes I didn't recognize. Phones synced to the truck, lighting up their location. And three small monitors cycling through a grainy surveillance feed, each one showing a different angle of places I had no desire to see right now.

My skin prickled. "What is all of this?"

A faint hum filled the space, and the image on the screen wavered, like the feed was struggling to hold steady.

Then it sharpened.

The air in the truck got heavier. It suddenly felt like I was no longer just watching through a screen but standing in the room itself.

The lighting was stark and clinical, bright and pouring down from above, casting deep shadows everywhere else. Metal tables lined the space, each of them bolted to the floor. Two bodies lay strapped to them, wrists secured, ankles bound. One body was still; the other wasn't.

Tubes ran from their arms and necks, disappearing into equipment just out of frame. Vials sat arranged on steel trays in careful rows, each one labeled.

Steam drifted lazily through the room, curling upward and softening the edge of everything. It gave the sense that something in the room was heating, reacting, changing.

An obscured figure moved in the background. Gloved hands came into view. One of the bodies suddenly went tense as something was administered, the reaction small but unmistakable.

My throat tightened.

Either Leo was sending this live feed into the truck to taunt me, or he kept around-the-clock eyes on his operation out of pure paranoia.

Now I understood what he meant when he said there was something I'd be dying to see. The sick fucking bastard.

Was he trying to take the bond away from other Guardians and Sacars?

I ran through everything I knew about the bond.

Choice stood out above everything else, the most sacred and defining part of its history. I had chosen. And choosing Leo was something that would never happen.

I had to be missing something.

"Kolton."

"Godsdamn it," he said, already knowing where my thoughts had gone.

"I know," I said quietly. "But we have to go back."

"He's going to try to take you from me," Kolton pleaded. The look on his face was wrecked, raw and desperate, and it cracked my heart clean in two.

"I will never choose him, Kolton. I will always choose you. You have to trust me on this." I ran my fingers through his orange hair. It stuck out at every angle, wild and untamed, but it was surprisingly soft as I smoothed a stray piece behind his ear.

He went still. Completely motionless in the way only a tiger was capable of. He studied me then, really studied me, and the intensity of it made my pulse jump. I had no idea what he was thinking, and that scared me more than his rage ever could.

"This is bigger than you and me, Kolton," I said. "I have an awful feeling about this. We have to stop it."

"You don't know who those people are. This could be a trick."

He was right. I looked back at the screen, watching. Waiting. I didn't know exactly what I was waiting to see. Maybe some sort of sign that this was, in fact, staged, or maybe I was staring, hoping to recognize one of the alleged victims. But instead, the more I stared, the stronger this sickening feeling grew.

The chip in my head was sending warnings throughout my brain, causing it to go through my entire body. I clenched my teeth, not enjoying the sensation it caused. But the sensation did make one fact very clear: the risk of this being staged didn't matter.

"I'm sorry." Was all I said. Knowing it would be enough.

He cursed some more. Colorful, frantic word choices before gritting out, "Can we at least get some fucking backup?"

"There is no time."

"Son of a fuc—"

I tuned out the rest of his curses and put the truck in reverse, grateful for the driving lessons Derek had given me, chaotic as they were.

The tires bit into gravel as I turned us around.

This was the right thing to do.

My hands tightened on the steering wheel, knuckles white, pulse hammering in my ears. Every instinct screamed at me that this was a mistake, that driving straight back into Leo's territory was choosing to walk straight back into a cage.

But the images from the feed burned behind my eyes.

Bodies. Restraints. Control.

Kolton went quiet beside me, the way he always did when his instincts took over. His jaw was set, eyes fixed on the road ahead as if he could already see Leo's estate rising in the dark. I could feel his tension through the bond, coiled and dangerous, barely contained.

"This isn't right," he said finally, lower now. "He wants you there."

"I know," I replied. "And the fact that something isn't right is exactly why we're going back."

The drive felt too short. The trees thinned, and the familiar outline of the estate came into view far sooner than I would have liked. Floodlights illuminated the area, cutting through the darkness. It washed the entire grounds in a harsh white light. As we approached, the gates began to open before we could slow, metal sliding apart with smooth, practiced ease.

No alarms. No hesitation.

Kolton noticed it too. I felt the shift in him, the way his attention sharpened, cataloging guards, angles, exits. There were too many of them. Too organized. This wasn't a response.

It was an expectation.

We rolled through the gates and came to a stop where they clearly wanted us. The truck doors opened before I could reach for the handle. Armed guards flanked the vehicle, calm and efficient, weapons visible but not raised.

Leo stepped forward as if he had been waiting just inside.

"Sky," he said pleasantly. Like this was a social call. His gaze flicked briefly to Kolton before returning to me, dismissive and uninterested. "You came back."

"I had questions," I said.

A smile touched his mouth. "Of course you did."

He gestured toward the estate with a casual sweep of his hand. "Let's not do this the hard way. You're exhausted. Come inside."

Kolton shifted beside me. I felt his anger spike, sharp and immediate. "She's not going anywhere without me."

Leo considered him for half a second, then looked back at me. "I have no intention of separating you two," he said smoothly. "That would be counterproductive."

Relief flickered in my chest, small and unwelcome.

"So, I'm staying with him?" I asked because this wasn't adding up. Kolton and I had a plan for when they separated us again. We were to stay mentally connected to one another. I would pull on the bond, whether conscious or unconscious, and he would do the same. With both of us having chosen each other, there was no way Leo could separate us. My Sacar flower essence lived in Kolton, and I wasn't letting go of it.

But it didn't appear we would need to worry about any of that...which felt wrong.

Leo nodded as if I had just confirmed something he already knew. "Naturally."

The guards moved in, escorting us forward. They were not rough, but they were unyielding. Weapons were removed. The truck was taken. And then we were guided into the house, through corridors that twisted downward, deeper into the compound. The air grew cooler with every step.

I stopped short when we reached the holding level with the cell Kolton had been kept in before.

"This isn't what you said," I snapped.

"It is exactly what I said," Leo replied calmly. "You'll both be contained. Together. Just not in the same room."

Kolton lunged at him and was immediately restrained, several guards stepping forward without urgency but with absolute control. I moved toward him and was blocked just as quickly.

I reminded myself of our dream bond, Bailey, and the earpiece in Kolton's ear. We were at an advantage. We had a plan. We just needed to stick to it, no matter how badly Kolton wanted to tear this place apart.

"This is a precaution," Leo continued. "Nothing more. He is unpredictable. You are not."

The doors to two cells slid open.

Kolton was pushed into his cell first. I caught his eyes just before the bars slammed shut, separating us. The flash of fury in his gaze did nothing to hide the fear underneath.

"It's okay." I mouthed to him.

They guided me into the cell across from his and locked it. It was a final, hollow sound that echoed through the corridor.

"And since I haven't figured out how you got him out last time," Leo said, "I'll be keeping this with me and me alone." He held the key up for emphasis.

Well. There went our Bailey advantage.

Leo lingered for a moment, studying me through the bars. "Get some rest, Sky," he said quietly. "Tomorrow, I'll show you everything."

He turned and walked away, his footsteps unhurried.

The lights dimmed slightly. The guards dispersed.

Silence settled around us.

CHAPTER THIRTY-ONE

The only good thing about being back in Leo's dungeon was that at least Skylar was with me this time. They also hadn't figured out that we had a mongoose who could sneak around the estate without alerting the guards or that I still had the comm device in my ear.

The joke was on me, though, because if I had to hear Derek sing Miley Cyrus one more time, I was going to rip my hair out and try to choke myself with it.

I can only hope that Derek relayed the message of where we were now.

I wished I could turn the fucking thing off.

I watched Skylar through the bars of my cell. She sat with her back against the wall of her own prison, arms tightly crossed. Her expression showed the kind of fury that foreshadowed a massacre with many bodies left behind. She looked pissed. Not irritated. Not annoyed. Pissed. As if she were quietly planning the downfall of every person who had ever wronged her.

Maybe she was.

And maybe I should not have liked it as much as I did. Most people would assume she was too soft for that. Too gentle. Too sweet. Hell, I made that mistake once. I made assumptions about her right up until the moment she slapped the shit out of me and knocked two of my teeth loose.

The memory made the corner of my mouth twitch. I fought back a smile.

Then I decided to lead her into a very familiar state of mind of my own.

Feeding into the rage.

"Your foundation is cracking, my Sacar," I said, breaking the heavy quiet. "Those walls you were locked behind do not exist anymore. They started to crumble the second your sister got you out. And you know what I think?" I took a breath, steadying myself. "I think you should crush those pieces beneath your boots as you climb out. Be free. Tear it all down."

She stared ahead, expression unreadable, but something flickered in her gaze. Something brave. Something dangerous. Something that wanted to sweep me up with her when she finally tore those walls apart.

"Tell me again exactly what he said to you while I was knocked out," I pushed, keeping my voice low.

"He said he had something to show me. So, I am waiting to see what it is."

"Skylar, I swear," I started, but she lifted her hand, cutting me off with that single motion.

"Do not start. I am thinking."

I bit my tongue until the copper taste of my blood hit my mouth. I wanted to pull her close and promise her I would end anyone who dared put their hands on her. At the same time, I wanted to sit back and admire her beautiful mind as it tore through possibilities.

Footsteps echoed down the hall.

A lion guard.

I pushed off the wall, and the guard hesitated mid-step. He looked at me with a quick flicker of uncertainty, as if something about me suggested that he should approach carefully. He didn't seem to understand the instinct, but it was clear that he wanted to heed it anyway.

I recognized it for what it was. It was an energy I gave off to everyone. A warning.

A truth he should have feared.

But he ignored his instincts and moved toward Skylar's cell.

"Don't you dare," I growled, but it wasn't anger that reverberated through my voice. It was something older. Something deeper.

The sound made him falter before he reached for the lock.

That was his second mistake.

He paused again, as if he wanted to get one last jab at me before opening Sky's cell. As if he thought he had any power here.

Then he finally unlocked her door.

Skylar did not move.

The guard waited a moment before reaching to grab her. That was enough to set my blood boiling.

"Do not touch her," I growled.

He ignored me, but I watched him hesitate when she didn't cower away from him.

He expected fear.

He expected obedience.

He would get none of those things.

Skylar slowly lifted her eyes to him, so calm that she made even *my* muscles tense. She looked like a storm right before it was about to break. Quiet. Controlled. Deadly.

"Get up," he snapped.

Skylar arched a brow at him, unimpressed. "No."

His jaw flexed. "I said—"

"You heard her," I cut in. "She said 'no.'"

His attention snapped to me. Perfect.

He turned, hot irritation visibly sparking across his face. I smiled.

"What?" I taunted. "Want to try your luck. Come over here and try grabbing me. Let's see who wins."

Because I felt Skylar through the bond, I knew she was up to something. Her fingers twitched in preparation. It was barely noticeable unless you were in tune with her every move, her every breath, the way I was.

The guard took one irritated step toward me, shoulders squared to accept my challenge.

I balled my fists tight, bracing myself.

Bring it, bitch.

His hand drifted toward the gun holstered on his belt. It was lucky for us that he reached for his gun and not the combat knife clipped on the other side. That was exactly where Skylar struck just as he gave me his full attention.

Her hand shot out, quiet as a shadow, fingers brushing the clip. The knife slid free without a sound. He never felt it leave his belt.

By the time he realized she had moved at all, she was sitting just as she was before. Hands in her lap. Calm. Innocent.

Innocent enough for him to give her his back, facing me again.

He unholstered his gun and pointed it at my chest. "Got something to say now?"

I started laughing. It quickly turned hysterical.

"Fucking lunatic," he muttered, holstering his gun and turning back toward my Sacar.

Skylar's fingers shifted, and with a tiny flick, she sent the knife skittering across the concrete floor, toward my cell. There was a single muted scrape. Just enough sound for me to hear it, but luckily not enough for the idiot in front of her.

He turned as I casually stretched my leg out and covered the blade with my boot. My pulse kicked up, violent and satisfied.

She found a way to arm me, and the lion had not noticed a thing. Gods. That only made me want her more.

"You think you're something," the guard muttered in my direction, still unaware of what just happened. "You're not. You will learn—"

"Oh, I've already learned," I said. "You're slow as fuck."

His face went red.

Before he could respond, the sound of thundering boots rolled down the hall. Reinforcements. Lots of them.

I quickly crouched down, lifted my pant leg, and slid the knife into my boot.

The guard straightened, stepping out of Skylar's cell as if he had been doing everything exactly as he should be.

She shifted her weight, just slightly, preparing.

I did the same.

Her eyes found mine.

A silent exchange.

We had a plan now.

A small one.

But enough.

The sound of boots stopped just before the men reached our cells.

CHAPTER THIRTY-TWO

"Up."

The command was firm, with the kind of tone that expected instant obedience. I fought the urge to roll my eyes. They loved their commands.

I stood slowly, my muscles stiff from sitting too long. The main door to the underground entrance buzzed. A heavy lock clicked, echoing down the corridor before the door slid open.

Men filled the hallway. Too many. Rifles raised. Every barrel aimed straight at my skull.

The sight sent Kolton into a frenzy.

He launched at the bars of his cage, claws scraping against metal, before he started pacing, half man, half beast. Orange fur rippled across his skin in patches, stripes flickering like wildfire as his features shifted and contorted. His growl built from low thunder to a full-blown storm.

"Shhh. Shhh." I kept my voice low, calm, like I was soothing a cornered animal. "It's okay."

His gaze snapped to mine, wild and desperate.

"It will be okay," I whispered again, this time for me. "They need me alive. Remember that, if nothing else."

He didn't shift back completely, but the rumble in his chest softened. His pacing slowed. He was still coiled tight, but at least he was breathing again.

I ached to touch him—to thread my fingers through his hair, to feel his warmth beneath my palms, but the bars reminded me of what I could not have. The sudden memory of his mouth on mine flashed through me, hot and dangerous.

He felt it. I know he did. His growl deepened into something possessive, almost broken.

"What the hell's wrong with him?" one of the guards muttered, voice heavy with disgust.

They would never understand what lived between us. They couldn't sense the invisible tether humming between our hearts.

"Let's just get this over with," I said, mostly to distract myself.

I stepped into the corridor. Every movement earned the click of a safety, the shuffle of boots. The sound of tension was thick enough to taste.

We moved in formation—me in the middle, guns framing my shadow on the floor. The air smelled of bodies with too much aftershave, grease, and gunmetal.

I expected to be led toward the main staircase, the usual route for interrogations, but instead, we turned right, heading deeper underground.

The path narrowed, walls closing in, until we reached what looked like a dead end.

No door. Just smooth stone.

Three men waited there, pressed close to the wall. They murmured to one another, then began pressing their palms against different bricks. One. Two. Three. The wall responded with a faint grinding sound, like stone awakening after a long sleep.

A hidden mechanism.

Interesting.

I watched every movement, memorizing the sequence—the order of which brick was pressed first, which hand they used, how long each touch lingered.

I might not have Kolton's claws and strength, but I had my mind.

And my mind never forgot a pattern.

I heard the hiss first, like air being released for the first time in ages. The sound slithered through the corridor, charged and mechanical, and then the wall began to move.

Stone and brick scraped against each other as it slid apart.

Bright, fluorescent light spilled through the widening seam, sterile and white, cutting through the dimness of the corridor like a blade.

It was familiar. Too familiar.

My stomach bottomed out.

Hands shoved at my back, forcing me forward as the secret passage yawned open. A staircase stretched below, carved into the stone. The walls were lined with exposed wires that hummed faintly with electricity. The air changed as we descended—becoming thicker, colder, with that unmistakable metallic tang of recycled air.

Down and down some more we went.

The lights buzzed overhead, flickering in rhythm with the echo of boots on concrete. Each step took me closer to something I wasn't ready to face. Something my body remembered, even if my mind refused to name it.

Then we stopped in front of a room. The men fanned out, forming a loose semicircle. I was left standing alone, staring straight ahead. For a moment, my brain refused to process what I saw.

No.

No.

No.

How—how could this be?

We destroyed it.

We blew it up.

We *all* made sure of it.

But the truth sat right in front of me, blooming in rows upon rows of impossible color.

Sacars. The sacred flowers.

Every stem was identical. Every bloom perfect. The eight-point symmetry of their petals glowed faintly under the harsh lab light, just as they did the first time I saw them in the facility. The air hummed with that same electric stillness, like the room itself was holding its breath.

The faint, sweet scent hit me next—vanilla. Soft. Deceptive. I knew that smell too well.

Bailey's voice flashed through my mind, *"Did you know you have a crack under your bed?"*

The faint scent I couldn't place.

It was all because of this.

All because *this* was down here.

Right beneath us the entire time.

"What do you think? Beautiful, isn't it?" Leo asked, appearing from inside the underground greenhouse.

I couldn't speak. Words escaped me, like water slipping through my fingers. My mind stuttered, refusing to form anything that resembled language.

"What was thought to be extinct," he said, adjusting his suit coat, "was right under our noses this whole time. Granted, it came in the hands of a slimy human, but that is a small price to pay for unlimited power and control."

"This is how you plan to undo the bond?" I croaked. Horror and sorrow coated every word.

He gave me a single look that told me everything, followed by a slow nod.

I wanted to scream at him, yell at the top of my lungs, "Why are you doing this?" But I knew. I knew the dynamics all too well. Clan members are born Guardians. And within them, a Primarc stands above the rest to lead. A Sacar can choose either a Guardian or a Primarc. A bonded Guardian can rival a Primarc. Sometimes even surpass one, which can drastically shift the dynamic of a clan. But a bonded Primarc...that is the highest power there was—authority, strength, and the bond amplifies both. That's what Leo was after.

Power.

"This will never work," I managed. "Whatever you think this is going to do, whatever outcome you have in your head, it will not work."

"And why is that?"

"Because I won't let you. We will stop you."

The laugh that tore out of him was unhinged. It was evil and delight in his own madness. It was a sound that belonged to someone completely broken.

"You cannot stop this, Sky. It is already done." Leo swept his arms wide, presenting his creation like a masterpiece. Pride gleamed in every twisted line of his smile. "Look around."

My mind raced. Calculating. Pulling fragments of everything I had ever read about the flower and its origins.

She tampered with sacred rites.

A ritual was performed...

The vanilla-scented flower was said to be a divine omen, blessed by the gods.

Magical abilities....

Magical.

Magic.

No.

I forced myself to really look at my surroundings. Now that I understood Leo's plan, the details came into sharp focus. The flower matched the mark over my heart. Eight petals. A round center holding the thin, delicate flower together. My mark was an odd tan, brownish color.

Nothing visually remarkable at all, yet its scent could captivate anyone who breathed it in.

It was why Dayken always said Onyx smelled like vanilla. The flower's essence lived in our blood. And Leo needed that essence to bond with me. But I had already given it to Kolton.

"There is no stopping this," he said again. Softer this time. Almost devout in his madness.

"I can. I will." My voice trembled, but I did not move. "My sister and her Guardian will be here any moment."

"And they will walk straight into a trap."

No.

Onyx was too smart to make a mistake like that. She did not walk into anything blindly. And Dayken was a leader who listened to his instincts and always had a backup plan tucked away.

They would be all right. They had to be.

"Do not underestimate my sister," I said, my voice no longer shaking. "She is fiercely protective of me and has survived far worse than anything you can concoct." I pointed at the flower. "You used this to create a poison strong enough to knock her out. She will burn through it in seconds. There is no stopping her."

I stepped forward, letting heat climb through my chest.

"But there is at least one thing that can stop you."

I pointed at him, letting my anger fill the air between us.

"Me," I said and lunged.

My body moved on instinct, fast and without hesitation, but then I heard a whizzing sound cut through the air. A burst of pain exploded in my thigh.

I was shot. Someone shot me.

I looked down to see an all too familiar dart filled with the silver formula designed to incapacitate Onyx and me.

Another miscalculation on my end.

I glared at Leo with an expression that asked, *Really?*

He just shrugged.

"You will be mine, amore mio. As I said, there is no stopping this."

Chapter Thirty-Three

The memory of being strapped to a table surfaced in my mind, unwelcome and intrusive. More memories came in hazy, sporadic images. Empathy for bodies on tables I didn't know slammed into me, and suddenly, the thought of being back in that hellhole of a facility made my stomach churn. The sound of metal instruments hitting a tray, the soft murmur of curious voices, and the bright, blinding light that was always overhead. I could see the brightness even with my eyes closed. There was no escaping; it was as if even the light mocked me. The reminders of a past I wanted to forget were rare, but for some reason, they were so strong right now that I could even feel the straps around my wrists and ankles. The bite of them cutting into my skin was too real, too familiar...why...

Why did it feel so real?

My eyes snapped open, only to be greeted by those cursed fucking lights.

No.

I was back there.

How?!

"She's awake."

"Hit her with it again."

That voice...no...not that voice...I hated that voice. That voice was not meant to be here. It belonged only in my nightmares.

"Wait..." I tried to stop them, but it was too late. I felt a sting at my neck, and then Leo's face appeared in my line of sight. The look in his eyes was one of...

Concern? No, that couldn't be right. This was wrong, all of it wrong. I needed to get out.

"Shhh, this will all be over soon, and then..."

He ran his fingers through my hair. I wanted to move away from his touch, but I couldn't. I was trapped, forced to endure his false affection as he said, "You will be mine."

I wanted to scream. But my energy...was fading.

I snapped awake, panic surging through me. My heart slammed against my sternum. I didn't have time to shake off the effects of the sedative. I forced myself to process my surroundings immediately, running everything through my head and discarding most of the input in rapid succession until only one fact remained.

This wasn't my room. Or the laboratory.

Leo.

I must be in his room. Everything was too intentional. Everything had a purpose. Dark walls. Expensive furniture with lines so precise it all felt curated. No clutter. No warmth. The faint scent of cedar clung to the air, sharp enough to make my nose itch. A single lamp cast a low, golden glow across the room, turning the shadows into long, stretched shapes on the floor. Heavy curtains blocked out every hint of outside light.

I turned my head slowly and froze.

Leo was right there, watching my every move.

I looked down and realized I'd been changed into a fresh, flimsy night-gown. The thin fabric clung to my skin, far too light to offer any real coverage. The audacity of it, the invasion of privacy, cut deep. Someone had touched me while I was unconscious. Dressed me. Decided what I would wear.

My fingers curled into the fabric for a moment, the anger rising hot in my chest.

But I swallowed it down. Leo would enjoy seeing that reaction far too much.

The chip in my head was rapidly processing possible outcomes until it looped through the same scenario twice, identifying it as the best course of action.

"You are awake." Relief bled into his voice. It wasn't meant for me, only for himself. It was the kind of relief a man felt when the person he had injured finally opened their eyes, and he could pretend he didn't cause any true harm. "How are you feeling?"

"I'm hungry."

"I'll get you a blood bag." He stood to leave.

"No." I reached out my arm, gesturing for him to move closer to me, toward the bed. He straightened and came closer but worry and hesitation caused his steps to falter.

I slowly lifted myself up onto my knees. "I want something now," I said, leaning into his space. I lifted my hand and slowly ran my finger down his neck.

"It's working," he breathed. Unsure what "it" was, I was left only with my assumptions.

"I...want to feed from you." I coyly tucked a piece of hair behind my ear. "I've never drunk directly from someone before."

"Yes, yes, this is good. Maybe then, maybe once you feed, that will be the final piece that's missing." He then pointed at my chest. "The final piece to removing *that*." he was pointing to the place above my heart, where my mark was.

He was suddenly very eager, undoing one of his cuff links and rolling up his sleeve to expose his wrist. I gently placed my hand over his. I let it linger, keeping my touch soft against his skin.

"That is what is calling to me," I said, gesturing to his neck. I watched as the main artery there thrummed underneath his skin.

"No. Not this time. Maybe once we are bonded, but until then." He lifted his wrist toward me, and I nodded in understanding.

It was clear to me that whatever they did while I was out, whatever procedure they performed, didn't affect me in the slightest. My mark was still present, and I could still feel Kolton through the bond. The only thing that was affecting me was the groggy feeling from whatever drugs they gave me, making me fatigued and sluggish.

But if he was under the impression that his plan was working, then I'd play along. There was no sense in destroying his delusion...*yet*.

I slowly slid my hand from his shoulder down his muscled arm, past his flexed biceps, and finally to his wrist. I made a show of gently raising it to my mouth, then licking my lips as seductively as I could, before I pressed them to his skin.

He watched me with awe and wonder in his eyes. I slowly opened my mouth and sank my fangs into his flesh. I took one deep pull from his vein and swallowed it quickly. It was thick and rich-tasting as it slid down the back of my throat. I needed the nutrients, having not actually eaten the blood bags they had given me before, fearing that they might have been tainted.

As I felt Leo relax his arm, his defenses slacking for a moment, I seized my chance.

With more force than I had ever used before, I locked my jaw around Leo's wrist, snapping my fangs hard enough to hit bone. I ignored his slew of curses as he attempted to throw me off him, biting down even harder. I knew, with every fiber of my being, that my jaw and teeth were strong enough to bite all the way through, and that was exactly what I planned on doing.

"Let go, you fucking bitch," he roared.

The sound of boots marching down the hall told me I was running out of time. I needed to move quicker. I clamped down as hard as I could, using every muscle in my face and tensing as Leo landed a blow to my head. I absorbed it, refusing to let go. He would have to knock me out, or kill me, before I willingly released him. This was my only chance.

With one more fierce thrust downward with my teeth, I felt the bone crack, and I broke through the other side of his wrist. He screamed in agony while I tore with everything I had. Blood sprayed everywhere, covering my face and the bed. It pooled in his lap. He screamed louder, roaring at me as he clutched the nub of his wrist to his chest.

The door crashed open. His clan members froze in horror at the gruesome sight before them. They looked from me, to him, to his hand, which had fallen to the floor, then back to him.

"Don't just stand there, you fucking fools!" he roared.

They attacked.

I was outnumbered. The next blow slammed into my head before I could react. My skull hit the ground, and the last thing I saw was the severed hand beside me, lying in a pool of blood. I couldn't help the small smirk that touched my lips as I once again lost consciousness.

CHAPTER THIRTY-FOUR

T he man in me screamed, and the tiger in me roared, the sound tearing from my throat warped and savage. Undiluted rage flooded my veins, pure and consuming as fire itself, as my connection to Sky was severed once again, leaving nothing but silence where she should have been.

What a foolish fucking idea this was. Coming back here was a mistake. They were going to take her from me. They were going to sever our bond somehow. I didn't know how that was possible, and I wished I had paid more attention in school, but seeing those people strapped to that operating table told me everything I needed to know.

For Skylar, it was different. That sight didn't evoke fear in her. It ignited anger. Revenge. She didn't want anyone to ever go through what she had endured.

And it was for that reason, and only that reason, that I sat here helpless again.

I roared once more, this time letting the tiger take over.

"Kolton, what is it? What happened?" Dayken's voice cut through my rage.

"They've taken her again," I shouted. My throat felt raw as I said it.

I couldn't wait for this thing to be out of my ear. It was annoying—and it itched—but it was also the only lifeline we had for getting out of here and getting Sky back at my side. My fingers kept drifting toward it, wanting to rip it out. Hell, I wanted to rip *everything* apart until I reached her.

"I don't understand why you went back there in the first place. We were almost to you guys," Dayken said for the hundredth time. His voice was steady but frayed from stress. He had been holding everything together for far too long.

"Skylar said there was something here that was important."

I fidgeted in the shadows, checking the corners again, pacing like caged prey. The corridor felt too narrow, too bright, too loud as thoughts of what they could be doing to her filled my head.

"You know what else is important? Keeping you idiots alive." His frustration crackled through the line. I could practically picture him dragging his hand across his face.

"Well, good news, they need her alive. They are trying to dissolve our bond." My jaw clenched. Saying it aloud sent a cold spike of fear through me, one I tried to swallow down but failed.

"And what if they succeed? What then?" he asked frantically. "You'll be dead." His tone softened at the words, but I heard the fear beneath it. The same fear chewed a hole in my chest.

"Don't pretend like you care about my well-being, okay? It's not a good look for you." The words came out more callous than I intended. Defensive. Exposed. I immediately regretted them.

"Oh, would you fucking stop, Kolton. This self-loathing shit has gotten old."

His anger hit me with such force that it felt like a physical attack.

It was deserved. It made me quiet my thoughts, forcing me to look inward, which was the last thing I wanted to do right now.

I bit back my retort—attempting to show restraint. My pulse thundered in my ears, and the walls felt tighter around me. But I couldn't shake the feeling that this conversation was long overdue.

"What conversation?"

Motherfucker! I said that out loud.

Heat crawled up my neck. Of all the times for my brain to slip, it had to be now.

I sighed loudly, but I couldn't help it. I was exhausted, stressed out about my Skylar. I hadn't slept or eaten in days, and now I had to pick a fight with Dayken. My energy was frayed to threads, and every emotion felt too close to the surface.

"It's not self-loathing, Dayk. It's the truth. I know you'd rather it had been me who was killed instead of your parents. You don't have to say it out loud. I still know." The words tasted bitter leaving my tongue. They had been rotting inside me for years.

Silence.

It slammed into me, confirming every fear I've ever had. My stomach twisted.

See, I knew it.

But when I listened closely, I heard his growl. It was low. Dangerous. It wasn't directed at me, but at what I implied. Then I heard him take a deep, steadying breath.

"So, what? You're in my head now? You suddenly know everything about how I feel, Kolton?" Dayken asked. His voice vibrated with warning, one that said I crossed a line I didn't understand.

"It's pretty obvious."

I leaned against the wall, then slid down it until I was crouched with my elbows on my knees and huffed out a breath. I hated this. Hated feeling like the unwanted one. The expendable one.

I had felt it all my life.

"Well, there's something that you've obviously missed or simply refuse to acknowledge. I love you like a brother. Always have. Always will."

His words knocked the breath from my lungs. I blinked hard, staring at the floor like it might offer emotional support.

It was my turn to stay silent. For real this time, I hoped. Now was not the time for my internal thoughts to share themselves.

I swallowed hard, unsure what to do about the sudden ache between my ribs.

"If you two love birds are done having phone sex, I have an update on the Urva Clan."

Ugh, Derek.

His voice sliced through the tension—unwelcome, unwanted. But at least I could turn my thoughts to something else for the moment.

"How did he get on this channel?" I grunted, pinching the bridge of my nose. My patience had thinned to a dangerous thread.

"I don't know how he keeps doing it, to be honest," Dayken admitted. I could hear the resignation in his voice, as if they had taken away his access multiple times now. A tired sigh followed, the kind that said he had already given up on trying to contain Derek.

When I didn't hear anything else from Derek, I started over. The words felt heavy, scraping me raw as I said, "I'm sorry it wasn't me. That you lost your parents as a result of protecting me. And because of my heritage."

Guilt rolled through me, familiar and suffocating. It's a weight I carried for too many years.

"I'm sorry I lost my parents too. They were great people, and I grieve them all the time. I grieved them even more when I was younger, which must have been difficult for you to watch. But I'm happy it wasn't you. Because we are brothers in heart, and that will never change." Dayken cleared his throat. "Now, let's hear what Derek has to say because I'm pretty sure I can hear him marching this way."

My imagination provided the distant sound of his footsteps. They were loud, stubborn, and impossible to ignore.

I nodded, even though he couldn't see it. The gesture was all I could muster in the moment. My body felt too full, too warm, too tight. My mind, which was a constant mess, just had another equation added to the chaos.

Dayken...didn't hate me.

If anything...he cared about me. A lot. And that was not something I saw coming.

After the church, I'd been certain I'd proven exactly what I was. Something unstable, Sky had to endure rather than want.

But the way Dayken spoke to me...like I mattered...said something different.

Like I belonged here.

If he could see me that way...

Maybe I'd been wrong about myself.

Chapter Thirty-Five

I felt her. I felt her panic, her fear. She was calling out to me, whether intentionally or not, and I couldn't do a fucking thing about it. Worse, she was now lying across from me in a cell. They just dropped her there, on the floor. Where I couldn't reach her.

The mongoose was nowhere to be seen, and Skylar appeared to be bleeding profusely.

At least, I thought it was her blood. But my own was roaring through my ears, making it impossible to focus. I clutched my head, about to smack it again to straighten it out.

My vision flickered from sharp to enhanced. From human, to blurry, back to sharp. The back of my neck, where my bond mark sat, burned.

"Skylar," I called out again, for the hundredth time. "Sky, wake up, please."

I tried to link our heartbeats, but hers was so faint I could barely feel it.

The sound of footsteps grabbed my attention. It was a lion who was sometimes on guard duty down here. I recognized him, but I didn't know his name. He was in his human form, murmuring and following the instructions given to him through the comm hooked to his ear.

"Mmhmm. Yup. On it." The keys dangled from his hand as he approached Skylar's cell.

"No." I stood up from my spot on the floor. "Get away from her."

He didn't flinch or pay me any attention.

The metal of the knife Sky had gotten me was a cold reminder against my back. I slowly slipped it out.

I was still locked in my cell, but when you spent as much time as I did bored and alone in a forest, you picked up tricks. Habits if you will. Throwing knives at the targets I carved into trees was one of mine.

Let's see if I still had it.

I just needed one shot, straight through the bars and into the back of his neck.

Piece of cake.

I moved closer to the bars, slowly, quietly, my tiger stealth unmatched. *They never heard me coming.*

Ever.

He stuck the key in the lock and prepared to turn it.

The blade left my hand, easily slipping between the bars, and hit its target spot on.

The lion crumpled to the floor.

One down, but there goes my knife.

"Skylar," I tried again. "I'm sorry, okay. I'm sorry for never listening to you. I'm sorry for always trying to stop you from doing what you thought was best. I'm sorry for trying to control you. Just wake up, please. I need you. I can't do this without you." The confession was out before I could even think about pulling it back.

So what? Why did I care about admitting the truth? It was something that needed to be said.

She was everything. Brilliant, powerful, and beautiful. Oh, so beautiful.

My world, my universe, my Skylar, lay completely and utterly motionless.

I heard the faint sound of more footsteps.

Here we go again.

"Well, I was hoping to do this the easy way, but it looks like I will have to force the bond."

Leo.

That fucking piece of shit.

He was speaking into the phone pressed to his ear, his lackeys trailing behind him.

His cold, detached eyes locked onto the dead body in front of Skylar's cell. Without a flicker of recognition or remorse, he simply told one of the guards behind him to remove the body. He completely ignored me, his attention quickly going back to Skylar. As he turned, I noticed the hand not holding the phone was wrapped up in...

Wait.

He did not have another hand.

And it all clicked together.

My fierce, beautiful Sacar. That had to be her doing. It made complete sense.

It explained why they were so pissed when they dumped her in the cell. Why they were speaking in urgent, hushed tones. And why she was drenched in so much blood, especially around her face.

My entire world was covered in our enemy's blood because she took his hand off.

Pride coursed through me, and I smiled. It was big enough to catch Leo's attention.

"Missing something?" I taunted.

He did not take the bait. He just moved toward Skylar's cell, across from mine, giving me his back.

"Get your eyes off her," I snarled, trying to pull his attention back to me.

"Shut up, tiger. You're next," he said, finally addressing me as he ended his call and crouched down to get a better look at Skylar. Her pale, delicate form barely moved, just her chest rising and falling with each breath.

"Perfect! I don't care. Kill me. Kill me right now and be done with it. But leave her alone. She doesn't deserve this, and you don't fucking deserve her!" I roared with everything I had.

"I deserve EVERYTHING!" He roared back before I could even finish, his lion front and center. "Everything! It should have been me that she chose! ME!"

My grip on the bars was too tight. I could almost swear I felt them bend to my will.

"It was a mistake that you were there that day. A FUCKING mistake!" he spat at me, each word coming out more aggressive and frantic than the last.

If Skylar were conscious, she would have argued that there was no such thing as mistakes when it came to the bond.

"She chose me," I growled at him. My tiger distorted my vocal cords, making me sound manic.

He laughed in disbelief as he spoke. "You haven't figured it out yet, have you? He told me he made Sky the smartest, most calculating creature to walk the face of this earth. All that power, all that value. The advantages that come with being a bonded Guardian are fucking wasted on you!"

If he meant to insult me, to make me feel unworthy, it was wasted. No one hated me more than I hated myself, but there was one fact that remained.

"You don't think I know that? I have no clue how we bonded, or why. But I don't give a fuck. I will always protect her. No matter what. So, I will say it again. Do whatever you want with me; just leave her alone."

"No."

He moved to open her cell. She didn't stir at the clanking of the keys or the grinding of metal as the lock turned. Her breathing didn't even change when the cell door slammed against the bars.

No movement.

I tried again, "Don't you need me dead for whatever you've got planned?! Come on, kill me! Come in here and try to sever the bond the old-fashioned way, you coward. You know that mark will disappear if I die!"

"Oh, make no mistake, you will die. But I need her to choose me. The timing must be perfect. Not that you could even begin to comprehend any of it."

I was at a loss for words. I was reeling, left powerless to do anything but watch as he pulled something from his pocket and rubbed it against her chest. His disgusting fingers massaged the top swells of her breasts, right where her mark was.

I was screaming, and my tiger was roaring. The sound of our combined voices hurt even my ears, but it was nothing compared to the hurt, pain, and rage in my heart.

My fists were clenched so tightly that my claws punched through my palms, and I heard my own blood splatter onto the floor.

Suddenly, I couldn't feel her anymore. The back of my neck burned with agonizing pain, and I watched as the mark over her heart began to fade.

I screamed, but there was no roar from my tiger this time. He was buried too deep. This pain was all mine. My screams. My fear seeping out to be absorbed into the walls.

"Shut that obnoxious beast up," Leo commanded.

Before I knew it, I was shot with something. I stared desperately at Skylar as I hit the ground. I caught the glint of something shiny on her chest, where the bonding mark should be, but I could barely make it out.

And then, I was unconscious.

Chapter Thirty-Six

"Kolton?"

"Skylar!"

I ran toward her, even though her voice wasn't that far. The distance kept shifting—one second, she was close enough to touch, the next, she was swallowed by haze. The world beneath my feet flickered between sand and smoke, everything half-formed and wrong.

"Sky?"

Then the world jerked.

I was yanked back into the basement—the one I knew too well. The place where I stalked and waited for my prey. Screams echoed off the concrete, haunting and familiar.

"Tell me." My voice was low, quiet enough to make it sound as menacing as I felt.

"If I knew, I'd tell you, you psycho." He laughed, but there was a tremble in it.

My fist connected with his face before he finished laughing. He staggered, blood running slowly from his lip.

"I saw you with them," I said. "Tell me where the rest of you are."

"Never."

I gripped his hair tight, yanking his head back and forcing him to meet my eyes. "Then this will hurt," I promised.

I knew exactly what came next. My movements were slow, deliberate, and methodical. I started with the shoulder—snapped the clavicle, then the humerus. I sliced through the muscles and tendons. I grabbed a shirt that was hanging out to dry and twisted it tightly around the wound to keep him conscious, as his screams slid into delirium.

"The other one's next. Tell me where they are."

"N-no," he said, but it came out as a plea as he squirmed, unable to crawl away from me with his one arm. Pathetic excuse of a human. I knew there was no need to tie this one to a chair. He needed arms for that, anyway.

"All right," I said coolly. "Your funeral."

"You're very thorough," a voice said from behind me.

I whirled around—Skylar.

No!

NO!

"You can see this?" The words were ripped from me, half roar, half plea. I wanted to run to her and clutch her to me. But at the same time, I wanted to push her away so she couldn't see my dark past.

She didn't flinch. Her gaze swept over me—calm, calculating, dissecting me piece by piece.

"I take it you did this while you were looking for me?"

The words were lodged in my throat. I couldn't answer, couldn't breathe. The nightmare playing out behind me was nothing compared to the look in her eyes. All I managed was a small nod.

"And what?" she asked, her voice firm. "You're concerned about what I might think of you?"

Her icy blue gaze was steady—watching me, analyzing me, seeing far too much.

I couldn't answer. The thought of her witnessing this—of her seeing what I'd done—was my worst nightmare come to life. She couldn't know this side of me.

What if she left?

What if she broke the bond on purpose?

What if she chose Leo instead?

I wouldn't survive that. I wouldn't even be able to breathe unless my mark still matched hers.

The screams behind me filled the space as I stared at Sky, desperate to find words that refused to come.

"And let me guess," she went on, ignoring my silence and inner turmoil, "this is also why you freaked out at the church? You don't think you deserve to bring me pleasure? You don't think you should torture me in the best possible way? You don't think I could have possibly enjoyed every second of that time spent together?"

I looked away, unable to meet her gaze. She was hitting too close to home.

She tsked at my silence and grabbed my face, forcing me to look at her.

"I once watched a man remove my sister's kidney and drop it into an empty jar," she said, her eyes back on mine. "They did it so they could study how long her organ would survive without a host. It lasted a week—FYI. Then, once it started to decay, they removed the new kidney she had regrown in that time and put the old one back in. They stitched her up and observed to see if her body would fix it."

She paused and pointed behind me before continuing. "So, I'll ask you this once—what could you possibly be doing over there that I haven't already survived myself or watched happen to my own sister?"

I just stared at her in disbelief. Absolutely stunned.

This couldn't be right. Was she—was she okay with this?

"But I-I killed—"

"My enemy," she interrupted softly. "You killed my enemy."

Then she took a step closer to me, forcing her to tilt her head back in order to meet my eyes. Her delicate, angelic hand rose and wrapped itself around the back of my neck, her palm flattening against the place where my bonding mark sat. The softness of her skin seeped into me, steady and grounding. She then took my hand and guided it to her chest, pressing it over her heart, where her own mark pulsed faintly beneath her skin. I pressed harder, feeling the rhythm—slow, deliberate, alive.

"Our enemy, Kolton."

"You're okay with this? You're not disgusted by the fact that I tortured and murdered countless people?"

She actually took a moment to think before asking, "Innocent people?"

"Not by my definition." I exhaled, "If I caught even the faintest hint of your scent—anything that reminded me even remotely of you—I'd hunt it

down until I found a facility worker. I tried to get information from them. I really did."

As if on cue, the gurgling scream behind me began to fade, dying with the man's last breath.

"But that would happen." I pointed to the man who was now dead because he didn't give me any concrete answers before succumbing to my torture. "It was how I knew to head to Michigan. I was hunting one of them all the way from California."

"I love that you never stopped looking for me. I love that you always want me near, even when you shouldn't have. I love how feral you are, and that part of you never frightened me. I love that, no matter what you've done, you're still the only place that feels safe. Actually, I think I might lo—"

"No." I pressed my fingers to her lips, cutting her off. "While I'm relieved that what you just saw didn't scare you off, I don't deserve those words coming out of your mouth."

I could see the protest flickering in her eyes, but I didn't let her voice it. "Plus, we need to wake up. You're unconscious on the floor in the cell across from mine, and you're not responding to my call. They hit me with something too, but I'm going to fight it. I need you to do the same."

I pulled her against me, rough and desperate, feeling the breath rush out of her chest as I squeezed.

"Your mark was starting to fade. He put some shit over your chest, and your bonding mark…"

"Don't worry." She pushed at my chest, forcing enough space between us to meet my eyes. "I know how to fix this. Trust me, okay? I will never leave you."

I nodded, because I did trust her. I trusted her so much it hurt. But the stakes were extremely high, and this was too much for my precious little Sacar to take on alone.

Skylar stepped closer again, and before I could say anything else, her hands slid up my chest. My protest died as light but steady fingers moved up my body, like she had already decided something I was still trying to talk myself out of.

"Sky..." I started, but the warning died in my throat.

She didn't stop.

Her fingers curled into my shirt, and she pulled herself against me, rising onto her toes. When her mouth brushed mine, it was soft, testing, like she was giving me the chance to pull away.

I didn't.

Gods help me, I didn't.

My hands found her before I could think better of it. I lifted her instinctively, and her legs wrapped around my waist like it was the most natural thing in the world. My grip tightened under her thighs, anchoring her against me.

The kiss broke, and for a heartbeat we just breathed together, sharing the same air. The cool skin of her arms brushed around my neck, and her lashes lowered. Her lips were so close I could feel the shape of her next breath.

Then I moved. One arm held her effortlessly while the other slid up, curling around the back of her neck and guiding her closer. She didn't hesitate. Her mouth met mine before I could even think to change my mind, and the sound that tore from my chest was a low, helpless moan.

Gods, I loved her lips. Soft. Unhurried. Tasting of something that wasn't blood but still felt like sin.

"Kolton," she murmured between kisses, her voice a rasp that shot straight down my spine. "I'm hungry."

Fuuuck.

I nipped at her bottom lip, trying to focus, trying to hold on to reason, but it was already slipping through my fingers.

"Wake up," I breathed, my words brushing against her lips, "so we can get out of here. Then you can feed from me all night…" I pulled back to lock eyes with her. "While I fuck you."

Her response was a delightful purr, divine, hungry, and a little savage. It vibrated against my tongue.

She kissed me harder. Rougher. Her fingers tangled in my hair and yanked, forcing me to tilt my head exactly how she wanted it. My pulse hammered so loud, I could barely hear her whisper against my jaw.

"I want to bite you," she groaned. Her mouth trailed down my chin, purposefully dragging her lips lower.

My control splintered. I wanted her to. I wanted her teeth, her claim, the sting that would make her mine all over again.

Could she even bite me here, in this dream world we'd built between us?

Only one way to find out.

No.

Not like this.

"Wake up," I said again, voice cracking. The words scraped out of me like a plea.

"But I want you."

Well, fuck. I was done for. Every nerve in my body was tuned to her, my chest tight, my cock straining against my pants, reason barely a whisper.

And then…she was gone.

The air went still. My hands were empty. The void she left behind was worse than the hunger.

Time for me to wake up.

CHAPTER THIRTY-SEVEN

I slowly came to, with desire burning deep in my soul.

Kolton.

My thoughts were groggy and sluggish, but he was the only thing on my mind.

I cracked my eyes open and was greeted by cold, hard concrete. Realization slammed into me fast and suddenly.

I told Kolton I knew how to fix this, and while I did have a plan, I started to doubt its feasibility when I looked down at my chest.

A sob ripped out my throat...

Kolton was right; my mark *was* fading. It was duller in color, and the tips of the petals were missing.

How?

How was this possible?

I once again ran through everything I'd memorized about the history of the bond when I noticed a strange ointment smeared across my skin. It had a strong vanilla aroma, along with a pungent chemical smell that stung my nose.

No.

I pulled on the bond.

Kolton.

Kolton!

KOLTON!

I pushed up onto my elbows and looked around until my gaze landed on a crumpled heap of lean muscle and orange hair in the cell across from mine.

"Kolt..." I rasped, barely able to make a sound, but it was enough for him to stir.

I tugged on the bond again, harder this time. He rolled onto his back with a groan. "I'm going to kill every last one of them."

"Not...John...I like...him."

"Well, he's the first to die then," he muttered as he rose onto his hands and knees. "Also, you're the one who kicked him in the head."

I smiled before I could stop myself. I could feel my body healing, repairing, expelling the drugs they gave me, and stitching itself back together. I tried pulling on the bond again.

"I'm right here, Skylar. I'm not going anywhere. I'll be right here...always."

A single tear slipped from the corner of my eye, and when I looked down, the color was already returning to my bond mark, the strength of our connection flowing through me.

"Let's get out of here," I croaked as my voice slowly grew stronger.

"BAILEY!" he roared.

Minutes, hours, seconds passed—honestly, who knew. I just lay there on my back, gathering my strength and gently pulling on the bond, despite Kolton being right there. I was determined to rebuild it, reinforcing the invisible strings that tied us together. Leo could try all he wanted to dissolve our bond, but Kolton was mine, and I would kill anyone who tried to take him from me.

While we waited, Kolton explained that Derek and Chase were going to be the fastest to get to us because they had the aerial advantage. And that Bailey was still in the area doing...well, no one really knew what Bailey was doing.

According to Kolton, my sister was frantically enraged at the latest news about my bond almost being severed. Kolton wouldn't give me the specifics of what was being said in his earpiece, but I knew my sister well enough to know they were not kind words.

Eventually, the familiar sound of tiny claws on concrete reached me, and relief spread throughout my entire body, down to my bones.

"Hi! Derek is a god now," Bailey said as she shifted and stood before us in all her naked glory. "But he said he was willing to postpone his god duties to help you guys." She held up a tiny disk in her hand before suddenly throwing it at the wall. "The god said just one tiny circle is fine."

If that silver disc was what I thought it was, she should *not* have thrown it like that. I lulled my head to the side, turning to look at Kolton. He had his hand pressed to his ear, listening to the comm device.

"No," he said before letting out a string of curses followed by more nos. I could only imagine what Derek was telling him. I smiled again. I couldn't help it. I'd come to love this dysfunctional family so fucking much.

I watched Kolton scowl as he listened to the instructions only he could hear, but Bailey suddenly crouched in front of the bars to my cell, pulling my focus away from him.

"Hi, my friend. I've missed you, my best, best friend. Can we share a Twix later? There are two, and there are two of us."

"Sure, Bailey. You got it."

It hit me then just how much she'd been doing to help us this whole time. She tried to alert us to the crack in the floor of Kolton's cell. She'd tried to warn us, telling us the flower was there—right under our noses—in the only way she knew how. And now she was the reason we had a chance. The reason Kolton wasn't spiraling. The reason we were getting out of here...*again*.

"Bailey," I said softly.

She tilted her head, waiting.

"You've done such a good job. Truly amazing. I am so proud of you, and I hope you know how happy I am that you are my friend."

Her lips trembled, and her eyes turned glossy. The way she reacted made me think that no one had ever spoken a kind word to her in her entire life. My heart melted when she whispered, "Bailey is happy."

I reached my hand through the bars, clasping on to hers, and she squeezed back.

"All right, this damn, fucking psychopathic bird wants us to blow a hole in the wall. No, *bird*, I'm not calling you that," Kolton grumbled, then looked at me. "Despite me telling him that we are *underground*."

Bailey released my hand and stood proudly despite her nakedness and said, "Mongooses can make very, very good tunnels. Tunnels are so, so, so fun."

"Yeah...well that's great, *really* great, but how are we going to get out of these cells? The keys are gone," Kolton noted, but he wasn't talking to me or Bailey. I waited, but the silence stretched too long. "Oh, wonderful. The 'tech whiz' is now a locksmith. I'm calling bullshit."

"Kolton," I hissed. "Be nice."

"Fine," he grumbled. Then, into his earpiece, "*You* shut up."

My grumpy tiger.

"Fine, hit it!" he barked before looking at me. "Brace yourself, my Sacar."

I sat up and backed into the corner of my cell, just as an explosion ripped through the underground prison. Walls rattled, chunks of cement fell and shattered on the ground, blowing up dust and more debris. I shielded my face with my arm, not wanting to lose an eye—they took way too long to grow back.

"You okay?" Kolton called through the settling dust.

"I'm good. Bailey, you good?"

But she wasn't there anymore. I looked around the destruction but didn't see her; she was...gone.

"Where is Bailey?" I asked. Kolton just shrugged. I reached through the bars, lifting rocks and chunks of cement, just to be sure she hadn't shifted and her little mongoose form wasn't crushed under the debris.

"Kolton, help me. I want to make sure she is okay."

He didn't move. I was just about to scream at him when he said, "Derek says she's with him. They are coming down now."

And as if summoned, a brown falcon shot through one of the holes in the cement wall. It tucked its wings tight before beating hard as it swooped inside. A second later, a sleek black falcon followed, its feathers catching the light from the flickering emergency bulbs overhead. They cut through the chaos like living arrows, weaving past the crumbling walls until they landed in front of my cell.

"Derek! Chase!"

The sound ripped out of me with raw excitement, coming out as something between a laugh and a sob. I felt the noise vibrate in my chest before I even realized I made it. Relief hit me so hard, my knees nearly buckled. I had missed them so much. Their presence felt like sunlight forcing its way into a room that had been sealed for days, warm and overwhelmingly safe.

Then a little mongoose scampered through a tiny hole in the wall. Once it hit a stable patch of debris, she shifted. "See, tunnels are so, so much fun! HI, GOD!" Bailey said, clapping excitedly.

"Derek, I told you not to tell her to call you that," Chase admonished as he and his twin shifted back into their human forms.

Derek just shrugged. "And forsake my people? Never!"

"Will you two asshats unlock the fucking cell doors?" Kolton growled, having officially lost his patience. But damn, he was hot when he was angry.

Chase approached my cell after taking a small pack from Bailey's outstretched hands. "Thanks, Bay. Can you grab the pants at the tunnel entrance?"

"Of course. God, do you want pants too?"

"No, I'm goo—"

"Yes! Grab his pants. Why would you even ask him?!" Kolton snapped.

Chase ignored the chaos behind him and instead focused on picking the lock. He gripped a tool in each hand, and I tried not to stare as his forearms flexed with the dexterity he needed to shimmy it loose. Once I heard the now familiar thunk, I shoved the cell door open and wrapped Chase up in a quick hug. He squeezed me back, causing Kolton to let out a furious sound.

"Hey!" Kolton punched his cell bars as he yelled, "Knife Fingers! Get your hands off her!"

I scrunched my eyebrows, releasing Chase before asking, "'Knife Fingers'?"

"Yeah! Show her those fucking things," he said, gesturing to Chase's hands.

Chase looked at me, then back at Kolton. He looked down at his hands and then shrugged before saying, "No clue what he's talking about."

"You motherfu—"

"Come now, my children," Derek interjected. He had his hands raised, accepting imaginary praise, as he stepped over debris. I hugged him too. He squeezed back so hard I grinned.

He gives the best hugs.

I glanced over at Kolton once Chase got his cell unlocked. His hair was wild, and his beautiful yellow eyes glowed, reflecting each blink from the emergency lights. Yes, he looked extremely scary while in a jealous rage from me hugging other men. But I knew that no matter how intimidating, possessive, or unhinged he appeared—there was one important fact about him that could get easily overlooked by an uninformed observer: he would never hurt me. Even with his fangs showing and a growl rumbling in his chest, I knew he'd never let any harm come to me.

Never.

I knew it in my heart like I felt both our heartbeats. Sure and steady.

Chapter Thirty-Eight

Time to fuck shit up.

I would make them rue the day they even thought to mess with me, my family, my clan, or my Skylar.

I extended my hand to help Skylar step over a massive chunk of cement in the middle of the corridor, which had cracked clean off the wall from the explosion. Dust still drifted all around us. The doorway to the stairs that led up into the main house was blocked as a result of the blast, barricading us from the lions on the other side.

I could smell them. Hear them. Their low snarls and scraping claws. They were confused as they tried to figure out what happened and why they couldn't get in.

There was no way Skylar and I could fit through the tunnel Bailey had dug. It was way too small, but we were absolutely capable of fighting our way out. They still thought it was just the two of us down here. They didn't know we had a mentally unstable bird and his smart-ass twin, both of whom were built like a brick shithouse. Plus, one very delusional mongoose and a beautiful, powerful vampire. And me.

All of us wanted the exact same thing. These fucking lion heads detached from their bodies.

"Ready?" I looked over my shoulder at our ragtag crew.

They nodded in unison, like they had done this a million times.

I shifted into my tiger form, which was clearly stronger and more superior than my human form, and pushed a chunk of cement aside with a low growl. Heat flooded my veins. My spine cracked into place. I roared a final warning, just as they managed to get through the door.

The lions poured in without hesitation.

Skylar took out the first one with a quick, fluid kick to the skull. Chase grabbed the next by the hair and dragged him away from the fray, giving himself enough room to beat the shit out of him without distraction. Derek punched one straight in the nose, and his blood sprayed across the wall. Bailey used one of the concrete blocks for leverage, vaulting onto a lion's back before climbing up his shoulders and snapping his neck. She jumped off just before he crumpled to the ground.

And me? I went for their throats. Fast. Efficient.

My vision tunneled. Everything vanished until I was left with pure instinct.

Another wave of lions rushed in, teeth bared, claws out. We cut through them fast. Chase dropped one with a knee to the ribs. Bailey flipped another clean over her shoulders. Derek was chuckling like a lunatic every time someone swung at him.

And Skylar...

Skylar was fighting in a nightie. A literal nightie.

Spinning, ducking, snapping a lion's arm like she was doing a morning exercise. The fabric clung to her. It was torn in places and streaked with blood that was not hers. She looked deadly and delicate at the same time. Something primal in me purred its approval.

Hell, my tiger loved all this bloodshed and even enjoyed fighting with the Guardians at my side.

These were my companions.

My people.

My Sacar.

After the second wave, we waited for more lions to come through. After a few moments with no sign of movement on the stairs, I shifted back and looked for my pants.

"Derek, toss me that weapon," Chase yelled.

Derek scooped a handgun off the ground and threw it to his brother. It spun through the air, barrel over handle, before Chase easily caught it by the grip. The move was so effortless it seemed like they had been practicing it since childhood.

Chase cocked the gun before looking at me and nodding once.

No more hiding. It was time to go upstairs. Having just escaped up these stairs less than two days ago, I knew the route well.

I felt a light touch on my arm, and I looked down. Beautiful ice blue eyes greeted me.

"I think we should head down, actually," Skylar said, motioning to where the lions had taken her yesterday.

I tilted my head in question.

"There are Sacar flowers down there, and we need to see if there's an easy way to destroy them. We can be quick."

"We could get pinned down there," Chase said. He brought up a good point, but I trusted Skylar to make the right decision.

"Then we'll fight our way out, just like we did here. We have weapons now. They won't be expecting that. It gives us an advantage."

Chase nodded in acknowledgement. We changed direction, heading down the tunnel toward the hidden door Skylar mentioned, but it was no longer there, having been destroyed in the explosion. When I turned to look back at her, I took a moment to take her in. Gods, she was stunning, her hair blown back from her face, her breathing slightly heavy.

She noticed immediately that I was staring.

"What?" she asked, pausing at the top of the stairs.

"Have I ever told you how beautiful you are?" I murmured, low.

She reached out, trailing a delicate finger down my abdomen.

"You may have mentioned it," she said, stepping closer. "But I wasn't listening. Tell me again."

I caught her hand and twisted it gently behind her back, using her forward momentum to pull her flush against me. My erection pressed against her stomach, and her eyes narrowed, her breath turning ragged. I took a slow inhale, breathing in her sweet scent. It destroyed me every time.

"See what your touch does to me, my Sky."

A sharp metallic clatter echoed down the tunnel, making us freeze. Someone was assembling a weapon or dropping a magazine. Footsteps followed the sound, faint but growing closer.

Sky tilted her head, listening with that eerie calm she got whenever danger approached.

"They are regrouping," she said quietly. "We need to move."

Her hand flexed in my grip, not pulling away, letting me have this one stolen moment. "You can tell me what my touch does to you later," she whispered, soft enough to ruin me.

"Yes, tell her how you like your intercourse later! We have lions to kill," Derek chirped, already checking the safety on his stolen rifle.

"I don't think they let anyone spend too much time down there; probably to protect against contamination, which would explain the constant live feed," Skylar said.

"They're not here,"

"Check that hole in the wall!"

"The Primarc has more coming."

Loud shouts and the sound of boots had us quickly running down the flight of stairs, heading deeper into the damp, dark underground of the estate. Our footsteps were hurried, almost frantic as we took the steps two at a time.

Once at the bottom, the sweet smell of vanilla grew stronger. There were remnants of debris and rubble from the blast littered across the floor. Some of it even made it past the doorway, managing to strike a few rows of flowers. Unfortunately, it wasn't enough to damage any of them.

I glanced up to where the cameras had been positioned, recognizing the angles from the screens in the truck.

Two of them now dangled from the wall by their wires, taken out by the blast. I quickly looked around for more but couldn't see any.

"I can't believe a supposedly extinct flower keeps popping up all over the place like a damn weed. How annoying. Why can't you just stay dead, you motherfucker," Derek said as he approached one of the beds, smashing a flower with his fist.

"Derek," Skylar said, trying to pull his attention away from the flowery nuisance. "I saw on a security feed that there were people trapped down here. Can you check on them? I'm pretty sure one of them was still moving."

"Incoming!" Chase yelled from where he was posted at the bottom of the stairs.

The sound of a scuffle and muffled impacts indicated that Chase was dispatching them, but who knew how long he would manage on his own.

Derek sprinted past the rows of flowers, dramatically waving the steam and humidity away from his face like he was swatting flies. "My brother, hold it down while I go rescue a damsel in distress," he called as he ran. "Wait, it was a woman, right, Sky?!"

His voice faded the farther he went into the massive room, so she didn't bother answering him. She just turned to me with a smile and a slight shake of her head.

I growled, not liking how she found the bird's antics amusing.

"Bailey, Kolton, help me move this table," she yelled, ignoring my outburst.

It was more like a massive concrete trough than a table. In addition to the flowers, it was also full of a grainy, sand-like soil. With a heave, the three of us sent it toppling to the ground, scattering the dirt and wretched flowers like discarded trash.

"Okay, now let's get it to the door," Skylar said, her objective finally becoming clear. "One, two, three." We grunted as we heaved it back upright.

"Chase, we're coming your way," she called over her shoulder as we started pushing the table in his direction.

"Well, this," Chase shouted with a huff, followed by a heavy smash. "Son of a bitch..." Another impact. "Won't stay down."

He went quiet before I heard a sound that reminded me of fabric shredding. Then silence.

"Here, let me help," Chase said, appearing after finally dispatching the lion he'd been scuffling with.

Once the greenhouse table was positioned in front of the entrance, we moved to grab another one, further barricading the door.

"Okay, that should buy us some time," Skylar said as she started looking around the room for a better solution.

"What now? As much as I like Derek's idea of smashing each individual flower, I don't think we have time for that," I said dryly.

"Smash flowers!" Bailey clapped excitedly.

Chase just patted her head like he was proud of her sudden explosive enthusiasm.

I rolled my eyes before turning my attention back to Skylar. She was smiling. Her brilliant mind must have come up with another idea.

CHAPTER THIRTY-NINE

"Kolton, come here," I said, wanting him close for what I had to say next.

He was at my side immediately, a blur of orange attentiveness. He always came when I called. Always.

Memories flickered through my mind. Him snapping to attention the second I opened my door and called his name. Him abandoning whatever he was doing in the gym the moment I needed a spot on a set.

Kolton always came.

The concerned look on his face as he made his way to me was so sweet and endearing that I wanted to kiss him. And not a quick peck either.

I wanted the kind of kiss that ended with me pressed against his body, his hands in my hair, and his mouth stealing my breath, making every coherent thought I had disappear. My body responded before I could stop it, heat curling low in my belly, but I mentally shook my head and focused on the task at hand.

"Is there anyone listening on the other end of that comms device in your ear?"

He scrunched his eyebrows together, as if deep in thought, then he nodded as he received a response through the device.

"Is it Onyx?" I asked. Something told me my sister wasn't far, even though we didn't have the same connection to each other as we did to our Guardians.

Another nod.

I cleared my throat and spoke loud enough so Onyx would be able to hear me through Kolton's comm.

"Onyx, tell everyone to meet us at the compound. Meet us at home. I know it must terrify you to leave me here, especially after we've been separated for so long, but I want you to know that I've got this. Trust me. You have taught me how to be strong, no matter what. You inspired me to be the best I can be, and now it's my turn to teach you how to trust. Trust me. I love you so much."

Kolton's eyes hardened, not liking the instructions I just gave my sister, but then they...*softened*. The expression that settled over his face was new. There was a love and openness I had never seen from him before. He nodded to me in agreement before his gaze went distant as he listened to my sister's response, words meant for me.

Eventually, he said, gently, "She said she loves you too."

I knew that couldn't be everything she said, but he relayed the most important part. That was more than enough for me. I would see her soon, and I would hug her so tightly that she would feel everything we couldn't say. All the words we lost during my captivity here.

Kolton's expression shifted, anger flickering over his face as he straightened. "We need more of those exploding discs. And where the hell is Titus? I haven't heard him in my ear, and no one has mentioned him." His voice was tight with worry.

Chase answered before I could speak. "We don't know. We haven't heard from him since the incident at the old church. By the time we got there, it was just DeStephano Clan members sniffing around. No fox footprints or anything."

Kolton's jaw worked, the muscles ticking. His frustration was obvious even without him saying anything.

Dread reared its ugly little head before settling in my chest. I hoped I didn't get him into trouble after involving him in my plan to get close to Kolton while he was tranquilized.

"I can make something. Not as small or compact as one of those discs, but it will work. I'll just need a few things."

I started ticking off the supplies I needed: fertilizer, sterile cleaners, watering tubes, and any metal pipes they could find. A greenhouse was the perfect place to be when you wanted to build an impromptu explosive device.

Chase and Bailey took off in opposite directions, rushing to gather the items I asked for before the next wave of DeStephano Clan members attacked.

"Wait. You know how to make a fucking bomb?" Kolton asked, giving me a look that was equal parts shock and admiration.

I just shrugged. I honestly thought that it was common knowledge, but apparently not.

Kolton's arm shot toward me. He grabbed me around the waist and dragged me against him. His kiss was hot, claiming and searing me to my very core. He sealed his lips to mine like he wanted to leave a permanent mark there, ruining me for anyone else. It was a silent vow. A promise that no one would ever kiss me the way he did.

And it was true. I was ruined. The taste of him lingered on my tongue, addictive and dangerous, and I leaned into him without thinking, wanting—needing—more.

"I think I'm obsessed with you," he murmured against my lips when he eventually pulled away.

"Bomb making does it for you, huh?"

He gave an aggressive nod, and I couldn't help the chuckle that slipped out at the serious look on his face, even while he was being playful. I loved this side of him, too.

The feral, unpredictable side of him was sin and danger. It tempted me in ways I couldn't begin to describe or even fathom. But this version of him, soft, sweet, and with just a touch of ridiculousness, had my mind wandering to places I would never expect.

Yes, we were bonded. Yes, he would always be at my side. But now, I wanted his heart and his soul, not because the bond demanded it, but because he chose me, just as I had chosen him.

It had me thinking about a future with him. It made me want forever.

CHAPTER FORTY

"There was nothing back there, just an empty room. No sign of anything malicious, maybe storage at one point?" Derek said as he returned from looking for the other captives.

Not good. That was probably going to haunt Skylar until she figured out where those experiments were taking place...if what she saw was even real...

"Onyx said we are to hang back and let you guys handle this," Dayken said in my ear, interrupting my thoughts. "While I think that's the right move, especially if we want to avoid a war, I still have Danielson Clan members posted all over the forest. We're here if you need us."

"Don't bother," I said. "I plan on using that forest for something else later, and I want it cleared."

If there was a response, I didn't hear it. I was too busy watching my intelligent, graceful Sacar craft a mother-fucking bomb in front of me.

A bomb.

Like it was the most ordinary thing in the world. Watching her made my dick stir.

Mine, my tiger purred in my head, low and satisfied, as heat curled along my spine.

No shit, Sherlock, I thought in response, as if it were a question. As if I would ever allow her to belong to anyone else. Of course she was mine. I would kill—had killed—and would continue to kill anyone who tried to come between us.

Mine didn't even begin to cover it.

She was stunning and brilliant and fierce, and somehow, she was still bonded to me. My chest tightened with the thought, a fierce possessiveness that lived deeply within both man and beast.

"He's purring," Derek whispered, or rather whisper-yelled, like he physically couldn't keep it inside him. He tilted his head toward me, eyes wide with the theatrics of someone uncovering a new discovery.

"That's new," Chase replied, looking like he was cataloging the information for future study.

"Hey, kitty, kitty. You gonna make some wittle biscuits now that you've calmed down?" Derek cooed at me in just enough of a singsong voice to piss me off.

Chase quickly elbowed him, a subtle reminder that upsetting me could easily bring back the growling, feral tiger. But the day Derek took a hint would be the day hell froze into solid ice.

"He just likes that I can make bombs." Skylar paused mid-pour, lifting her eyes to mine with a wicked glint that fried every circuit in my brain. "Bomb kink. Who would have thought?"

"Checks out, actually," Derek said without missing a beat.

I had gotten used to them talking about me like I wasn't standing right here. Honestly, I preferred it. I hovered in the background whenever my tiger took over, letting him push to the surface. It felt easier. Quieter. More natural. Like slipping into a second skin of pure instinct.

"I hear more footsteps coming." The words slipped out in a low growl before I even realized I said them. My tiger was much better than I was at honing every instinct, every sense, hearing each step get closer and closer. "We need to hurry."

Skylar did not look up, but she tightened her focus. Her hands moved faster, still careful, still precise, but with a new urgency.

Then my tiger went silent, listening so intently that the world seemed to narrow. I shifted my stance a little, angling myself between her and the direction of the noise without stepping into her space or interrupting her work. I stayed close enough to shield her if someone broke through, but far enough not to risk her accidentally detonating something before she was ready.

The rush of movement happened too fast. I could not have stopped it even if I tried. The massive tables came crashing into the room as three lions and two men barreled into the space, guns firing. Their aim was locked and lethal, clearly operating under kill orders.

A bullet nailed Chase in the shoulder, and the impact sent him flying to the floor. Skylar quickly crouched over her work, turning her body into a shield. A second bullet slammed into her, hitting the lower left side of her back. Her pained gasp slashed through me like a knife.

I roared in fury. "STOP."

And surprisingly...

They did.

The lions froze mid-attack, just feet away from Derek and Bailey. The two men also went still. They did not lower their weapons, but their fingers went slack on the triggers.

I embraced the energy coursing through me. The power, the command. I pulled hard, letting the instinct take control. I let it flow through me, then sent it out, like an edict written into the air itself.

There was no going back now.

"Lower. Your. Weapons."

And they did.

The order hit them so strongly, so absolutely, that resistance was not an option. Their weapons quickly clattered to the floor.

I turned my back on them and dropped to my knees in front of Skylar, brushing the thin fabric of her nightie aside to see where she'd been shot. Her body was already forcing the bullet out, but I was still fucking pissed.

I rose to my full height, ready to grab the gun that damaged my precious Skylar and shove it up the lion's ass, when I noticed Derek watching me.

He was crouched beside Chase, his palm pressed to the bullet wound, staring up at me with wide eyes. He was speechless, probably for the first time in his life.

"Holy fucking shit," Chase breathed through clenched teeth.

I ignored them, scanning Skylar one more time. The wound was already closing, skin knitting itself together as the bullet worked its way free. But my chest was still tight, and my hands still shook with the need to break something.

"Sit down. Shift back," I ordered the lions. "Derek, stop staring at me and tie them up. You need to move quickly."

I turned back to Skylar, lowering my voice. "Skylar, my world, are you almost done?"

Apparently, I was the only one capable of giving orders at the moment. *How fucking terrifying is that thought?*

Very terrifying. I wasn't cut out for this shit like Dayken was. He was a natural-born leader; the Primarc title was never a question for him. Me, on the other hand...

Skylar was staring at me with a mix of shock and admiration on her face that helped me shake away my spiraling thoughts.

I suppose I could handle it all for a moment longer. Just for her.

"Almost done," she said. "I just need something to cut this with—"

Chase was there in an instant, supporting his wounded shoulder and providing help with...what did you know...his fucking talons out.

Fucking Knife Fingers.

Skylar's giggle and his answering smirk made me want to punch his fucking lights out, but now wasn't the time.

"Cut right here," she said. A slice, and then she added, "Perfect, all done."

CHAPTER FORTY-ONE

The second Kolton issued his command to the lions, the very moment the words left his mouth, the room changed. Not metaphorically. Physically.

The air trembled, vibrating against my skin, causing my instincts to bow without my consent. Every lion in the room stilled.

I'd read about this kind of thing before. The rare, impossible moment when dominance wasn't just presence—it was law.

And I knew instantly that there was only one possibility for someone to control multiple Guardians like that.

Kolton hadn't just commanded them.

He had commanded the entire room.

Every ounce of power in that space bent to him.

He was a Primarc.

It wasn't the kind of power you inherited. It was something you were born for.

And I was bonded to it. To *him.*

My heart soared with pride as I realized what this meant for him. My poor tiger, who had been lost for so many years, abandoned without his family, without his Sacar…was now one of the most powerful beings to exist. I had no idea if this was something he wanted or if he ever hoped it would happen to him. All I knew was that only good things could come from this.

"Kolton," I whispered as Chase walked away to help his brother. Kolton just looked at me in question. The fact that his eyes didn't contain any shock or surprise told me that he already knew he held this power and had either been hiding or suppressing it. I planned to find out which one it was.

"You knew." It was a statement, not a question.

"I had a feeling," he replied softly, to not let the others hear.

"A feeling? I would say that it's a little bit more than a feeling, Kolton."

"Are you angry with me?"

"No, of course not. I just wish you had told me."

"And when, my dear Sky, would you have liked me to do that? When they tried to take you from me? When they actually took you away? Or when they attempted to destroy our bond?"

"Oh, will you lose the attitude? You know what I mean."

"I promise you, I was not trying to hide anything. It's just a lot to process. I haven't figured out the full implications yet. And to be honest, I still don't understand it."

I studied him for a second longer, weighing everything I didn't have time to unpack at the moment. Whatever this was, whatever he was becoming, it would have to wait.

That was going to have to be enough. For now.

We had a mess to clean up anyway. Or a mess to make, depending on how you looked at it.

"Okay. I need to move this over there by the flowers."

I carefully lifted my makeshift bomb, which was rigged to go off once the slow drip finished. If I'd timed it right, we had about thirty minutes.

"Derek, take this tube and run it through that trough over there. Chase, do the same with this one."

"On it!" they said in unison and immediately moved to follow my directions. No questions, no hesitation.

Bailey was crouched down angrily yelling at the lions that were tied up about shooting her best, best friend.

Meanwhile, Kolton was purring again, the sound low and comforting. He also seemed to be fighting back a smile, almost like he couldn't help himself.

"Okay, let's get out of here," I said. "We've got about thirty minutes, and I bet Leo is upstairs waiting for us. Chase, Derek, Bailey, take the tunnel. He won't hurt me, but I can't say the same for you three."

I glanced at Kolton, who was completely unfazed by the threat of death or harm. There was a brief sense of reluctance from the other three Guardians as we reached the makeshift tunnel near the cells. Their instinct was to protect, not run away.

"Are you sure we should go?" Chase asked.

"Yeah, you two might be all superpowered up with bombs and shit, but we can still help fight," Derek added, and Bailey nodded in agreement, dancing on her toes and clapping her hands in excitement.

"No. This is the safest option for all of us. Leo probably hasn't been able to confirm if you were here, and we should keep it that way," I said.

We agreed to meet them in the next city over. I reminded them to move quickly so they could get far enough away to avoid getting caught in the blast.

I watched as they shifted and went back through Bailey's tunnel.

Kolton and I turned toward the stairs that led to the main floor, leaving the flowers and the ticking time bomb below as we went to face our enemy.

I paused before the stairs, looking down to see a clan member dead on the ground, one that Chase had taken down. I crouched down and started to undo his belt.

"What the fuck are you doing?" Kolton hissed at me.

"Oh, relax." I swatted his hand away from my shoulder. "I need a weapon and means to carry said weapon."

I paused my belt removal task to gesture at my attire.

Which was a nightie.

My reasoning seemed to have appeased him because he visibly relaxed and allowed me to continue my task of arming myself.

I quietly made my way up the steps with Kolton on my heels, carefully maneuvering around the rubble from the first explosion. We went slowly, listening for sounds or any clues that would indicate what was waiting for us up there.

Relief flooded me when we finally made it to the main floor, with no scents or signs of an ambush waiting for us. Leo must have called in reinforcements, which meant we needed to move quickly.

"Lead the way," Kolton said from behind me. I headed in the direction of the front entrance, cutting through the dining room, then the living room, when I heard a familiar voice that forced me to stop in my tracks.

CHAPTER FORTY-TWO

"Hello, Skylar," Crowe said from where he sat on a high-backed chair in the corner of the room.

How?! How was he here?

"We have much to discuss, you and I," he went on, as if there was nothing extraordinary about our paths crossing at this moment.

My mind ran through all the possibilities of how he could be here, but one, and only one, was even remotely plausible...

Someone let him out.

My heart cracked at the sight of him, and my stomach ached. Not out of fear, but from pure distress. Because for him to have gotten out meant either someone betrayed us or someone died in order for him to escape.

He must have seen the realization on my face because his tone turned mocking. "Oh Skylar, you silly little vampire. Haven't you figured it out? Is that chip defective now?" He ridiculed me as I took in the criticism and tried to tap into my chip, cataloging events and rifling through everything that had happened up until this point.

When I come up empty, I said, "Must be. Please enlighten me."

"Haven't you ever wondered why I know so much, why I always knew where to look and where to be? Surely, you've figured out who I am."

I paused, not wanting to reveal that I truly had not figured it out, for fear of appearing weak.

"I am Lunce's son."

That...

That didn't make sense.

Lunce was the first-ever vampire.

This was another trick of his, surely.

"That's not possible, you lunatic. Lunce was born during the Roman Empire. And has never been seen since. Not to mention you are not a vampire!"

"I was born in 1334. Just before the Black Plague. I survived, but you are right, it's not because I'm a vampire. Not because of the immortality my great-grandmother created. No. Not that. I have no fangs. No speed. No strength. I am just *this*." He gestured to his aging face, eyes fever-bright. "I eat food, I bleed, I sleep. I age—much slower than average, but I still age. I am utterly human. A genetic dud."

"So, you expect me to believe that?" I tried to process his words. "And what? You tortured us, had your lackeys kill innocent people for what...a pity party?"

"When my brother announced that he was going to have a child," he continued, completely ignoring my question, "I needed to know if it, too, would be like me. Imagine my surprise when your sister arrived, a pure vampire."

He was talking about my father, my *real* father, as if he were scum. He spoke with such callousness, trying to get me to react emotionally instead of with logic, but I couldn't suppress the questions that rose to the forefront of my mind.

What was he like?

Was he kind?

Did I look like him?

What about my mother?

His voice hardened when I still didn't give him the reaction he wanted. "So, I got closer. Embedded myself. Years later, *another* child—and *again*, not a dud. So, I killed him. And his wife. Took you both and froze you in stasis so I could study you properly."

I felt the bile rise up my esophagus, but I swallowed it down. "You *froze* us?"

"For centuries. You were mine. Every cell, every drop of blood, every answer I was denied. But technology evolves, doesn't it? Unfortunately, my funds dwindled. So, I adapted. I thawed you out, dressed it up as government research, and let the human warmongers help me finish what I started."

A wide grin split his face as he said, "You were never free. You were always in my possession. From the moment you were born all the way to your fake parents."

Pieces began to fall into place, creating the full picture of why Kolton and I bonded as babies. It was because I *wasn't* a baby. I was hundreds of years old at that point; it all made sense.

I wanted to weep. All the years Onyx and I had lost. All that time spent frozen, robbed of the existence, the life, even the time I was meant for.

But then, my chip helped me come to a sudden conclusion. If Onyx and I hadn't been stolen, if we had lived in the time period we were meant for, I would never have gotten to where I was now. I would not have found my Guardian, my friends, my family.

Sure, everything I'd known was a lie up until I met them, but was that lie worth it?

I thought so.

I looked over my shoulder at Kolton, who stood tall and proud. His muscles were flexed and ready for a fight. His jaw was clenched despite being able to see the outline of his fangs in his mouth, making his lips appear puffy. Perfection, absolute perfection.

I couldn't fathom anyone else but him being my Guardian, in any lifetime. It has to be him. Always.

The realization hit hard and fast. *No.* I didn't give a fuck what Crowe had to say. I had my tiger, my sister, and my friends now.

"You probably thought telling me this sob story would soften me, make me weak, maybe even get me to see things your way. You are wrong." The subtle glint in his eyes told me I had hit the nail on the head. "Because all you've succeeded in doing is making me want to kill you myself, instead of letting someone else do it."

His smile was wicked, filled with pure malice. "Oh, my lovely niece, I made you so brilliant."

"Shut the fuck up," Kolton yelled. "You didn't make shit—she was *born* brilliant, and you hate that fact." He clasped his hand on my shoulder, pulling me back against his body, needing the physical connection.

A slow, menacing laughter broke the air.

"Agreed, and she's far too brilliant for your dumb ass."

Leo stepped into the room with a lazy smile on his face. His gait was unhurried, almost casual, as his eyes flicked between Kolton and me, calculating. He stopped beside Crowe and clapped him on the shoulder with his remaining hand, easy as old friends meeting up for drinks. The familiarity made my stomach turn.

They stood too close. Too comfortable. Like monsters who had planned for this moment.

Rehearsed it.

I could end him now. I had my newly acquired gun holstered at my back. Plus, my movements were faster than anyone in this room.

But...could I do it? Could I end his life? I knew if I couldn't, Kolton would gladly do it for me. He might even be forming his own plan right now.

"I see the mark is still there, Leonardo," Crowe mocked. "Couldn't pull it off after all, huh?"

"There was a slight complication during the procedure," he said dismissively. "She burned through the elixir faster than we anticipated."

"I told you when you captured her that she would have already built up a tolerance to it...but *no*, you didn't want to listen to me." He sounded like he didn't care either way. "Pity what's to come as a result of your arrogance."

Crowe knew...he knew I wanted to end Leo. And he was okay with it.

I was either doing Crowe a favor, or Leo was never that important to his larger schemes.

Did he know I was armed? Was he hoping I would start a war between the DeStephano and Danielson Clans?

Possibly, but there was one thing I knew for certain he wasn't aware of.

He doesn't know that Kolton is a Primarc.

That fact alone changed things. If Leo got taken down, the lions wouldn't be alone or left to fend for themselves, regardless of what Kolton decided—it meant something.

"You can't have her, and neither can you, you fucking joke of a Primarc."

Crowe arched a brow at Kolton, then looked to Leo to see if he was going to respond. He just glared at Kolton, leaving Crowe to deal with the conversation.

"She already is mine. It will just take time, but we are connected. She will feel it soon."

I read him like a book. His eyes flickered slightly, and his pulse was heavy at his throat. The subtle scent of fear hit my nose.

I immediately recognized what he was doing. He was baiting me, trying to get me to test it, to search for the connection. But I wasn't going to fall for it.

That was what he needed. He needed me to be the one to choose, to reach out for him. He needed me to pull the rubber band for him.

Ha, that will never *fucking happen.*

"Leo, I'm going to tell you this once and only once. Stop this non-sense. Stop trying to come between my Guardian and me. Let us walk away before any more blood is shed," I pleaded.

He laughed, actually genuinely laughed. It caused my heart to sink, saddened by what I knew I must do.

"Never," he snarled before pointing at Kolton. "This worthless piece of shit doesn't deserve to be a bonded Guardian. *Never* has."

He turned to me before continuing, "You need me, Sky. Admit it. Admit that you need someone stronger, more powerful, wealthier than him. Reach out to me, just once, and then we can end this madness, and you can transfer the essence from that feral tiger to me." His tone lost some of his menacing anger as he pleaded, "Pick. Me."

I made the mistake of looking at Kolton; his eyes were full of hurt, pain, even disgrace. Leo's words made him doubt himself, his worth, and that enraged me.

Everything suddenly clicked into place. The events leading up to this, the carefully chosen words he used during my time here, how he tried to manipulate the flower to sever the bond.

Leo needed Kolton here because if he couldn't force me to choose him, he planned for me to somehow reach out to him, accidentally or otherwise. When that happened, he would have immediately killed Kolton, permanently replacing him as my Guardian. Whatever they had done to tamper with our bond, however they tried to weaken it by des-ecrating the sacred flowers, it was always going to end with them killing him. They wanted to murder my beloved tiger, my cherished Guardian, the love of my life...Kolton.

Fuck it.

Everything happened in quick succession.

I pulled the gun from behind my back. I aimed and pulled the trigger. The bullet hit its mark, embedding itself in the center of Leo's forehead.

Crowe dropped to the floor, hitting the ground hard. Kolton lunged after him, but I quickly realized his plan. Crowe reached into his pocket, clearly anticipating one of us to get close to him.

"Kolton, no!" I grabbed his arm and yanked him back, which gave Crowe enough time to duck out of the room.

"He wants us to chase him," I said. "*Don't*. He has something on him that will knock us out or some other kind of trap. I just know it."

Kolton looked like he wanted to argue but eventually nodded in agreement. He peered down at Leo's lifeless body before saying, "I'm shocked you didn't shoot Crowe instead."

"I couldn't risk accidentally bonding to him," I replied, motioning to Leo.

"Good call," Kolton said, pulling me toward him. His grip was crushing. "Are you okay?" he asked, more for his own sake than anything else.

"Yes, more than okay, actually," I said calmly as I looked up into Kolton's beautiful, bright yellow eyes.

"You are terrifying, you know that."

"So people keep telling me."

"Come on, let's get the fuck out of here."

"Wait. I need to run to the kitchen real quick."

CHAPTER FORTY-THREE

W e stood at the front of the mansion, on the massive concrete patio with stairs that led to a terrace. The moon and stars shined bright above us, casting a soft glow over everything. This was where it all started, where I found Sky standing strong next to our enemy. Now it was time to burn it all down. Again. But this time for good.

"We're outside," I said into the earpiece, hoping someone was on the other end.

Dayken's voice came through seconds later. "Good, glad you made it out. Any immediate threats?"

"Crowe," I bit out. "He was here. Got out somehow and ran off. No clue where to."

Dayken unleashed a string of curses straight into my ear. His anger came through loud and clear, felt as much as heard through the comms.

"I couldn't make out the other voice in the room, but I knew something wasn't right...it was fucking Crowe?"

"Yeah. Might be worth sending any nearby wolves after him. See if they can catch a trail."

A brief pause.

"On it," he said a second later. "You guys stay safe in the—"

I let a claw grow out on one of my fingers and used it to dig out the earpiece, making a bloody mess in the process. I was pretty sure I punctured my eardrum, but I saw the silver device at the tip of my claw and knew I would have sweet relief once it healed.

"What the fuck, Kolton! What did you just do?" Skylar shrieked as she saw the blood dripping from my ear. "I could have taken that out for you."

I shrugged. Then I pulled her against me and kissed her, cutting off the rest of her argument.

Gods.

She melted into me for half a second before going still, like she didn't know what to do with it. I didn't give her time to figure it out. I didn't want her thinking. I just wanted her here.

Alive.

I pulled back just enough to look at her. Really look at her. No blood pouring from her chest. No lifeless body in my arms. No empty bond clawing through me.

She saw everything I was. Every broken, ugly piece of me.

And she stayed.

That did something to me. Something I didn't have a name for yet, but I felt it settling in my chest all the same.

"So..." she said, a little breathless now. "What does this all mean?"

I didn't answer right away.

My gaze lifted, catching on the last of the lions as they fled into the forest. Panic drove them, their movements frantic, desperate. They had to know their Primarc was dead. Had to smell the explosives waiting to bring this place down.

Good.

Let them run.

My eyes shifted to the pair Derek had tied up in the subbasement. Not tied anymore. Either someone freed them, or Derek really was that bad at knots.

I tracked them as they disappeared between the trees, my body already leaning into the hunt before I could stop it.

They had shot her.

My jaw locked.

Every instinct I had screamed at me to go after them. To make them pay for it. To finish what they started.

But Skylar's soft hand reached for me, and that simple gesture cut through the noise in my head. She was still right here. Still breathing.

Not dying. Not gone.

Here.

I forced myself to stay where I was, dragging my focus back from the forest. The mission had never been about chasing every last lion. It was about getting Skylar back and ending this place. Burning out everything rotten at its core.

Not all of them chose this.

Not all of them deserved to die for it.

My chest rose with a slow breath as I let the urge to hunt slip through my fingers.

I looked back down at my Sacar, into her ice-blue eyes.

Nothing else mattered. Not the lions. Not the past. Not the blood still drying on my skin.

Just her.

"I honestly don't know what all this means," I said. "But I know I'm done letting this place exist."

I ran a hand through my hair, hating the uncertainty but forcing myself to stay strong for her.

"We'll figure out what comes next once we're back at the compound. I'm not staying here any longer than we have to," I added.

"Why? This land could be yours. You're a Primarc, after all. You can't deny that any longer."

"Your home is where your sister is, and my home is where you are," I said. "So we're going home to the compound."

A tear slid down her cheek.

"No, none of that." I brushed it away. "I'm still not some romantic idiot. I plan on fucking your brains out in that forest as soon as the rest of the lions are gone. And once I make sure the bird brains and that mongoose are off the property too."

Her eyes went from teary to slitted and full of desire in less than a blink.

"Come on," I said softly. "How long until that sexy ass bomb you made explodes?"

"It should go off soon. That's why I turned on all the stoves in the kitchen without lighting the burners before we came out here. I needed the gas to fill the main floor to make sure there would be nothing left."

"Gods, that brain of yours is so fucking sexy." I grabbed her face like the lunatic I was and kissed the top of her head. She giggled, and I wanted more of those soft, perfect sounds.

"I love your laugh."

"You do?" she asked.

I nodded like an idiot.

She beamed up at me, and my heart thumped wildly in my chest before her expression turned serious. "We should probably get off the patio. The further we are from the building, the better."

She tugged on my hand and led me into the middle of the backyard.

We waited.

Nothing happened, so we waited some more.

"Hmmm," she murmured. "Looks like we have more time than I accounted for."

She turned suddenly, rising onto her toes and crushing her lips against mine. My reaction was instant. I didn't think about it. I didn't stop to question it. I just moved.

I lifted her, wrapping her legs around my waist, and she instinctively locked them behind my back. She weighed nothing as I walked toward the tree line, abandoning watching the place blow up and instead cradling her close to my chest.

I broke the kiss only so I could watch where I was going. I nearly tripped when she started kissing and nipping at my neck. I growled and felt her smile against my skin.

I picked up my pace as we got closer to the edge of the property. The forest waited ahead like a dark curtain ready to close around us. The explosion hit a heartbeat later.

The shockwave slammed into me hard. An echoing *boom* tore through the night, violent enough to rattle my bones and force the air from my lungs. The ground seemed to buckle beneath my feet as heat licked at my back and debris rained down behind us.

I didn't stop walking.

I adjusted my grip on Skylar, sliding my hands to her ass and giving it a squeeze. Each step I took was steady yet relentless. The world could be ending behind us, and that still would not slow me down.

She didn't flinch either.

Skylar stayed pressed against me, fingers curling at my neck, shoving aside the collar of the shirt I stole from inside to give herself better access. Her mouth was warm against my skin, and she kissed along my throat like nothing else existed.

And maybe it didn't.

The fire, the mansion collapsing behind us—all of it faded into nothing but noise and light and smoke. All I knew was her weight in my arms, the forest ahead, and the certainty that nothing back there mattered.

She was restless by the time I reached the edge of the forest, rubbing against me as I walked, pulling my hair for a better angle. Before my foot even touched the leaf-covered dirt, she struck.

I nearly fell to one knee.

The sharp little pinpricks of her fangs sank into my neck. Her tongue lavished my skin as she made sure not a single drop of blood slipped past her lips.

"Fuck yes, Sky. Take what you need from me." I could feel every pull, every moan as she swallowed my blood. She enjoyed the taste of me. Me…and only me.

Then one of her hands drifted down between our bodies, rubbing my erection through my jeans. I found a whole new vocabulary of curses. She must have liked my foul mouth because she began rubbing harder, and before I knew it, I was about to cum in my pants. I grabbed her wrist to stop her, and she pulled away from my neck. There was a slight coating of my blood on her lips as she looked up at me with questioning eyes, wondering why I stopped her.

"I'm going to cum," I said, and she smiled that adorable, fanged smile. I nearly lost it. Was it possible to come just from looking at her? Because that was about to happen.

I lowered her to the ground, pushing her back down to the damp earth, and crawled over her.

"Not exactly what I had planned, but I can't wait another fucking second."

"Then don't," she purred. She was so perfect, so beautiful, and so, *so* mine.

I dropped down to kiss her, crushing her to me. She arched her back to meet my chest, and I dug my erection into her. Her answering moan let me know I hit the right spot.

"More," she begged. I loved the sound of it, so I ground against her again. Her back arched further, and she began frantically pawing at my shirt, trying to feel my skin. The moment her hands touched me, my tiger took control for a second, growling in appreciation. Her nails clawed down my abdomen and then back up my chest.

"Off," she commanded, and who was I to deny her? With one arm on the ground, I braced myself and yanked the shirt over my head with my free hand.

"Mine," she said as she took me in. Her pupils narrowed into slits, her fangs fully elongated, and her short hair flayed around her. She was a sight to behold.

"Yes, yours, my Sacar."

I kissed her again, this time slow and deep. I tried to be gentle because I thought that was what she wanted, and I wanted her to feel everything I couldn't say in that kiss. But Skylar was having none of it.

"I've waited long enough, Kolton. I've wanted you from the moment I opened my eyes on that operating table, and now that I know you, the real you—"

She paused, placing her hand over my bare chest, just above my heart. "I want you on a much deeper level. You will give me what I want, right?" she said in that playful tone I'd come to love.

"Yes, Sky. I will give you anything and everything."

"Forever."

Forever? She wanted forever?

Because of the bond, she was stuck with me, but surely, she wouldn't want *me* forever. She would get bored with me, find me insufferable, and eventually lose interest.

No, not forever. She couldn't truly mean it.

She put her hands on my face and met my gaze. "I lo—" she started, but I quickly silenced her with a kiss. I began grinding against her again, hitting just the right spot to make her squirm.

Pleasure. I could give her pleasure. That I knew how to do. The future was uncertain, and I couldn't hold onto promises of forever. That thought seemed too dangerous to hope for, and I couldn't let it live free in my mind.

So, I locked it away in the vault with my demons and other bad thoughts while I focused on bringing her the best orgasm of her life.

CHAPTER FORTY-FOUR

I writhed in his arms, desperate, needy, wanting more. I *needed* more from him. He was holding back; I could feel it. I could read him better than anyone, and he was at war with himself again. Wanting me desperately one moment, then scared the next. I wanted to take back what I just said, but at the same time, I meant those words with all my heart. They were for him and him alone; he could crush them or hold them dear.

Wanting to take his mind off what I said, I decided I was done with foreplay, as I had read it was called. I pushed him off me, and he gave me the exact look of shock and confusion I expected.

"Sky, I'm—"

Before he could finish that sentence, I rose up and pushed his shoulders, forcing him backward until he fell to the ground. Once on his back, he realized what I had planned, and his confused expression turned to molten desire.

Yes. This is how I want him to look at me.

Not with fear, but with the look he gave me when I knew he was thinking wicked, naughty things.

I straddled his thighs. "You are not giving me what I want," I teased. "So, I'm going to take it."

"Yes...take. Take it," he purred, in a low sensual voice that brought goosebumps to my skin. I made quick work of undoing the button on his jeans and pushed them down, barely sliding them past his hips. His erection was on full display, hard, thick, and so large that I started to question if we were even anatomically compatible. But my heart still raced, and my fangs shot out of my mouth. I wanted to lick it, to feel every smooth edge against my tongue, so I did.

"Fuck!" Kolton half roared, half groaned. His explosive reaction only made me want to do it again, so I did.

He was shaking, and his leg twitched ever so slightly. He moved my hair out of my face so he could watch me. This time when I licked, I went slowly and focused on the tip, which I noticed got me the strongest reactions from him. The amount of foul language pouring from his mouth told me I found the right spot to focus my attentions.

"Sky, I'm going to cum all over that pretty mouth of yours if you don't stop."

"Is that a bad thing?" I asked, genuinely unsure.

His head fell onto the ground with a heavy thunk. He covered his eyes with his forearm, looking like he was contemplating how to respond. I didn't like being unable to see his face, so I crawled up his body, abandoning my exploration of his erection.

His answering purr, and the low rumbling from his chest, let me know he liked my body on top of his. When I was finally hovering over his covered face, I moved his hand away so I could see his eyes.

He looked utterly tortured.

"What is it?" I asked.

"I just—I forgot how inexperienced you are and how taking you on the forest floor probably isn't the best idea. But I'm not noble enough to stop now."

"Good, because if you don't stop your little pity party and start fucking me, I'm going to—"

He flipped me onto my back before I could finish the thought. He kissed me, his tongue tangling with mine, and I moaned. He aligned his cock perfectly with my core and thrusted ever so slightly, the tip easily slipping past the hem of the skimpy lingerie Leo kept me in.

"This is going to hurt a little," he said as he broke the kiss and moved the flimsy piece of fabric aside. Feeling the head of his cock pressing against my entrance sent sensations all through my body. Like fire in liquid form. It coursed through every vein, and I wanted more. So much more.

"Hurry, Kolton, please," I pleaded.

He hummed, a low, amused rumble. "I like that." He kissed me again, deeply. "Beg me again. I think I found a new kink."

I could not believe he was teasing me at a moment like this. I clawed at his back, trying to make him move. When he still refused, I begged, just as he demanded.

"Please, please hurry and fuck me."

He smiled against my mouth. He reached his hand down, wrapped it around his cock, and he rubbed himself up and down my slit in slow, deliberate strokes.

I writhed and moaned.

"Again," he demanded.

Masochist asshole.

"Kolton. If you don't fuck me right now—"

He thrust inside me before I could finish the threat. Pain and pleasure shot through me all at once, and I cried out.

"Shhh, shhh," he whispered against my forehead as he kissed down my face. "I told you it would hurt."

"More," I demanded in a low moan.

"I have to go slow. I do not want to hurt you."

"More...*now.*"

My nails dug into his back, pulling him closer. I did not want the gentle version of him, not tonight, not after everything. I wanted the raw, untamed Kolton.

He must have heard the need in my voice. Felt it. Understood it.

Without a word, he drew back his hips and slammed into me again. The back of my head pressed deeper into the forest floor, leaves damp beneath my skull as he drove into me again and again.

"Yes," I cried.

"So, this is how you want it?" he asked, and I nodded, breathless. "Good. I am going to ruin this sweet little pussy. It is mine now and only mine."

His filthy words only made me more wet, more needy. The tension inside me coiled tighter with each thrust. My nails dragged deep lines down his back, no doubt drawing blood, but he did not seem to mind. His pace stayed ruthless. He grabbed one of my wrists and pinned it above my head, leaving me trapped beneath him while he kissed and nipped down my neck. His grip was ironclad. Tight, rough, and demanding.

I was a mess of sensations. Restrained. Bitten. Worshipped. Overwhelmed by the pleasure he was pouring into me. My moans grew loud. They carried through the trees, and the nearby birds took flight.

"You like that?" he growled. "You like it when I fuck you hard into the dirt. My filthy little Sky. Only I get to see this side of you. Do you understand me?"

I nodded, unable to even fathom being with anyone other than him.

He consumed my every thought, every breath, and now every gasp and moan of pleasure. It was all...him.

Kolton released his grip on my wrist and traveled his hand down my body as he continued his relentless thrusts, building the pressure and bringing more pleasure as he did.

His hand finally landed on my sensitive clit, and when he began rubbing it with the pad of his thumb, a burst of sensation exploded through my body.

I cried out in pure, undiluted pleasure, and his answering praise was everything I craved.

"That's right, my Sacar, cum for me. I'm right there with you."

He pushed himself up to meet my gaze. Pleasure clouded his yellow eyes, which were half-hooded. He looked at me with such fierce desire my orgasm nearly doubled. "Yes, that's right. Keep cumming around my dick. I'm going to—fuck," he roared, and I felt him cum.

His body shook, and his movements slowed. As I came down from my high, so did he. He collapsed onto me, nearly crushing me with his weight, before he shifted slightly to the side. I hadn't minded the weight, though. I liked the heavy pressure of his body against mine.

"Kolton," I murmured.

"Hmmm?"

"That was perfect."

He lazily kissed the side of my neck. "Good," he purred.

CHAPTER FORTY-FIVE

I did not want to leave Skylar's warmth. I was lying on my back in the dirt with her draped across my chest. Her breath brushed against my throat, soft and shaky, and I wanted to keep her tethered to me like this forever. But the realization that I had just taken her virginity on the cold, damp forest floor left a sour feeling in my stomach. I could not say I regretted it. I would never regret being inside her. But guilt curled in my chest at my lack of control. I had acted just like the feral beast Leo accused me of being before she had shot him.

"Come on, we should get home."

She simply nodded. For a moment, I felt a strange tinge of disappointment that she didn't ask to stay here, curled up together, for longer. Not even for a second. But then she slid her delicate fingers up my chest and then ran her nails back down, grazing my nipple. My eyes fluttered shut, and a deep rumble escaped me.

I could no longer remember what I had to be disappointed about.

I stood up before helping her to her feet, steadying her when her legs trembled ever so slightly. She tried to pretend that nothing was wrong, but her body told a different story. Pride swelled in me, but I pushed it down. I had to focus. I plucked stray leaves from her hair and wiped a few smudges of dirt from her neck and shoulders.

The forest felt heavier now. Darker. I wrapped one arm around her waist as we began to walk in the direction of our meetup spot with Derek and Chase. We took the long way, weaving through thicker brushes, cutting through shallow ravines, following animal trails that only a feral mind could map. I stayed hyper alert, listening for any snapped twig or shifting shadow. Skylar kept close, quiet. She was still glowing from her recent orgasm, but she was tired enough that her silence felt natural.

Halfway through the forest, a set of headlights blinked twice ahead of us. The sound of shifting gravel told me exactly where the car was. This was where Dayken told me the twins would pick us up right before I ripped the earpiece out. Instead of Derek and Chase, though, we found a different Averie Clan member. A girl with short auburn hair and a freckled nose stepped out of the car and waved.

I couldn't remember her name, but I was pretty sure she was the twin's cousin. Sweet-faced, but I'd bet her mind was as sharp as her talons.

She tossed me the keys. "Your ride. Courtesy of the falcons. Nobody followed me."

"Good." I pocketed the keys, and the moment she turned her back, I ducked my head under the car to look for any signs of a tracker. I would not risk anyone tracing us.

Not tonight, not ever.

Call it caution, call it paranoia, but I trusted no one.

The girl pretended not to notice. Members of the Averie Clan were smart enough to not ask questions they didn't want the answers to.

I helped Skylar into the passenger seat before walking around to the driver's side. I started the car as the falcon shifted and took off into the sky without another word. She was observant enough to realize neither of us was in the mood for a chat.

The drive back to the compound wasn't too bad. Having already crossed a majority of the distance on foot, we were only a little over an hour away from Sparta.

When the familiar security gates came into view, Skylar's entire face lit up. Relief. Hope. Something bright and unguarded, and so completely Skylar.

My chest tightened at the sight.

Before I even pulled the car to a stop, she was out the door and sprinting toward the compound entrance.

Onyx stood there waiting with Dayken at her back, her constant shadow. Skylar let out a sound that could only be described as half madness and half joy, yet somehow pure delight. Her energy burst out so fiercely that the air around us felt warmer.

I rubbed a hand over my heart without meaning to.

She made me feel things I was not used to. Made me feel things I did not want to name.

Because everything I had ever named had been taken away from me.

And I did not want to lose anything else…

Dayken approached me, leaving the sisters to their reunion and forcing me to abandon the dark thoughts in my mind.

"Welcome back," he said, extending his hand to me. I looked at it, contemplating what to do. If I took his hand, did that mean that I accepted what he said before as true? Would a handshake make everything good between us?

I was unsure how much weight the simple gesture could hold, but I stuck my hand out in return. He grabbed me in his hard, firm grip and pulled me to him. I crashed into his solid chest. He patted me once on the back and said softly, "I'm glad you're okay."

Emotions lodged in my throat, and the stupid thing felt very tight all of a sudden. Like it didn't want me to be capable of speech, but I tried anyway.

"Thanks, man." It was all I could manage before I clasped him on the back in return.

"Come on. Let's hear all about what happened." Dayken released me and motioned to the front entrance, where the sisters were having a well-deserved moment.

CHAPTER FORTY-SIX

My sister.

My strong, loyal, beautiful sister was finally in my sight, and I ran. I ran with everything I had. She was running toward me, too, and when we collided in a tangle of arms and tears, it was the most glorious feeling in the world.

Onyx was squeezing me so tightly it was hard to take a breath, but that was okay. Who needed air when your body was capable of healing any injury? What couldn't be repaired was how much time I'd lost with my sister.

"I've missed you so much," she said against my hair.

"Thank you for trusting me."

"I never doubted you, Sky. Not for a second." She looked so genuine, so concerned, as her brows furrowed together. "If anything, I was afraid for a different reason."

"What?" I asked.

She ran her hands through my hair, cupping my face before finally meeting my eyes.

"I was afraid that you would realize just how strong you were on your own. Without me." Her voice wavered as she continued, "I know it's selfish, and I have no right to think that. You are strong. I've never doubted that. I'm just terrified that one day you'll realize you don't need me. That you're okay on your own. And when that day comes, I don't know what I'm going to do. You are a part of me."

I shook my head and said, "Stop. Stop those thoughts right now. I might not always need you to rescue me, but I will always need you by my side. I will always need your hugs. I will always need you to look me in the eye and tell me everything's going to be okay. I will always need *you*."

Tears streamed down my face, blurring my vision, and Onyx was in the exact same state. She clutched me to her chest again and let out a choked sob that sounded painfully familiar.

"I'm just so happy you're okay. I'm so proud of you."

I smiled and let her hold me for a moment before sighing and pulling back from her comforting arms.

"There's something I need to tell you, though," I confessed, as we started walking into the compound.

"What is it? You can tell me anything."

"Crowe was there, at Leo's estate," I said, and concern instantly flared in her eyes, followed by a rage that promised violence and retribution. But she didn't interrupt me. One of the many reasons why I loved her so much.

"I have no idea how he escaped Alicia's cells or how long he was working with the DeStephano Clan. He was able to get away again, but not before he told me something."

"Go on," she commanded.

"Let's wait until we're somewhere private," I said as we descended the stairs to the basement where our rooms were. Onyx's door was first. We opened it and silently slipped inside. I flopped down on her perfectly made bed while she stayed standing, tense as she waited to hear what I had to say.

I told her everything. Crowe's claim about being Lunce's son *and* our uncle. How he stole us from our parents before killing them. That we were both so much older than we thought because he froze us and left us that way for centuries. I told her how he never inherited the immortality and strength Decima, our great-great-grandmother, created with her magic and the Sacar flower, and that was the reason for his experiments. For the torture.

As I repeated everything Crowe told me, it still sounded as insane as when I first heard it. And yet, at the same time, it all made perfect sense.

I watched Onyx closely and noticed the pieces clicking into place as she came to the same conclusion. His hatred had always felt too personal; we just never understood why. The resentment he held against us was much more than a simple prejudice. It carried so much more weight and history than we ever could have expected.

"I want to look at the Otacilia family tree. To at least confirm his claims about being Lunce's son," Onyx said quietly.

I nodded, not wanting to tell her that I had already seen it. Memorized it. The chip in my head made sure of that.

When I reached back into that part of my mind, his name was there, clear as day.

Lunce's offspring:

Corvin Otacilia

Alaric Otacilia

Corvin meant crow.

And Alaric was our father.

It fit too well, every piece sliding into place with sickening ease. Still, letting Onyx do her own research, allowing her the time to come to her own conclusions, felt kinder.

"I don't remember our real parents at all. You would think I would have some type of memory."

I could hear the distress in her voice, and I watched her brows furrow as she tried to pull on a memory that would never come. I gently ran soothing circles across her back, trying to tether her back to me in the present.

Because I had not finished with my revelations yet, and my next one might truly break her. I wanted the crease to ease in her brow, and when she looked at me, I seized the moment.

It was now or never.

"And there's something else," I said softly.

She straightened immediately.

"While we were in the facility, he did things to my head. A lot of brain surgeries. Scans. Electric shock." My throat tightened. "They were trying to get my brain to connect with, to absorb, the chip they implanted in my frontal lobe."

I could see Onyx's shock and rage, but she did not interrupt. She never did when it mattered.

"The chip is still there. It helps me make decisions. It lets me read faster. Process information at speeds normal people, even vampires and shifters, can't." My voice cracked, and I swallowed hard. "But it also put us at risk. And I'm so sorry."

"Now it's your turn to stop," she said, holding up her hand. "You think I don't know they were doing things to your head? Don't you think I noticed how fast you tore through all those books? How much you had to slow down whenever you read aloud to me, how intentional you were with every word?"

Her eyes softened. "I'm your sister, Sky. Of course, I noticed. And you never put us at risk. I know you would never."

I jumped up from her bed, and I hugged her again. I felt like that would speak louder than any words. It was silly of me to think my incredibly observant sister wouldn't have noticed the changes happening to me.

I pulled back from the hug, looking into eyes that were identical to mine, and suddenly realized how much I must have missed while I was held captive.

"How's Alicia? Any news? What about Peach? Is she hanging in there?"

I wanted to ask about Aurora too, but it didn't feel right. Not yet anyway. I wasn't as angry as Onyx or Kolton were. I knew she had a good soul. I was just disappointed.

But I knew it was still a very hard subject for Onyx.

"I haven't talked with Peach much, to be honest. I've been a little preoccupied," she said sheepishly.

"Understandable."

Then an idea struck me.

"Onyx. I have an idea."

"Of course you do." She smiled, genuine and bright, practically glowing as it spread across her face.

We were all gathered in the security room. It was a familiar, comforting sight. All of us back together again. Laughing, smiling, catching up on things that happened while I was stuck at Leo's place.

"We need to talk to Aurora and see what she knows about Crowe. What she saw and heard, maybe if she could repeat some of the conversations they had. I can analyze them for clues," I said as I rubbed my temples, already sorting through possible timelines in my head.

"We also need to start interrogating some of the Mack Clan members to see who let Crowe out. Pinpoint the exact day and time, then we can find out who was guarding him when he escaped," Chase added, typing rapidly on his tablet as if the answers might leap out if he worked hard enough.

Kolton cracked his knuckles, grinning like he was gearing up for a fight. "I do love a good interrogation."

"Absolutely not, Kolton," Dayken said. He did not even look up from the map he was examining, which was spread across the table. The fact that he didn't want Kolton to conduct the interrogations, even without witnessing what Kolton was capable of, spoke volumes. Dayken exhaled through his nose and lifted his gaze to Onyx. "My Goddess, can you handle the interrogations? We need to remain diplomatic. Can you keep the peace between our clans but also scare them shitless?"

"Of course." She smiled at him, already standing a little straighter, clasping her hands behind her back with almost prim delight.

Kolton scoffed and threw his arms out. "What the hell? I can scare them shitless."

He looked ready to protest, likely claiming that he would be the better choice. Dayken's shoulders tightened, preparing for an argument, but right when I thought it was about to escalate, Kolton instead grumbled, "You are just playing favorites."

He said it in an almost playful tone, his mouth twitching at the corner, and that gave me hope...hope that maybe he and my sister could get along, find a common ground. Because they were the two most important people in my life.

"The twins stay back, though. I don't feel like dealing with them," Dayken added like an afterthought, already moving pieces on the map.

"Didn't want to go anyway," Derek muttered from the couch, not even looking up from whatever game he had resumed playing on his phone the second no one was watching him.

CHAPTER FORTY-SEVEN

I t was nice, just Kolton and me in the car. Even with Crowe on the loose and a possible traitor in our midst, there was something comforting about being alone with him. I glanced down at my lap, feeling another wave of relief at being back in a pair of comfortable jeans again. The jacket and boots felt good, too, solid and familiar. It was such a stark contrast to the clothes I had been forced to wear while I was with the DeStephano Clan.

I reached over, resting my palm on Kolton's thigh. I meant the act as something simple, appreciative, and grounding. I completely misjudged how he would react. The growl that rose from his chest was low and raw, threaded with desire. It sent a shiver straight through me.

"I was just thinking, it's nice we are alone."

"Were you now?" he purred. "What else were you thinking?" He glanced over at me, taking his gaze off the road to look at me with those searing yellow eyes of his.

"You are so beautiful," I confessed, not for the first time.

"You keep complimenting me like that, and we won't make it to your friend's place."

His words caused my mind to scramble. What started as innocent appreciation quickly turned to...need. I needed to touch more of him.

"I was also thinking, I need something from you."

I reached out again, rubbing my hand up his thigh until I hit his very hard, very large erection. I looked down to see that the outline of it was visible through his pants.

"Fuck..." He groaned.

I pressed harder, adding a little more friction. And his hips jerked forward.

"Holy shit, that feels so good. You are going to make me cum in my pants."

"Well then, I'd better get it out so that doesn't happen."

His eyes flashed to mine. His pupils were slitted, and his double fangs started elongating from his gums.

I didn't need his words; the look in his eyes told me everything. I kept rubbing his dick while I used my free hand to release the button of his jeans and undo his zipper. I reached in and freed his cock, and gods, was it glorious.

He cursed, throwing his head back into the headrest.

I gripped him in my fist and ran my thumb up and down his head, loving the feel of the ridge there. Kolton shook with each swipe.

"Fuck! Now I'm going to cum *on* my pants instead of *in* them."

"I can fix that," I said, licking my lips.

The car jerked to a sudden stop. I sat up straight, releasing his cock to take in our surroundings. Kolton had pulled us over to the side of the road, onto a dirt path. It was probably an emergency offramp or something, but it was completely secluded.

"Wha—"

He reached over and undid my seat belt, pulling me toward him. He didn't stop until I was forced to scramble over the center console and onto his lap.

Before I knew it, I was straddling him.

"As much as I am dying to come in that beautiful, perfect little mouth of yours," he began as he started slowly unzipping my pants. "In fact, I probably won't think of much else until that happens. I need to be inside you. Right now."

I barely got my pants and underwear past my knees when I realized I was still wearing my boots.

Kolton didn't care. He just spun me around and lowered me until his shaft was pressed against my ass.

"Kolton," I moaned.

"My sweet Sky, we haven't even started yet." He lifted my ass, gripping his shaft, and slowly lowered me down onto it.

"Oh gods," I loudly moaned.

"That's right. See what happens when you pet a tiger. You become his plaything."

He held my arms behind my back, so I couldn't use them. My feet were on the floor between his legs. The pressure this angle caused was so intense I was pretty sure I was shaking.

Kolton started pounding into me relentlessly. Keeping my ass up, and then pulling out and slamming back in.

"Fuck! Kolton, I'm going to—"

"Yes, you are, but not yet. I'm not done playing with you," he purred in my ear as he slowed his rhythm. He released my arms, and I tried to brace myself on the steering wheel, but he wrapped his hand around my throat and pulled me against him. My back was flushed with his chest, all while he kept that slow, steady rhythm.

"I'm gonna—" I tried to say, but he gave my neck a little squeeze as he trailed kisses down my cheek.

"Not until I say."

I needed him to let me come.

Let's see if I can get him to come first, then.

I ran my hands up my stomach, lifting my shirt. I pinched my own nipple and moaned.

"Oh fuck, Sky." He started pistoning into me faster, harder. "You know you are my undoing, don't you?" He reached down and used his finger to circle my clit, causing me to cry out. "Now, Sky! Cum now. All over my dick."

I felt his release first, but I was right behind him. My body trembled. Everything felt too sensitive, but not enough at the same time. As I came down from the high, I collapsed onto Kolton. Boneless, weightless, and utterly content.

That was amazing.

"Fuck, that was amazing," Kolton said, echoing my thoughts.

I chuckled. "I was just thinking that."

He peppered my neck with light, soft kisses as a low rumble purred from his chest.

"More," I said as I shifted, turning my body so I could kiss him. He smiled and then laughed. A genuine, beautiful melody, and I was awe-struck.

"What?" He looked concerned, and I realized I was staring.

"Sorry, it's just that I've never heard you laugh like that before. It's magical."

He seemed unable to accept the compliment, so I just relaxed back into him. I didn't want to move, but I knew we needed to get going. There was too much at stake to be selfish right now.

I cleaned up, pulling my underwear and pants back on, then shimmied over to the passenger seat with only mild grumblings from my adorable, ruffled-haired tiger.

I reached over and held my hand out; fingers splayed in a gesture for him to grab it. He just stared at it, as if what we just did wasn't more intimate than simply holding hands. When he didn't take my hand and just kept scowling at it, I reached over and grabbed his instead, squeezing hard.

There, that's better.

CHAPTER FORTY-EIGHT

It felt amazing to see my dear friend Peach again after so long. I clutched her tightly, and she squeezed back just as hard. A shaky breath escaped me, and when I drew in another, I was wrapped in the scent that was uniquely hers. Warm vanilla with the softest hint of lavender. Comforting. Familiar. Peach.

I didn't realize how much I had missed her until that moment.

"Have you gotten any updates on Alicia?" I asked, finally pulling out of the hug.

"Only a small one this morning, and it wasn't great," she said as tears started welling in her beautiful purple eyes.

"Wh-what did they say?" I felt myself getting emotional with her, and I hadn't even heard the news yet.

"They can't keep her blood pressure steady. It keeps spiking, and then it will stabilize, but then it will drop low. They haven't seen anything like it." The last part was said with a sob that escaped her throat. My heart ached for her.

"Oh, Peach, I'm so sorry." I squeezed her hands. "She is strong, and she is going to get through this. I just know it."

"That's what I keep telling myself too." She dabbed her glossy purple eyes, trying not to smudge the black mascara that coated her perfectly fanned lashes.

"Enough about us, though. I know you came here to question Aurora. Let's hurry up and get you some answers," she said before turning to one of the bear shifters. "Can you lead the way?"

That was why I loved her. She had a beautiful soul, but she was still all about business.

We moved through a maze of corridors and underground tunnels, walking for miles until we finally reached a completely different building. Peach resided miles away from this place, but Alicia made sure to keep her enemies close, just not close enough to endanger Peach.

She built these underground tunnels for multiple reasons. They weren't easy to navigate, but they gave Peach plenty of options if the Mack estate was ever attacked.

We could have driven over here like we did last time and come in through the main entrance, but I was enjoying catching up with Peach, and we walked and talked.

I filled Peach in on everything that had happened to me since I was taken. I told her about Leo's death and how Crowe got away. She already knew he had escaped the Mack Clan cells, since that was the first call Dayken made when he found out. But what she didn't know was the revelations he shared about Onyx and me.

Kolton trailed close behind us, keeping near but respecting the space and time I wanted with Peach.

"He's Lunce's son, but he was born without any vampiric abilities. Just slowed aging. Very slow, actually."

"Wow, who would have thought that lunatic was a part of our history?" she said as she twirled a strand of her long blond hair around her finger. It was an almost nervous, uneasy gesture. "But what does that have to do with me? Why does he want *me*?"

"You aren't a descendant of Lunce's bloodline. Your line traces back to a made vampire. So, he thinks that separation, and the differences in your genetic code, are the key to him finally gaining immortality."

"I wish I knew more about my family's history, but everyone has always kept it so hush-hush. I don't see how it should matter, though, whether one is made or born. We are all vampires and still treated sacred."

"Yes, but we are only sacred because there are so few of us. Imagine if he could figure out how to make more."

"True."

The flowers' intended use was to save a dying boy. Instead, that boy went on to sire the first vampire and the first shifter.

Given what we know about history, that flower has the ability to create immortality.

But no one knows what that woman did.

There are no recipes or instructions to follow.

It's said the ancient magic involved in the process has long since died.

So, not only is it concerning that Crowe has figured out how to sever a bond using the flower, but I can only assume he is also very close to figuring out how to create a Sacar as well.

Peach paused, taking a deep breath as her purple eyes shimmered with worry. She tried to mask it with a tight smile. "We're here."

It was a similar design to our compound, but it was much larger, more up-to-date, and modernized with automatic sliding doors. The doors opened to reveal the familiar rows of plexiglass cells. There weren't very many of them, and they were all empty except one, which had a beautiful gray wolf inside it.

"One of the bears tried questioning her to see if she saw Crowe escape or if someone might have let him out, but she won't shift back. And she isn't responding in her wolf form either," Peach said, her tone sad, as if it pained her to see Aurora like this.

I crouched down in front of the cell, while Peach and Kolton stayed back. I pressed my hand to the glass and said, "Aurora, I have something to tell you. Something that may be a bit contrary to what you've heard up until this point."

I waited for her to acknowledge me, to do something to indicate that she could at least hear me or sense my presence. When she didn't move, I continued, "You showed me nothing but kindness when up until then I had known nothing but cruelty. You gave me a room and a soft bed when I was only ever given bars and concrete. You gave me books—willingly, without any strings attached. Everything in my life before that had come with expectations and conditions. Maybe you did it all out of fear, or maybe it was fake, but to me, those moments were real. I felt the goodness inside you. And I just want you to know that I forgive you."

The air thickened, heavy with things unsaid. There was a soft hum from the overhead lights, filling the silence. It was the kind that made my ears ache with the empty stillness.

"Yeah, well, I don't."

"Kolton!" I hissed. My voice was low, but sharp enough to slice through the quiet. I whipped my head around to glare at him, and he just shrugged in response.

The wolf didn't move, didn't whine, didn't even change her breathing, but I knew she heard me. I could feel it, sense it. She was in there, just being very, very stubborn.

"Now, we need your help. I need you to tell me everything Crowe ever said to you."

Silence. Still nothing.

I sighed. "Please, Aurora. Please. I need you, just as I needed you at the farmhouse."

She let out a low, soft whine. If it wasn't for my advanced hearing, I probably wouldn't have noticed it. It was sad, so sad.

"I know it's got to be hard to face us, but I also know you can do it. Please shift back and talk to us. You could have valuable information and not even realize it."

She raised her head and tilted it, ever so slightly, so I went on, "Yes, critical information actually, and it might be enough to save us all, but I need you to repeat Crowe's words, exactly as he said them, so I can listen for clues."

She shifted back to her human form. She didn't meet my eyes, but gods, it was great to see her again. Her long brown hair was a mess. Her brown eyes, which were normally so kind and gentle, looked lost and broken. The only read I could get from her, the only thing I could feel, was *shame*. Utter and absolute shame.

Poor Aurora. My heart just broke for her. I didn't know how to fix this, how to undo this for her. But I did know one thing: if she wanted out of this cell, she needed to figure out what redemption looked like on her own.

Maybe that's what this was. The questions I needed to ask her. This search for answers about our enemy. Maybe it was more than that. Maybe it was a way out for her.

I could only hope.

I thought back to the hope she once gave me.

"Wow, this is so cool!" I spun around, taking it all in.

"This is my sewing area. It's in the basement, but I don't mind. Dayken had it remodeled for me so it's actually nice and cozy down here." Aurora beamed.

"It's so cozy! That's exactly how I would describe it."

She smiled, a genuine, beautiful smile, and I suddenly felt the need to hug her. But I didn't. I still needed to figure out how physical affection worked, and I felt, deep down in my soul, that moment needed to be shared between my sister and me first.

"Come over here. I will teach you a basic stitch for sewing, and we will hem some of my pants and dresses for you."

She patted a cushioned stool, and I practically ran to it.

Helping us with intel on Crowe was exactly what she needed to start feeling redeemed. I just knew it.

"He said that you were dangerous. That there was something defective with both of you."

I analyzed the words. He was deflecting, talking about himself. This was good. I could work with that.

"Keep going," I pleaded.

"He said it was crucial that he get you back quickly, that he needed to move fast, and that I wasn't giving him updates fast enough." Her voice cracked with her confession. "He used a word that I found odd. What was it...I think it was barricade. No, no, it was a blocker. He said there was a *blocker* that needed to be moved quickly."

Poor Aurora. She was tricked by a sociopath.

It wasn't her fault. Not really.

"This is good, Aurora. It tells me that he is racing against some kind of clock, that he has some type of timer he is up against," I said and fully sat down in front of her cage. "Keep going. This is great."

And she did. I dissected every little thing he said to her. There was some stuff that wasn't very helpful and some that might or might not mean anything, but it was mostly valuable information. She didn't see how Crowe got out, but she did wake up when a scuffling sound startled her.

"Sky," she said. "I'm sorry for believing him. I should have known you would never be capable of the horrible things he said."

A small smile pulled at the corner of my mouth, and I placed my hand up against the glass. Fingers splayed wide as I looked her in the eyes before saying, "It's okay, Aurora. You went up against our strongest enemy and lost. I don't blame you."

I know my words could have come across as harsh, but it was the truth, and I had a feeling Aurora wanted brutal honesty. She nodded in agreement to my words, and I knew I was right. Slowly, very slowly, she began to lift her arm. She touched her fingers to the glass first, lining them up with mine. Then her palm followed, and I looked up from where our hands met through the barrier to see a single tear slipping from her eye.

"It's okay," I said again.

"I miss you, Aurora, so please talk with me next time I visit, okay?" Peach pleaded. "Not that they let me visit very often."

She muttered the last part under her breath so low I had a feeling Aurora didn't hear it. But she nodded in agreement regardless.

CHAPTER FORTY-NINE

KOLTON

"We aren't going to catch him. The interrogations got us nowhere, and who knows where he is by now," Onyx said.

We had gathered in the main entrance, making use of the comfortable couches there. Onyx sat on the floor with her back against the arm of a couch, her head resting lightly against Dayken's leg. She looked exhausted, irritated, and relaxed all at the same time.

We were putting together our next plan of attack after sharing the information we had compiled from our different sources: Onyx from the

Mack bears, Skylar from Aurora, and Dayken from the Danielson Clan allies he had contacted.

Skylar nodded in agreement with her sister's sentiment. "And the fact that Aurora didn't see anything makes it even more challenging."

"How—how was my sister?" Dayken asked, then stopped himself. "You know what, never mind. We can talk later."

"Are you sure?" Skylar tried.

"Yeah, and just so everyone knows, I put the word out to the other Primarcs outside of Michigan too," Dayken said, getting right back to business. "All the clans in Canada, Wisconsin, Indiana, Ohio, and Illinois are now on high alert as well."

His voice carried a steady calm meant to ease the tension winding its way through the room. But I knew his sister's fate was weighing heavily on him.

"That is good. Really good," Skylar said quietly. "I'm still worried, though...his knowledge, his intelligence, and his resources.... Now that we know who he really is, it feels like we are at even more of a disadvantage. He has had decades to plot and plan, and we've only had the few months since our escape. It feels like we will always be one step behind him."

That was when Chase entered the room, wearing a stoic, unreadable expression. I was surprised to see Titus' sister, Nessalay, following behind him.

Her white hair caught the overhead lights, making it almost glow. She wore her usual sunglasses, even though we were indoors. I didn't like that because being unable to see her eyes always made it more challenging to get a good read on her. I trusted her about the same amount as I did her brother. Which was not at all.

The room fell silent as everyone slowly took note of their arrival.

Chase casually leaned against the wall, arms crossed as if trying to appear unfazed, just another guy escorting a guest. I was confident I was the only one who caught the way his eyes dragged over her, starting from her combat boots to the white hair cascading down her shoulders.

Did I see appreciation in his gaze? No, I must have imagined that.

"I can help with that," Nessalay said, pulling my attention back to her.

I pulled Skylar closer to me on the couch, wrapping my arm around her waist and tugging her to my chest. She softened instantly, melting against me. My instincts kicked in, strong and unapologetic. I pressed my head gently against hers as I held her firmly. Maybe I was being overly possessive, but something about Nessalay's presence sharpened the need to protect, to defend what was mine.

"Help with what exactly?" Onyx demanded.

Good. At least I wasn't the only one who felt the need to keep their guard up around this fox.

"I have knowledge. Just as much, if not more, than Crowe, and I am confident in my ability to outsmart him."

"How?" I asked.

"I will be keeping my cards close to my chest for now. I am sure you can understand why. I am currently outnumbered, and my clan is missing their Primarc. The little leverage I do have, I would like to keep secret." She was implying that someone in our compound was a possible traitor.

I hated to admit it, but she was probably right.

"Titus still hasn't returned?" Dayken asked.

"No. And I want my brother back." Her tone shifted. I could hear the determination in her voice, but there was also a hint of desperation. "You help me find him, and I will help you get Crowe."

"What's to stop this from ending up completely one-sided? How are we supposed to know if anything you provide will even be helpful to us?" I asked, hoping she might give us at least a hint of what she had to offer.

"Maybe she doesn't know how these things work," Derek said to me before he turned to address Nessalay.

"Let me break it down for you. In order to make a deal, first, you need—"

"Derek, enough," Chase snapped. "You know damn well she knows how deals work."

Silence filled the space in response to Chase's outburst.

I had not spent much time with the twins recently, but I had grown up with the Danielsons, and the brothers were always around. I could confidently say that I had never heard Chase talk to Derek like that. He normally laughed at his jokes or ignored them, if anything. This behavior was so at odds with how Chase normally acted.

"I do know how deals work, yes. And I would like to strike one." Nessalay straightened, squaring her shoulders. Confidence radiated from her, despite still not offering us a single detail.

Yes. She was definitely Titus' sister.

"Make your offer, Ness. We are all friends and allies here," Dayken said, once again proving himself a proper Primarc. His voice was smooth and diplomatic, a tone I should probably learn how to use someday.

Nah.

Nessalay didn't hesitate as she stepped closer to our ring of couches, confidently entering our small circle. She took her sunglasses off, and we were all hit with her eerie-looking red eyes.

"Before I begin, I want you all to remember that I am the bookkeeper for the entire Sharp Clan. I would also like to add that my brother and I consider the sacred bond between a Guardian and their Sacar to be the highest of honors that one can be granted in life. I love being a Guardian, and my brother and I have traveled the world in search of Sacars, in the hopes that we, too, may one day become bonded Guardians."

She let her declaration linger, and we were all stunned. I had always seen the Sharps as greasy, deal-making, shady creatures. I found it hard to imagine them actively seeking to protect anyone, let alone a Sacar.

I looked at Skylar to see if she sensed any dishonesty in her words. She felt my gaze and turned to me. The softness in her expression told me that she believed every word coming out of Nessalay's mouth.

Well, I trusted Skylar more than anything in this world. If she believed her, then so did I.

"And?" Dayken said after a moment, prompting her to continue.

"And, with all of that in mind, I will provide you with a list of locations I believe Crowe would likely use as his current hideout. I will do this under the condition that you not ask me how I've gotten this information. Most importantly, once I have given you this information, you will help me search for my brother."

"Well, as noble as your intentions are, we are going to need some time to think about this," Onyx said. She then raised herself from her seated position on the floor and extended her hand to help Dayken up from the couch, which she did effortlessly.

Freakishly strong, that one.

"I don't have time! Did you not hear me? My brother is missing."

"Oh, we heard you," Dayken said. "And as my Sacar just said, we need to think about your offer. We'll discuss it as a group. I don't make rash decisions, Ness, you know this."

"Come on, everyone. Let's regroup in the security room," Onyx suggested, already heading in that direction.

"I can stay here with her," Chase said.

I couldn't help but arch a brow at that. The security room was his domain, his nest. There was no way he was going to let us all in there without him.

"You don't want to weigh in on this?" Dayken asked.

"I trust my brother's judgment," Chase said, and he looked at his twin as they silently exchanged...something.

Derek nodded and followed after Dayken and Onyx with Skylar right behind him.

Since I was the last to leave the room, I was able to overhear Chase say, "So, you're the one who I've been dealing with on the shipments. The one who has been charging for items we never received."

"As I told you in my email, I do an inventory check every—"

I was soon out of earshot and missed the rest of the exchange. I quickly made my way to the stairwell, letting the door slam shut behind me.

Maybe it wasn't appreciation I saw in Chase's eyes; he was probably just sizing up his opponent.

Yeah...that made way more sense.

Chapter Fifty

"So, what are we thinking?" Dayken asked once we were all seated at the conference table in the security room. Tension hummed beneath the low lights.

Onyx spoke first. "I don't like it. I will never blindly trust a stranger, and that is basically what she is."

"Now, now," Skylar said gently. "Titus and Nessalay both fought with us when Crowe attacked the compound. We know they aren't working with him. They took out too many of his men. Logically, it just doesn't add up."

She made a good point. My smart, beautiful Sacar always thought of everything. I wonder if she thought—

"Ugh. Stop purring. It's creepy." Derek groaned.

I flipped him off. Also, I had not realized I was doing it.

"Okay, fine," Onyx conceded. "But how the fuck does she have potential locations for where he might be?"

"The Sharps make it their business to know everyone else's business," Derek said. "I wouldn't be shocked if she knew what color my shit was this morning."

"Eww, Derek. That's gross," Skylar said.

"Spoiler alert, it was brown," he added, only to be met with angry shouts. "Look, all I'm saying is that it's possible that Nessalay caught wind of something and got the details. She's stealthy." Derek leaned back, putting his hands behind his head. "Like a fox."

"It pains me to admit it," Dayken sighed. "But Derek is right."

"Hey—"

"It's likely that Nessalay did something questionable to get that information," Dayken continued, ignoring Derek's protest. "If she's asking for privacy around it, I think we should respect that."

"Okay," Onyx said slowly. "So, then what does 'helping find her brother' actually entail?"

"I don't know," Skylar said. "But I think that I might be the reason he went missing."

The room went silent. Every set of eyes turned to her.

She cleared her throat. "There were a lot of Leo's men at the church. They had taken Kolton down with a tranquilizer. Titus was the first to show up, and I made him help me get to Kolton so I could remove the dart."

"And?"

"He killed some of Leo's men in the process. Others saw it." Her voice dropped. "He hasn't been seen since." My chest tightened as she admitted, "I'm worried they might have killed him."

"Why didn't you tell anyone?" Dayken asked.

"That I thought I got Titus killed?" Skylar asked as she drew in a shaky breath. "What good would that have done? I was trying to survive myself. And it was just speculation. I have no proof. When Nessalay said he hasn't been seen, it just...clicked. I really hoped that he had gotten away."

Dayken placed his hands flat on the table. "All right. Then I say we make the deal."

Everyone except Onyx nodded, and all eyes turned to her.

She sighed. "Fine."

"A lot of people think my shit is white, you know."

"DEREK!" the entire room yelled in unison.

CHAPTER FIFTY-ONE

"**O**kay, Ness. We agree to your terms," Dayken said after we filtered back into the main entrance.

The vibe in the room felt off the second I stepped inside.

Nessalay was stretched out on one of the couches like she owned the place, legs crossed, posture relaxed. Too relaxed.

Chase was nowhere in sight. That set my nerves buzzing. Chase would never leave someone unattended unless they had his utmost trust. Never.

"Where is my brother?" Derek demanded, his voice cutting through the room.

Nessalay shrugged without looking up from her nails. "I am not his keeper."

The words were careless, but her tone was not. There was something practiced about it, like she already knew exactly how this would play out. I kept my gaze locked on her, instincts screaming that Chase had not wandered off on his own. Before anyone could push further, Dayken spoke.

"I have wolves ready to immediately assist in the search for your brother. But first, I need the addresses. Anywhere you think Crowe might be."

Her eyes flicked up at that. Quick. Assessing.

"Thank you, Dayken. Of course." She reached for her phone, fingers moving with unsettling speed and confidence. A few taps. A pause. Then, "Sent."

I heard Dayken's phone vibrate in his pocket a second later. That alone made my skin crawl.

"But," she continued smoothly as she set her phone aside, "I do not want wolves."

The room stilled.

"I want the eagles. Falcons. Hawks."

Derek bristled instantly, shoulders squaring, but Dayken did not rise to the bait.

"That is not my decision," he said evenly. "I do not dictate what the Averie Clan does. If they are willing to lend support, then we will discuss it. But as it stands, you came onto Danielson Clan territory and struck a deal with its Primarc."

Nessalay smiled, appearing all innocent. Her eyes told a different story. They gleamed with quiet certainty, like the outcome she desired was never in doubt.

It was almost as if she already had what she wanted, which likely came in the form of a black falcon who was currently missing from the room.

"Of course, Primarc," she said and gave a low, submissive nod. "I meant no disrespect in asking for more than you are capable of delivering. All I want is to find my brother, and an aerial view offers the best speed and accuracy." She paused, appearing to choose her next words carefully. "Maybe Chase would be willing to help if he knew that I uncovered a pattern he never stopped questioning."

There it was. Her move.

The Sharps were good. I had not given them enough credit before now. Her words meant something. I could tell by the change in Derek's body language. But I didn't have time to pry, as Derek quickly left the room.

"Again, I do not speak for the twins. It is their decision. For now, you have the Danielson wolves at your disposal," Dayken said, his tone final.

CHAPTER FIFTY-TWO

I watched as members of the Danielson Clan escorted Nessalay out of the compound through the loading docks.

We agreed to look into the information she gave us and reconnect later this evening.

Dayken huffed and dropped onto the couch, defeat clinging to him. But the moment Onyx stepped in front of him, everything about him shifted. He patted his lap, and she sat without hesitation.

She whispered something in his ear, and he smiled.

It did something to my chest, seeing her take even a fraction of the weight off him. They fit together in a way that just...worked.

The relief didn't last long.

"Dayken, you're needed in the security room." Chase's voice echoed over the PA system.

Onyx straightened, sliding off his lap so he could stand.

"Come on," I said to Kolton. "I want to see what this is about."

We moved quickly through the compound halls, our boots echoing against the concrete floors. The air felt cooler as we made our way back to the security room, tinged with metal and recycled ozone from the monitors that never slept. The closer we got, the tighter my chest felt.

It was not the emergency alert, which was a small relief. Still, concern gnawed at me.

The security doors slid open just as Chase's voice carried out of the room.

"Two SUVs spotted turning left onto the private drive. One red, one black. I believe they are headed in our direction. They have not slowed their speed or looked for a turnaround."

Dayken stood in front of the monitors, arms crossed, his attention fixed on the live feed. He leaned in slightly, eyes sharp and assessing.

"Alert everyone," he ordered.

Chase activated the microphone, and a moment later, his voice boomed throughout the compound. "Incoming. Everyone on high alert and standby."

"Who is it?" someone asked through the comm system.

"Can't tell. Windows are tinted."

"Should we throw them a welcome party?" Onyx asked.

"I'm in," Kolton replied. "Where are the grenades?"

We gathered at the bottom of the steps that led to the main entrance, waiting. We continued to watch the SUVs' approach through the security feed on one of Dayken's tablets.

As the two vehicles neared the compound, the red SUV slowed, hanging back as dust curled around its tires. The black one continued forward, rolling steadily toward the gate.

"State your purpose," Chase said through the gate's intercom once it pulled to a stop.

"I need to speak with the Primarc."

The sound of his voice made my stomach drop.

It was familiar. I turned to Kolton, searching his face, and I noticed his jaw tighten. He recognized the voice too.

"There are procedures in place for you to request a meeting with him," Chase replied evenly.

"Well, he hasn't exactly made himself available."

"Dayken is always available," Chase began. "And it is very easy to—"

"I am not here for Primarc Dayken Danielson," the man interrupted. "I am here for Primarc Kolton Teegra."

So, it *was* him. John found us.

"Fuck..." Kolton groaned.

"You know him?" Dayken asked.

Kolton just shrugged in response.

"Yeah," I said. "He was one of the guards at the DeStephano property while we were there. He was very helpful and kind." I left out the part where I kicked him in the head. "So, I would like to hear what he has to say."

Chase looked to Dayken, who nodded for him to open the gates. The black SUV pulled forward. The rest of the welcome party kept their guards up. Leo might be dead, but we had no idea if the rest of the lions were working with Crowe or why they would want to speak to Kolton.

Not that it mattered, I still didn't like this one bit.

"Dayken and I will hang back near the entrance," Onyx said. "We'll let you two handle this, but we'll be there if you need backup."

We walked outside just as the SUV parked in front of the compound, and John got out.

"John. To what do we owe the pleasure?" Kolton said "pleasure" like the word was poison.

"Look, I'll make this quick. The lions are without a leader right now. Our Primarc was killed by someone who we thought was our *new* Primarc," John said, looking pointedly at Kolton.

"I didn't kill him. It was my Sacar who put a bullet in his brain."

Oh, Kolton. No one needed to know that.

John looked shocked for a second but recovered quickly. "W-well," he started before clearing his throat. "Regardless, we don't know what to do. We don't know which of the clan properties to stay at or who the properties even belong to, and we have kids whose teachers' contracts expired the minute Leo died." John huffed out an exhausted sigh. "We need help."

"I don't know what to tell you. I didn't kill your Primarc, and I have no interest in taking over his territory."

"Then I'm asking you to reconsider," John said.

"No."

Dayken correctly judged that moment as the right time for him to step in. "I know a contract specialist who can help. She is the Primarc of the Randall Clan, and Kolton owes her an apology anyway. So, that works out great for me."

"But I don't know anything about contracts," John said.

"I know. Let me lend you some assistance while you all figure things out."

Admiration shone in my sister's eyes as she watched her big, giant softy of a wolf step up to help the lions who may have played a role in his parents' murder.

If I didn't completely and utterly respect Dayken before, he had it in droves now.

As Dayken and John continued their conversation about the next steps for the future of the lion clan, I decided to head back inside the compound. I had some research I needed to do on the property layouts for the addresses Nessalay had given us.

"Wait, Sky," John called before I reached the doors. "Don't you want to know how I was able to find you?"

I froze and turned back to face him.

"I guess I just assumed you knew where the Danielson compound was and decided to check here first."

He shook his head no. "I was sent a text with a link to this signal." He handed me his phone, which showed a dot lit up on a map. "I was told that if I followed this, I would find you."

My world narrowed, tunnel vision hitting hard. My heart raced as panic crawled its way up my throat.

"Who sent you this?" Kolton demanded with a growl.

"I don't know, but I was also instructed to share it with everyone I know. I didn't, obviously. But it was very odd. I thought you should know." John shrugged after he finished speaking.

Realization, dread, fear—they all hit me at once. My chip was processing everything at high speeds, leaving me a little dizzy.

One conclusion kept repeating itself through my mind:

Crowe had made his move.

I bolted back into the compound, Kolton right on my heels.

"Sky!" I heard my sister yell.

"I've got it, Onyx," Kolton barked at her.

I couldn't stop. My brain, which could normally handle multiple conflicting scenarios at a time, suddenly couldn't process anything.

For the first time in my life, I was stuck with a one-track mind, and I needed to move quickly.

I could hear Kolton chasing after me.

"Sky!"

I kept running.

"Skylar! Stop for one godsdamn second."

"No time. I need to get to—"

A rough grip on my arm halted me in my tracks.

"My Sacar, tell me what's going on." Kolton's eyes were pleading with me. I wished he'd always look at me so sweetly, but instead, those beautiful, bright citrine eyes were going to become full of anger as soon as I confessed my realization.

"Kolton, just let me fix this before you explode into a fit of rage, okay? I have to move."

He tilted his head, eyes narrowing in suspicion.

"I'm scared. If I yell, it will be out of fear, not rage. Now tell me what's going on," he demanded.

I sighed in defeat. He wasn't going to let me go until I told him. "It's the chip…"

"What about it?" His voice was cold, deadly. It was a tone I was familiar with, and I knew nothing good would come from it.

"Crowe just used John to tell me that he can always find me. I need to get to Chase immediately. I need his help reinstalling the blocker on my chip."

I saw the rage in Kolton's expression as the tiger tried to take over, but I pushed on, rushing through the rest so I could hurry to the security room. "Crowe must have disabled it while I was unconscious at Leo's place."

Kolton roared. It took every ounce of my willpower to remain firm, squaring my shoulders instead of giving into the urge to cover my ears.

"That *thing* needs to go! Now. It's not safe. You are being irresponsible by wanting to keep it." Kolton's fury was palpable. But I wasn't backing down.

"You want to lecture me about safety and responsibility when you refuse to help the Guardians who came to our door, practically begging you to lead them. You turned your back on them, and you have the nerve to lecture *me*?"

Now I was furious. I pushed aside my terror at the fact that I was broadcasting our location to anyone Crowe shared that link with while I took my rage out on Kolton.

"I have no interest in being a Primarc."

"Too bad!" I screamed. "Because you *are* one. So, step up. And don't talk to me until you're ready to take your head out of your ass."

I turned, prepared to storm off but fully expecting to feel his grip on my arm, stopping me. Only, there was no rough tug on my limbs. And there was no sound of his heavy footsteps behind me.

Well...I guess I did tell him not to speak to me.

I just didn't think he'd choose now to actually listen to me for once.

Chapter Fifty-Three

"Chase, I have a favor to ask."

"Anything."

"Um. Well, see, there is this chip."

"Oh, I know. I saw your login activity in my audit trail when you touched the firewall configuration setting. Nice try attempting to delete it by the way, but my backup goes to an on-prem server and the cloud."

Damn. I still need to learn more about the cloud...

"Wow. Well, all right. So—" I cleared my throat, unsure how to ask for help now that he already knew. "I-I was curious if you could help me install a firewall back onto the chip."

He looked at me with his impossibly dark black eyes, studying me in a way only Chase could.

"Sure," he said simply as he started to clear his workstation.

I sighed in relief that he wasn't going to pepper me with endless questions or lecture me about taking the chip out. He was giving crazy big brother energy right now, and I wanted to give him the biggest hug.

"You are kinda the best. You know that?" I said as I plopped down into the chair next to him.

"I know," he said, and I couldn't help but giggle.

He started pulling up the programs I told him to while also trying to locate the signal on my chip. It was buried, and the encryption key was hard to crack, but it wasn't impossible. Chase was enjoying the challenge.

"I never asked, but why don't you and Derek have your own compound?" I wondered while we waited for the programs to run.

"Birds don't like enclosed spaces. We need to be free in the sky and trees. We have a few cabins in the woods, but nothing like this."

"Well then, sitting in the security room all day must be torture for you."

"Yes and no. I like computers more than I like the clouds." Chase cleared his throat. "My brother and I have always been a little different from the other birds because of something we went through."

"Not that I want to pry, but Nessalay mentioned something."

"I'd rather discuss my brother's bowel movements than talk about her right now."

I chuckled softly and threw my hands up. I could read him well enough to know that if I kept prying, he would shut down. So, I left it alone.

"Well, I'm happy you are here—" I started before the door crashed open behind us.

"What the fuck?" Kolton roared.

I stared at Kolton, then looked back at Chase, who just shrugged before saying, "Good luck with that," then put on his noise-canceling headphones and rolled his chair back to his desk.

Chapter Fifty-Four

"I have no interest in being a Primarc," I said because that was the truth.

"Too bad!" she screamed at me. "Because you *are* one. So, step up. And don't talk to me until you're ready to take your head out of your ass."

I watched as she stormed away from me, resisting the urge to grab her again.

She didn't want to take that fucking chip out of her head?

Fine.

Then it was time to play dirty. I turned and started practically sprinting down the hallways until I found my target. My boots slammed against the floor, my pulse roaring in my ears.

"What was that about?" Onyx asked frantically when I finally found her, her voice sharp with panic.

"It's that fucking chip."

"What about it?" came Onyx's cold, even response.

Holy shit. We were more alike than I realized.

"It's going to get her killed. She thinks that fucking piece of shit, Crowe, tampered with it when they were trying to remove her mark."

"Motherfucker!" Onyx roared.

Finally.

Now there was someone else just as angry as me about this.

"We have to remove it."

"When does she want to do it? Now? I can have Dayken make some phone calls."

"Well..." I ran a hand through the tangled mess of my hair, trying to smooth it like that would help calm my nerves. It didn't. "She doesn't necessarily want it removed."

Onyx just crossed her arms over her chest and glared at me. When she didn't say anything, I couldn't take it any longer.

"What?!"

"I'm happy you love my sister so fiercely. I'm sorry for not seeing it sooner," Onyx said.

"Love?" I scoffed. "I'm her Guardian, and I'm scared shitless for her. I do not love her." The words felt wrong the moment they left my mouth, but I couldn't dwell on that right now.

"Interesting," was all Onyx said. "Do you know how much I know about tigers?"

Odd change of subject.

"I would imagine not much, but I don't think I like where you're going with this."

"Oh, shut up, it's not bad." She waved her hand dismissively at me. "I actually know quite a lot. Like, way *too* much."

Onyx began rattling off facts on different tiger species. Weight. Height. Appetite. Habitat for each one. By the time she was done, my jaw was on the floor, mainly because this was not how I thought this conversation was going to go at all.

"Do you know why I know all this?" she asked, and before I could respond with *because you did your homework on me*, she said, "Because Sky loved reading about tigers. She would read the same passages over and over again. She would trace her fingers over the images in slow, methodical motions, like she would never see them again and wanted to treasure the memory. It took me a little while to realize what she was doing." She paused, just long enough for what she said to sink in. "She was downloading it to her mind."

She put her hand on my shoulder and said, "Tigers, Kolton. Tigers were the first things she downloaded onto that chip you want removed so badly."

I didn't have words.

I think I actually would have reacted better if Onyx had just slapped me instead of leaving me so emotionally stunned. And in my shocked state, I came to a realization.

I needed my Skylar. I needed her to forgive me for my selfishness. I needed her to give me that smile of hers and tell me everything was okay, like she always did. Like she could make the world steady again just by looking at me.

"I had no idea," was all I could say.

"Well, now you do." Onyx's voice softened, just barely. "And now you also know that all those thoughts in that fucked-up head of yours are circling back to one thing. You love her."

I opened my mouth to argue, but she cut me off.

"And you may not realize it yet, but what you two have is special. And I'm not talking about the bond." Her eyes locked onto mine. "She adores you. Don't fuck it up."

And with that, she punched me in the arm before walking away.

I was running again, but in the opposite direction this time. I needed to find my Sacar.

I hit the stairs to the basement with quick, efficient steps, my boots barely making contact as I hurried downward.

Move faster. My tiger chanted. *Find her.*

I'm trying, damn it.

The sound of her giggles hit me, and instead of being comforted by the noise, rage flared. I didn't like knowing she was nearby and happy with someone else.

Who was making her so happy right now?

It should be *me.*

I'm her tiger. I'm her Guardian. It's me. Me.

All the selfishness I had sworn I would rein in surged forward, front and center, and there was nothing I could do to stop it.

I opened the door to the security room harder than I intended.

"What the fuck," I yelled.

I saw Skylar sitting next to Chase in the middle of what looked like an intimate conversation.

Too friendly.

Too close.

With big smiles and crinkled eyes as they looked at each other.

Be rational.

Take a breath.

I couldn't.

"Good luck with that," Chase said as he turned back to his desk, clearly not interested in engaging with me. "I'll get to work on this in the meantime."

"Outside. Now," Skylar growled as she shot up from her chair.

Fine with me. At least that meant she'd be away from him.

I waited for her to reach the doorway before I stepped into the hallway.

"You need to calm down," she said in a low hiss, and I wondered if she was whispering so no one else would hear.

"Make me."

"What?"

"Make me calm down, because you are the only one who can." I was pleading with her, but I didn't care. I didn't give a shit how pathetic I looked right now. I needed her to soothe that deep ache inside me. Something that only she knew how to do.

Her eyes searched my face, irritation warring with something softer. Something dangerous.

"I can't keep saving you from yourself, Kolton," she said quietly.

"It's not about that," I said, my hands curling into fists at my sides. "It is about you smiling at someone who isn't me."

Her jaw tightened. "You do not get to decide who I talk to."

"I know." The words came out rough. Honest. "But that doesn't stop it from tearing me apart."

Silence stretched between us, thick and charged. I could hear my own breathing. The tiger paced just under my skin, restless and possessive and entirely unapologetic.

"You are spiraling over something that isn't worth spiraling over, Kolton. *You* have to fix this. I don't have a magic wand to wave to make all the negative thoughts in your head disappear. Only you have that power," she said.

"But what if—" I cleared my throat, terrified to ask, but knowing I needed to. "What if I can't ever get my mind right? What if I'm always this jealous asshole? What if I always resort to violence? What if I'm always selfish? Then what? You'll just walk away from me? I won't get to touch you again? I-I don't..."

"Kolton, no. No, stop that. Of course, I'm not leaving you. I'm right here." She grabbed my face tightly, fierce and demanding. "I am here, always, but that doesn't mean I'm your salvation or that I'm going to fix your brain. I'm going to call you on your bullshit. I'll love you fiercely while I do, and I'll wait for you to come to your senses. Like I think you were trying to do just now, but you got derailed a little," she said with a small smirk playing on her lips.

I exhaled deeply.

She was right. I came down here to fix things, and then I lost it.

Fuck.

"I love you." The words were out before I could second-guess myself. "I love you so fucking much. You are all I think about, all I care about, and all I want in this world. I'm not good at this." I motioned between us like that would explain the things I was trying to say.

"I don't know how to put others' feelings before my own, but I do know this—you come first, in anything and everything. You are the only one who does. You are mine, and I am consumed by you. Please don't leave me because I can't get it right, just...just give me time?"

A stray tear rolled down her cheek, and I suddenly wanted to smash everything around me. I replayed everything I just said, trying to figure out what bad thing I said to make her cry.

She exhaled slowly, then stepped closer and lowered her voice even more. "As long as you stop running away from how you feel, I will always be by your side, Kolton Teegra of the Teegra Clan."

I swallowed hard and said, "I'm not running anymore."

Her gaze softened, just a fraction. Enough to undo me.

"Then prove it," she said.

And I rose to the challenge. I slammed her into the wall, a little rougher than intended, but she only let out a breathless gasp as I did. I pulled her head to the side, and she clawed at my back in response as I nuzzled her neck before kissing my way down her throat.

"Room," she gasped.

Oh, right, we were in the hallway.

I picked her up, and she locked her legs around me. I made my way down the hallway and kicked open the door to her room. I then had to kick the door shut when it bounced back off the wall. Once I heard the thud of it closing, I threw her on the bed.

She rose to her elbows, and I was in complete awe of her.

"Fuck, I love you."

"Prove. It."

"Done," I growled, but as I went to her, she stopped me.

"Wait," she said as she held up her hand. "Take off your shirt."

I ripped the thing off like it was preventing me from breathing.

The look in her eyes as she raked her gaze over my body nearly undid me. It certainly had my dick straining against my zipper. I wished I could see what she saw when she looked at me like that. Her attraction to me was tangible, and it made me want to pry open her mind to understand it better.

"Now your pants."

I hurriedly undid them, shucking them off with force while I waited for her next instruction. I was hers to command after all. Hers to do with as she pleased.

I stood bare before her and watched as her fangs descended. The small tips poked into her bottom lip, her ice blue eyes practically glowing with desire for me.

It was still hard to imagine that I could be desired by someone this badly, but dear gods, I would cherish it, cherish her.

"You are mine, Kolton Teegra. You know that, right?" she said in a breathless, yet commanding, tone.

"Yes, I am yours."

"Stroke yourself as you say it."

Fucking hell! I was going to burst all over the floor. It was going to be awkward to clean up, but I did as she commanded. I took my hand and gave my dick a long, slow stroke up to the tip, then back down.

She moaned as she slipped her hand under her sweater before it traveled up to her breast. I stepped forward, needing to be inside her tight pussy, but she stopped me again.

"Say it," she commanded.

"I'm yours." I gripped the head of my cock tightly, trying to stave off my pre-cum.

"Good boy," she purred. "Come here and kiss me."

She barely finished the sentence before I was on her. I gripped her neck and ran my thumb over her throat as I broke the kiss to nip at the side of her neck and then her collarbone.

"Did you like commanding me, my Sky?"

She nodded.

"Good, because that's all you're getting tonight."

With that, I took my nail and let it extend into a claw, slicing her sweater down the middle, then cutting the front of her bra open. I moved the fabric out of the way and quickly brought my lips to her perky, perfect nipple, sucking and then nipping until it grew even harder. All the while, I used my hand to toy with her other breast.

"Kolton," she begged. I knew what she wanted, but she was not going to get it yet.

She reached down and grabbed my dick, pumping it as she did. I growled loud and hard, almost cumming in her hand.

All right. It looked like it was time now. I shredded her jeans and spread her wide before me.

"My beautiful Sky, I'm going to fuck you for the next hour straight, so you never question my love for you again. Do you understand me?"

She nodded, and I thrust into her. Hard and fast. She screamed in pleasure, and I leaned down to kiss her, thrusting my tongue into her mouth to tangle with hers as I pounded into her. I swallowed her cries as she pleaded with me to let her cum.

"Fuck, you feel so perfect. I'm not going to last much longer," I purred against her neck. "So tight, so right."

"Cum, I'm going to—" We shattered together, the force of it fierce and consuming, leaving me dazed but still aware enough to cling to her warmth, unwilling to let it go.

I propped myself up onto my elbow so I could look down into her ice-blue eyes. She was glowing, and I just stared in absolute awe of her.

She looked so beautiful like this. Pale porcelain skin with a slight flush from her climax. The short, chopped ends of her hair spread across the pillow.

"I thought you said an hour?" she asked with a small giggle.

I smiled, something I found myself doing more and more lately.

"Oh, we are not done, my love," I purred.

She laughed softly and lifted her hands, threading her fingers through my hair.

I stilled for half a second.

A ridiculous thought hit me—*should I cut it?* Would it be easier for her to run her fingers through it if it were shorter? Less tangled? Less messy?

My brow furrowed slightly as I leaned into her touch, anyway, chasing the warmth of her fingers against my scalp.

Then the thought shifted, as realization stuck. It wasn't about my hair.

It was about her.

It was about how instinctively my body responded to the smallest things she did. How quickly my mind started trying to *adjust*, to *optimize*, to make even something as insignificant as running her hands through my hair easier for her.

That...was new.

My hand slid along her waist, pulling her closer without thinking, like I needed the contact to ground myself.

Because this was no longer just about want. It wasn't solely instinct, desire, or the pull of the bond. It was something deeper—quieter but far heavier. I longed to make her life easier. Not just safer or protected, but better. I wanted to give her everything she had been denied.

Books stacked to the ceiling. Soft beds. Warm water. Silence when she needed it. Laughter when she didn't expect it. A life that didn't feel like survival.

My chest tightened slightly at the realization.

I wasn't just thinking like a Guardian anymore.

I was thinking like she was...mine to care for in every way that mattered. And I didn't know when that line had been crossed, but I relished in it anyway. There was absolutely no going back now.

Chapter Fifty-Five

Nessalay did not sit once the entire time we were in the security room.

She paced the length of the table like a caged animal, arms crossed tight over her chest, her movements controlled but restless in a way that made the tension in the room feel heavier with every pass.

Onyx tracked her movements like a watchdog, never taking her eyes off her. I could see the tension in my sister's muscles, how stiff she was, how on guard she was, as if she would strike if Nessalay made one wrong move. Meanwhile, Dayken sat at the head of the table, trying to keep everyone's emotions in check.

"We should already be moving," Nessalay said, her voice steady but edged with something sharper underneath. "Every minute we spend standing here is another minute Titus is out there without backup, support, or any means of reaching me."

I watched her carefully, trying to read what sat beneath the surface.

Nessalay was many things. Composed, calculated, and always two steps ahead. I didn't need to be in her presence long to pick up on that.

But this felt...bigger. It was a different side of her.

This was more urgent than I expected from someone like her.

And that made me uneasy for some reason.

"We're not standing around doing nothing," Chase replied from the other end of the table, his fingers moving quickly across his keyboard. "We're narrowing down locations. Your brother didn't just disappear into thin air."

"How is this not standing around?" Nessalay pressed immediately, spreading her arms out wide, to the group, "Because from where I'm standing, it looks like guesswork."

"It's not," Derek cut in, pushing off the wall. "We pulled everything we could from the security feeds before your compound's system went down. Then we tapped into the surveillance within the city where the church was. We pulled vehicle logs, heat signatures, and partial routes. There were only a handful of exits he could have taken without being seen."

"And we called in favors," Chase added. "Falcon scouts are already covering the outer perimeter of the church where he was last seen by Sky. We've got eyes on the main routes heading out of the estate. If Titus is being moved, we'll catch it."

"So no, this is not guesswork," Dayken said, summarizing for the twins. "This is a strategic and well-thought-out mission before we put boots on the ground."

Nessalay's gaze shifted between them, weighing every word. Without her sunglasses as a shield, her eyes appeared brighter and redder. When they locked onto Chase, they lingered a moment too long.

Chase didn't look away. His jaw flexed slightly before his tongue dragged once across his bottom lip, slow and deliberate, like he wasn't even aware of what he was doing.

Well...damn.

Did not see that coming.

"Well, it sounds like you have enough information and have narrowed down the location. Why are we still here?" she finally said.

Because we don't know who to trust.

The thought hit before I could stop it. It sat heavy in my chest, unwanted but impossible to ignore.

We had already been burned once. Crowe walking free proved that much. Someone on the inside had helped him. Which meant the smaller the team...the better.

"We're keeping this contained," Dayken said, his voice calm but firm as he leaned forward slightly. "Only the people in this room have the full details of your brother. No one else gets the full picture, and that is to your benefit," he reminded her. Because if it became public knowledge that the Sharps were without their Primarc, it would be an immediate war for her.

Nessalay's jaw tightened, but she didn't argue.

That told me everything I needed to know.

She understood the risk just as well as we did.

We all agreed to have three vehicles staged outside, ready to move the second we had something solid. Limiting it to just three teams, one team per vehicle, was enough to split us into teams without drawing too much attention and controlled enough that we could keep track of everyone involved.

Controlled.

That word should have made me feel better.

It didn't.

Because no matter how much we planned, how much we narrowed things down, there were still too many unknowns.

Too many things kept slipping through our fingers:

Titus.

Crowe.

The rest of the lions that had scattered.

The trader in the Mack clan.

And worse...

The people I saw strapped to those tables.

My stomach turned at the memory before I could stop it.

Cold metal. Restraints. Bodies that didn't move.

I had told myself I didn't know if it was real. That it could still have been a recording, fake, staged. A manipulation tactic. Something Leo wanted me to see.

But deep down...I knew better.

"There was nothing back there," Derek had said earlier after checking the lower levels. *"Just an empty room. No sign of anything malicious. Maybe storage at one point."*

It didn't sit right, and it felt wrong.

Because that meant whatever I saw had been moved. Or never existed, and to make it worse, I had no idea which one was more plausible.

And I wasn't going to be able to rest peacefully until I knew. Because this felt heavier and more personal as it sat in the back of my mind, constant and unrelenting, like a weight I couldn't put down.

Tortured vampires and shifters were out there...or *could* be out there.

Eventually, the tactical topic in the security room moved on to the subject of Crowe and where he might've gone next.

"I want a team actively searching for Titus," Nessalay cut in, breaking through my thoughts. Her voice had lost none of its intensity. "Not just tracking Crowe. We need to be searching for both."

"We are," Chase replied. "But splitting resources blindly won't help him. If Crowe has him, then finding Crowe is how we find Titus."

"And if he doesn't?" she challenged.

Silence followed that. It was brief but heavy.

Because that possibility existed too.

"We're not ignoring that," Dayken said after a moment. "We've already reached out to contacts outside the immediate network. *Discreetly*. If Titus surfaces anywhere, we'll hear about it. In addition to what we've already covered, if he isn't with Crowe, there aren't many other places he could be that we wouldn't have eyes on."

Nessalay studied him for a long second, then gave a single, tight nod.

Her dark skin, in contrast with her long, silky white hair, made her appear as an ethereal goddess as she stood tall and confident. She was a force to be reckoned with, and she was making it known that this wasn't an agreement.

It was a temporary alignment. But it was enough for now.

"Then move," she said. "Because standing here isn't bringing him back."

No one argued after that.

We didn't have the luxury to.

CHAPTER FIFTY-SIX

It had been over a month since Nessalay gave us the list of properties Crowe might be holed up in. And over a month since Titus went missing. After researching each possible location and scouting the ones he was more likely to use, we had finally narrowed the list to a single address.

It was time. Our official mission was to kill Crowe on sight and hope he had Titus, and we could rescue him in the process.

Kolton was unusually quiet while we geared up in the weapons room together. He wasn't tense or pacing back and forth. He was instead laser-focused in that distant, inward way he became when his attention narrowed on a single task.

I was reaching for ammo and strapping belts across my waist and chest. While he soon began to do the same. I stood across from him in the room, tugging my gloves on, watching the way his hands moved with practiced ease as he checked his weapons. He did everything the exact same way each time. Methodical. Precise. It was his routine that kept the chaos in his head under control. I stepped closer and reached for the strap at his shoulder, pretending to adjust it even though it was already perfect.

"You missed a spot," I said softly.

He glanced down at me, one brow lifting. "Did I?"

"Mmhmm."

I leaned in, not adjusting anything, just pressing my forehead briefly to his chest. His breath stuttered, subtle enough that anyone else might have missed it. His hand rose and rested at the back of my neck, thumb brushing my skin once. It was a gentle grounding touch, not just for me, but for him as well.

"You good?" he asked.

I nodded. "You?"

He hesitated. Not for long, but just long enough for me to notice. Kolton never lied with words. He lied with body language, body language he knew I could read effortlessly.

"Yeah," he said.

I smiled anyway. Not because I believed him, but because I knew what it would cost him to say otherwise. Admitting doubt made him feel exposed. Saying he was fine was how he kept control.

"Try not to maim anyone unless they deserve it," I murmured.

A low sound rumbled in his chest. "No promises."

I pulled back, meeting his eyes. "Then stay close to me."

His gaze softened, something fierce and protective burning in his yellow eyes.

"Always."

Moments later, we moved out. Chase and Derek, and some of their clan members, took point in the lead SUV. Onyx rode shotgun beside Dayken in the second truck. Kolton and I followed in the rear vehicle. The Mack Clan wasn't joining us on this mission. They stayed behind, focusing and bolstering the security at their compound to protect Peach. But we did have the Urva clan joining us on this mission, and I was looking forward to seeing Bailey again.

We arrived at the location in two trucks and the SUVs. The Urva clan, having joined us en route, made it a total of four vehicles. The moonless night engulfed us completely as the twins, along with new clans they enlisted, took to the air while others stayed on the surrounding ground. Wings beat silently overhead. Shadows slipped through the trees, silent on four legs. The coordination was seamless, the result of far too many late nights over weeks of planning.

We were taking a play straight out of Crowe's own book.

Contain. Isolate. Cover every possible exit or escape route.

I stepped out of the truck and shut the door, rolling my shoulders as I shifted the weight of my gun. Updates from the reconnaissance team murmured in my ear, constant and calm.

The mongooses had already confirmed that there were no under-ground tunnels beneath the property. Which meant there was one way in, and one way out. There was a narrow river behind the house, but it could only be crossed by boat.

There would be no elaborate escape plan for Crowe this time.

The house itself looked painfully ordinary. Dark blue siding with white trim. The lawn was covered with melting snow in uneven patches over dead grass. No porch, just a small set of steps leading to the front door. The kind of place you would never look twice at if you drove past.

But the ground told a different story.

Several tire tracks crisscrossed the slush near the driveway, showing recent and frequent passage. The signs of someone coming and going confirmed that it was real—this was actually happening.

A group of us quietly crept toward the front of the house, keeping low in case anyone was to look out a window. Onyx and Dayken stayed far enough back that they could quickly get to us but also keep a good view of the entire property. Bailey stayed in human form, clothed this time. She tilted her head as she studied the front entrance as she approached it. Then her face lit up.

"Oooh, wow," she said cheerfully. "The front door has lots of booms on it."

Chase sighed beside her. "Explosives."

"Booms," she corrected without missing a beat.

He knelt, carefully running his hand along the doorframe before pulling a small device from his coat. The scanner hummed softly as he passed it along the base.

"Copper wiring," he said. "With a trip mechanism on the handle. Bailey, check the windows."

"For booms?"

"Yes. For bombs."

She grinned before dashing off to the left side of the house, peering far too cheerfully through each window.

I lifted my gaze, scanning the perimeter. Derek was there one moment and gone the next, a massive shadow slipping soundlessly along the tree line. Overhead, I could hear wings fluttering as the bird shifters adjusted their positions, keeping watch to make sure no one would slip in or out without our notice. Every piece was in place. It was perfect.

Too perfect.

That feeling settled in my gut, slow and heavy.

"Windows are boom free," Bailey quietly announced. "Very rude of them, honestly."

"Copy," Chase said. "Front door is the only trap I'm seeing."

I stepped forward. "Can we disable it?"

There was an immediate response through the comm in my ear.

"Hold," Onyx's voice said. "Thermals are reading cold. There are no heat signatures inside."

My pulse ticked up. "Can you confirm that?"

"Confirmed," she replied. "No identifiable smells and no sounds coming from inside either."

Silence stretched between us.

Kolton's voice cut through the comms, low and controlled. "So, we don't know what we are disabling? Something's wrong."

I nodded in agreement, even though I didn't know if he was looking at me.

Chase finished disarming the door and cleanly snipped the wire. He stood and looked at me, waiting.

I took a breath. "Open it."

The door opened without resistance, just a quiet creaking sound.

The house smelled wrong.

Stale. Empty. Like the air had not been disturbed in days.

Bailey, Kolton, the twins, and I walked slowly as we cleared the house, room by room. Each time calling out, "clear," before moving on. Kolton, as predicted, refused to leave my side. We were cautious but also made sure to be thorough and efficient.

We all met back up in the living room. The whole house was completely untouched. The kitchen clean, almost sterile. Bedrooms bare. No personal items. No signs of panic or a hasty exit.

No signs of life.

My chest tightened with every step.

"This place was active all week. I saw it with my own eyes," Chase muttered. "I don't like it."

Neither did I.

Once we finished scouring the main floor, we moved toward the door to the basement, which was left wide open. I descended first, gun raised, heart pounding in my ears.

There was nothing down there.

Concrete floors. Empty shelving. A single light bulb hanging from the ceiling, currently switched off.

I turned slowly as dread pooled in my stomach.

"It's empty," I said quietly. I inhaled deeply to see if there were any odd smells lingering in the air.

Nothing.

No one spoke; everyone remained still, listening for any sign of movement.

We made our way back upstairs. All of us were puzzled and sharing our own theories.

Then I heard a quiet sound. A low hum, like an electronic circuit not working properly.

It was soft, but I couldn't quite place it. All I knew was that it immediately set me on edge.

I felt something wet trickle down my neck and lifted my hand to feel what it was.

"Sky," Chase said sharply. "Your ear."

His warning came a second too late.

"EMP!" Kolton roared through the house, already moving toward us.

Electromagnetic pulse?

I didn't have time to process Kolton's words. The world exploded, drowning me in sound and light. Too much.

Not a blast. Not an impact.

It was a pulse that vibrated over my skin. A tickling sensation coursed through my entire body. Then every comm went dead at once. The hum continued to rise inside me, turning into something sharp and invasive, crawling along my spine. I ripped the device from my ear, pain flaring as it tore free.

My head throbbed as the chip in my brain short-circuited.

Blood was everywhere, from where it was already leaking out of my ears and all down my neck.

Above us, glass shattered. The sharp, clear, crystal-like shards are raining down like a storm.

The lights throughout the house flickered on once, then died.

"Out," I shouted. "Now."

We sprinted.

The front door blew inward as we reached it, the force knocking me off my feet. I rolled hard, breath punched from my lungs, and I dropped my gun. It slid away from me across the concrete. Kolton was there instantly, hauling me up and shielding my body with his own as another blast rocked the house, this time coming from inside. He held me close to his chest, choosing to lift me off the ground and carry me as he sprinted.

The windows detonated outward, not with fire but with force, sending shards of wood, brick, and glass raining into the yard.

Outside, chaos erupted.

Kolton and I were blasted to the ground, his grip on my arm crushing but secure.

Birds of all shapes and sizes faltered in midair. Shifters on the ground stumbled, disoriented. The vehicles we left idling died where they sat, engines choking into silence.

This had been planned.

The house was just bait.

My heart hammered as I untangled myself from Kolton and shoved myself upright, wildly scanning around me.

"Status," I shouted.

Groans answered. Curses. But no screams.

Comms were completely destroyed, so it took a moment for everyone to confirm they were ok.

Once it was confirmed everyone was alive, I felt a prickling sensation go up my spine.

Another EMP?

As the thought hit, I turned to look around, and that's when I saw him.

Across the yard, at the edge of the tree line, a figure stood calmly watching the aftermath. Hands clasped behind his back. Unbothered.

Waiting.

Rage flooded me, hot and blinding.

"We were never meant to catch him," I whispered.

Kolton's hand tightened on mine. "No. He just wanted to prove that he's still one step ahead of us."

The figure turned and vanished into the trees, swallowed by darkness.

He left behind nothing but chaos and an empty, ruined house.

And the certainty that this was far from over.

CHAPTER FIFTY-SEVEN

I stood completely still, staring at Skylar on the operating table. My heart lodged somewhere in my throat.

Dried blood from her ear clung to her neck and chest like a thick, dark paste. I wanted nothing more than to throw her over my shoulder like a caveman and drag her to the nearest shower. Wash it all away. As if that would somehow repair my Sacar and make any of this okay.

My precious universe lay there, still clutching her head, trying to minimize the pain she was in.

"Hey, it's okay," she said softly, her eyes finding mine immediately. Even now...she searched for me first. "They're just scanning my brain. No one is hurting me."

I must have been growling for her to comfort me like this.

"But your head—"

"It's just a headache. It'll go away soon."

Her hand lifted slightly, like she meant to reach for me, but the wires tugged at her skin and stopped her short. My chest tightened at the sight.

She was comforting me.

How pathetic am I?

"I love you," I blurted, because my entire world was in pain, and I didn't know what else to do. For once, breaking things didn't feel like the answer.

"I love you too," she said without hesitation, her voice softer now. "Now, sit down and take a breath."

She held my gaze like she was trying to anchor me in place.

I nodded.

Didn't move.

Chase was frantically typing at a nearby table, his laptop flashing as screens pulled up and disappeared in rapid succession. I forced myself to focus on him, pretending I understood any of it.

Meanwhile, his annoying brother, who was somehow always the only fucking doctor around, was prepping Skylar for the scan, attaching wires and sticky patches to her skin like she was something fragile...something breakable.

I hated it.

I waited.

And waited.

My body locked in place, fear rooting me to where I stood. I couldn't even pace.

I was scared.

And my tiger didn't understand fear. It understood danger...rage...violence.

This...this was something else entirely.

"I've got it," Chase finally said.

I didn't know what that meant, but Skylar pushed herself up onto her elbows to look at him. She winced, her body faltering—

I was at her side instantly, one arm sliding behind her back before she could fall. She leaned into me without thinking, her weight settling against my arm like it belonged there, because it did.

My other hand came up, hovering for a second before I let my thumb brush along her cheek, trying to wipe away the dried blood.

Useless.

That shit wouldn't budge. Just sat there, mocking me.

Her fingers curled weakly into my shirt, barely there, but enough. Enough to steady me.

"Okay, thank fuck," Derek said, glancing at the screen. "Because these scans are coming back with giant white splotches, and they definitely did not teach this in medical school."

"I'm disabling it now," Chase replied.

"Perfect. That should give her brain time to heal. Then we can either do surgery to remove the damaged chip...or leave it and hope her brain heals around it."

He said it casually.

Like that wasn't completely insane.

Brain surgery. On Skylar.

A low growl built in my chest, vibrating where she rested against me. Her fingers tightened slightly at the sound, not in fear...in recognition.

"I want the chip to stay," Skylar said.

Panic slammed into me.

Why?

Not this again.

"Hang on." She lifted her hand, pressing lightly against my chest as if to steady me before addressing the room. "Imagine waking up one day, and your dick is just...gone."

Derek choked on his water. Chase immediately grabbed his crotch. My brain short-circuited.

"It would feel unnatural, right?" she continued. "Like you lost a part of yourself. Well...that's exactly what it feels like you're asking me to do."

Her voice softened, and her gaze flicked back to me.

"I love the chip. It helps me read, helps me think in ways other people can't. It lets me understand people before they even speak." Her fingers shifted against my shirt, grounding herself. "Please don't ask me to change."

Derek was on the other side of the table, removing wires and patches from her skin, when he paused to look at me.

"I would never," I said immediately, my hand flattening more firmly against her back without thinking, holding her there. "But I'm scared to death right now, Skylar."

"I'm also scared!" Derek snapped, finally finished with his removal task. "Just the idea of Captain Flappy being removed is terrifying. My poor baby." Derek turned away, pacing in the opposite direction, petting his crotch.

"Don't be scared," she said to me, not the lunatic who was actively talking to his dick. "I know the EMP damaged it," Skylar said, calmer now. "But I believe Chase can fix it. And I just need time to heal, and…feed."

Suddenly, my dick was no longer worried about being chopped off because it rose to full attention at the idea of her feeding from me.

"Well, the good news about the chip being disabled is that we don't have to worry about keeping the firewall up. So that will give me time to update the chip, reprogram it, and get it on a private, untraceable network. Assuming it has the capabilities. Which, given what I've seen from that thing…I'm gonna go with, yeah, it does."

Skylar beamed. A bright, beautiful smile.

"Thank you, Chase. You are best!"

"Hey! I carried you in here, and I helped with stuff." She chuckled at my jealousy and my sad attempt to seem important.

"Yes, yes, you are the best, too." Skylar cleared her throat before adding, "Speaking of best, have I mentioned that I'm hungry?"

"Out!"

The room cleared. Not because I believed I had the authority to order the twins around, but because they didn't want to witness what was to come next.

I scooped her up in my arms, and she instinctively wrapped her arms around my neck and leaned into my neck, inhaling deeply.

Purred, loving the feel of her in my arms and at my neck.

"Do it," I gruffed.

I'd barely finished the words before I could feel her pinprick teeth pierce my neck. My own double set of fangs punched down from the roof of my mouth. My tiger surging to the surface, wanting to protect her with everything we had, while she enjoyed feeding and getting substances from our blood.

Pride swelled in my chest.

Mine.

My world.

My universe, the sun, the moon, the stars in the sky.

Chapter Fifty-Eight

KOLTON

I didn't want to do this.

But what I wanted had never been part of the equation.

It never was. Fate had chosen differently.

Being a Guardian meant standing still when every instinct screamed at me to run—to disappear, to sink into the shadows where nothing could touch me. Where I didn't have to be this version of myself.

But that wasn't who I was allowed to be.

Skylar believed I could be more.

She saw something in me I had never seen in myself. A man who could fight demons and come out the other side without becoming one. A man who could protect instead of destroy.

And I loved her too much to let that belief die for nothing.

The image of her anchored me.

Curled up in our room, legs tucked beneath her, a book in her hands as she flipped through the pages faster than anyone should be able to read. Completely lost. Completely at peace.

Safe.

That was how she'd looked when I stepped out into the hall to deal with this.

For a second, I almost went back. Almost told myself this could wait. That I could have one more minute—just one—with her before everything shifted.

But I knew better.

There was no pausing this. No delaying what had to be done.

I wanted to get back to her. Fast. Before she noticed I was gone. Before that relaxed look on her face disappeared.

My gaze dropped to my phone, the screen glowing too bright in the dim hallway. I stared at it longer than I should have, thumb hovering, unmoving.

My chest tightened. My pulse pounded loud and uneven, each beat echoing in my ears like a warning I couldn't ignore.

This was it.

The moment everything changed.

After this...there was no going back. No pretending. No hiding behind half-truths and restraint.

Whatever came next would be real.

Permanent.

Fear settled deep in my gut. Not sharp or fleeting—but heavy. Solid. The kind that rooted itself into your bones and refused to let go.

I exhaled slowly, dragging a hand down my face.

Because the truth was...I'd already lived through hell.

I'd survived things that should have broken me. Done things that should have buried me.

And somehow, every single one of those moments—every bad decision, every scar, every drop of blood—had led me here.

To this.

I knew it with a certainty that settled deep in my bones.

This wasn't just another choice.

It was *the* choice.

Fate, destiny. Call it what you will.

My thumb finally moved.

It was time.

I pressed the green call button and lifted the phone to my ear, my jaw tightening as it rang.

Once.

Twice.

"Hello?"

"Hey, John. It's Kolton." I cleared my throat, forcing the tension out of my voice. "You got a minute?"

EPILOGUE 1
One Month Ago

I sat in my chair, my phone resting on the desk in front of me. I dragged a hand down my face as I listened to him ramble on speaker, his voice blending into a dull, repetitive hum.

If I were being honest, I wasn't listening. Not really. My mind was elsewhere, and I didn't give a shit what he was planning this time.

My gaze drifted to the stack of unsigned contracts piling up on my desk. Nessalay was definitely going to hand me my ass about that later.

I tuned back in just in time to catch...

Wait a second.

I straightened abruptly, my back going rigid.

Well, fuck...this isn't going to be good.

"And then I want you to go over there and tell them you overheard a conversation while you were on the phone with me," Leo continued. "Say you heard one of my associates talking about heading to a nearby hospital."

I stared blankly ahead, listening as he laid out the details. I'd done plenty of deceitful shit in my time, but this might be the worst one yet.

"Don't you think they'll see right through that?" I asked. Because let's be real, that group might be a chaotic mix of personalities, but they weren't stupid.

Chase, especially.

Smart as hell.

And the most dangerous of all of them.

"Not if your sly ass does it right," Leo shot back. "And, Titus, don't make me remind you what happens if you even think about screwing this up...or betraying me again."

Can't blame a guy for trying.

"I don't need a reminder," I said flatly.

"Good. Because I have Sky exactly where I want her, and I don't need you deviating from the plan. I need the tiger here. Immediately."

My grip tightened slightly on the edge of the desk.

"On it."

Epilogue 2

"Alicia Mack of the Mack Clan. Nice to meet you."

She was huge for a twelve-year-old—built like a bear. My uncle nudged me forward so I could reach her, his hand firm between my shoulder blades. Everyone always thought I was timid, so when I extended my hand to shake hers, I made sure my grip was firm. I didn't want her to think I was weak.

It must have worked, because she smiled. A genuine, bright, inviting smile—and all at once, I saw her in my future. My best friend. My partner-in-crime. Sleepovers, gossip, workouts. We were going to do it all.

Suddenly, a sharp pain lanced through my chest, knocking me back a step. I gasped, clutching my heart. I looked up to see if Alicia had shoved me, only to notice that she was gripping the back of her neck, wincing.

Then my heartbeat wasn't my own anymore. She must have felt it, too, because she looked at me—wide-eyed and stunned.

"Congratulations!" my uncle shouted, spinning toward the crowd. "They've bonded! The Mack Clan now has a Sacar under their protection!"

The room erupted in cheers.

Alicia released her neck, straightened, and grinned at me again. That smile felt like safety and sunlight.

"We're going to be best friends," she said.

"Yeah, we are!" I clapped, unable to contain myself. For once, I wasn't afraid. I'd just found my best friend—and my Guardian for life.

The memory dissolved, and I blinked as I refocused under the bright living room lights, surrounded by the familiar faces of the Mack Clan.

My phone buzzed on the coffee table. An unfamiliar number lit up my screen. I considered not answering for a heartbeat before finally picking it up.

"Hello?"

"Is this Peachabelle Vaughn?" the male voice asked.

"Yes, this is she."

A pause. Then the voice continued, low and carefully, "We've got some bad news about Alicia Mack of the Mack Clan."

GLOSSARY

Bond: A sacred connection is formed when a vampire transfers their flower essence to a chosen Guardian. An eight-petal flower mark appears at the back of a Guardian's neck and over the Sacar's heart. Bonds can form at any age but most often occur in preadolescence.

If a Guardian dies, the bond returns to the Sacar.
If a Sacar dies, the bond remains with the Guardian.

Guardian: Also known as a shifter. Guardians protect, hunt, and fight with enhanced physical abilities thanks to their sliced animal gene. Guardians can range from any type of predator species as a result of the original shifter Avont experimenting with his DNA.

Bonded Guardian: A Guardian chosen by a vampire for lifelong protection, marked by the shared bond symbol on their body.

Their bond allows them to sense their Sacar's emotions, location, and condition, creating a deeply personal connection rooted in absolute loyalty. Bonded Guardians' ability to protect, hunt, and fight becomes stronger and more enhanced with the need to guard their Sacar.

Primarc (pronounced Prime-Arc): The leader of a clan. A Primarc governs alliances, conflict, and the overall strength of their people. Chosen for power, intelligence, and influence, they maintain order and balance within the clan. Primarcs have a natural ability to control clan members and assert dominance and will over other clan members.

Bonded Primarc: A Primarc who is also bonded to a Sacar, carrying both leadership and protective responsibilities. The top tier in ability, power, and enhanced abilities.

Sacar (pronounced Suh-car): A vampire bound to a specific Guardian through a sacred, unbreakable bond. A Sacar is both a purpose and a lifeline to their Guardian, tying their fates together.

Vampire: An unbonded Sacar. Though more vulnerable without a Guardian, they remain powerful, with enhanced strength, speed, and regeneration.

Bonding Mark: A shared floral marking between Sacar and Guardian symbolizes their bond. The design features eight petals to represent eternity and unity, placed over the heart (Sacar) and base of the neck (Guardian). Its tone naturally complements the skin. Colors range from light tan to deep brown.

Clan: A structured group of shapeshifters led by a Primarc. Each clan is tied to a specific animal form that shapes their traits and combat style. Clans function as loyal, hierarchical families, forming alliances or rivalries with others.

Otacilia familia line

Decima Ana Otacilia & Husband (deceased)

Augustus Maximus Otacilia & Wife

Lunce Otacilia
&
Wife (unknown)

Avont Otacilia
&
Kleo Almica (Otacilia)

Corvin Otacilia

Alaric Otacilia
&
Seraphine Macino (Otacilia)

Child I Child II
Child III Child IV
Child V Child VI
Child VII Child VIII
Child IX Child X

KEEP READING

more is coming

The sister's story may be over, but the adventure isn't.

Stay tuned for Book III

Which will be about Titus and Peach.

What does it mean to use the flower to create life, and to destroy a bond?

Only one way to find out.

Keep reading!

ABOUT THE AUTHOR

S.M. Storm is a Michigan writer who loves all things dark, magical, and a little bit spooky. She's been writing her entire career, but her favorite experience has been this one, where she gets to weave together vampires, shifters, and the kind of slow-burn romance that makes you yell at the page.

When she's not writing, she's cheering on her son at soccer, rewatching her favorite comfort shows (with a fairy-tale ending, always), and dragging her husband into endless coffee shops.

Sacar is her debut novel and the start of **The Marked Bonds Series**, a paranormal romance and urban fantasy world full of secrets, bonds, and, most importantly, tension.

www.ingramcontent.com/pod-product-compliance
Lightning Source LLC
Chambersburg PA
CBHW061414160726
47995CB00003B/601